From *The Black Coat*

George had disappeared, and the hall was deserted and only dimly lighted. Anne went into her room, which was in complete darkness, and began to grope for a switch. She could not find one, and remembered at last that there was a lamp on the bedside table and a ceiling light with a dangling cord.

She moved into the center of the room and raised her arm, feeling for the cord, and touched instead a cold, inert hand.

Books by Constance & Gwenyth Little

The Grey Mist Murders (1938)*
The Black-Headed Pins (1938)*
The Black Gloves (1939)*
Black Corridors (1940)*
The Black Paw (1941)*
The Black Shrouds (1941)
The Black Thumb (1942)
The Black Rustle (1943)
The Black Honeymoon (1944)*
Great Black Kanba (1944)*
The Black Eye (1945)
The Black Stocking (1946)*
The Black Goatee (1947)
The Black Coat (1948)*
The Black Piano (1948)
The Black Smith (1950)
The Black House (1950)
The Blackout (1951)
The Black Dream (1952)
The Black Curl (1953)
The Black Iris (1953)

*reprinted by the Rue Morgue Press
as of July 2001

The Black Coat

A Murder Mystery Comedy by

Constance & Gwenyth Little

The Rue Morgue Press
Boulder, Colorado

Printed at Johnson Printing
Boulder, Colorado

The Rue Morgue Press
P.O. Box 4119
Boulder, CO 80306

PRINTED IN THE UNITED STATES OF AMERICA

About the Littles

Although all but one of their books had "black" in the title, the 21 mysteries of Constance (1899-1980) and Gwenyth (1903-1985) Little were far from somber affairs. The two Australian-born sisters from East Orange, New Jersey, were far more interested in coaxing chuckles than in inducing chills from their readers.

Indeed, after their first book, *The Grey Mist Murders*, appeared in 1938, Constance rebuked an interviewer for suggesting that their murders weren't realistic by saying, "Our murderers strangle. We have no sliced-up corpses in our books." However, as the books mounted, the Littles did go in for all sorts of gruesome murder methods—"horrible," was the way their own mother described them—which included the occasional sliced-up corpse.

But the murders were always off stage and tempered by comic scenes in which bodies and other objects, including swimming pools, were constantly disappearing and reappearing. The action took place in large old mansions, boarding houses, hospitals, hotels, or on trains or ocean liners, anywhere the Littles could gather together a large cast of eccentric characters, many of whom seemed to have escaped from a Kaufman play or a Capra movie. The typical Little heroine—each book was a stand-alone—often fell under suspicion herself and turned detective to keep the police from slapping the cuffs on. Whether she was a working woman or a spoiled little rich brat, she always spoke her mind, kept her sense of humor, and got her man, both murderer and husband. But if marriage was in the offing, it was always on her terms and the vows were taken with more than a touch of cynicism. Love was grand, but it was even grander if the husband could either pitch in with the cooking and cleaning or was wealthy enough to hire household help.

The Littles wrote all their books in bed—"Chairs give one backaches," Gwenyth complained—with Constance providing detailed plot outlines while Gwenyth did the final drafts. Over the years that pattern changed somewhat but Constance always insisted that Gwen "not mess up my clues." Those clues were everywhere and the Littles made sure there were no loose ends.

Seemingly irrelevant events were revealed to be of major significance in the final summation.

The Littles published their two final novels, *The Black Curl* and *The Black Iris*, in 1953, and if they missed writing after that, they were at least able to devote more time to their real passion—traveling. The two made at least three trips around the world at a time when that would have been a major expedition. For more information on the Littles and their books, see the introductions by Tom & Enid Schantz to The Rue Morgue Press editions of *The Black Gloves* and *The Black Honeymoon.*

CHAPTER ONE

THE TRAIN LURCHED, and Anne's knees slid against those of the girl sitting in the opposite seat. The girl giggled and rearranged herself, and Anne said, "I'm sorry—this car seems to be terribly bumpy."

"I'll say. I didn't sleep a wink all night."

"I didn't sleep much, either," Anne agreed.

She turned her eyes to the window and took a quick look at the girl on the way. Of course she hadn't slept—she'd been horsing around in the lounge car most of the night. Anne had heard her creep back to her berth somewhere in the early hours of the morning.

The girl cleared her throat and said, "My name's Anne Magraw. What's yours?"

"Why—Anne too. Anne Hillyer."

Miss Magraw gave a little scream. "Well, how do you like that!"

Anne smiled without enthusiasm. After all it didn't seem to be anything to get excited about. Plenty of Annes around.

"That's a good one, all right!" Miss Magraw laughed heartily. "Listen, we gotta celebrate us both bein' Anne. Come on down to the lounge car, and I'll buy you a drink."

"Oh, I don't think—" Anne began reluctantly. "I mean," she added, "it's too early for a drink."

"Ahh, come on!" Miss Magraw stood up and clutched at her arm. "It's never too early for a drink—especially when you got something to celebrate, like us."

Anne shrugged, laughed, and stood up, and they made their way down the swaying car. When they came to the lounge car, Miss Magraw stopped abruptly just inside the door and ran a roving eye over the occupants. She was obviously in search of someone, and after a moment she found him. She waved gaily and began to make her way toward him, and Anne followed slowly, wishing that she had not come.

The young man got to his feet and asked, "Where you been all morning, Sugar?"

"Look," said Sugar, "here's my new friend—she and I got the same name." She flashed a smile and proceeded to a simple introduction. "Anne, this is Dick. Dick, this is Anne."

Anne murmured, and Dick said, "Hi there."

"And now," Miss Magraw announced, "we gotta celebrate our names bein' the same this way."

"Sure you have," Dick agreed amiably, "and I gotta join you being as my sister is Anne too."

Miss Magraw gave a little scream of pleasure and settled herself into an armchair. "Call the waiter, Dick."

Dick held up a hand and told her in an aside, "They ain't waiters when they're on a train like this. You call them stooards."

"No kiddin'," said Miss Magraw. "You can call 'em King George for all of me—but get one. I want a drink."

Anne discovered immediately that the celebrating was being done without any reference to herself. The other two fell into talk that excluded her entirely, and she sat there, taking an occasional sip from a drink that she did not want. Her glass was still half full when the others ordered seconds, and they turned their attention on her long enough to exhort her earnestly to drink up and get on with the next one.

She did finish it at last, and became conscious at the same time of being a trifle nauseated. She was not accustomed to drinking in the morning, and she knew that she was a little nervous, anyway. She was just another small-town girl coming to the big city to try to make out. She had some connections, though—some nice letters and an invitation to stay at the apartment of one of her older sister's friends.

Dick's arm jolted her elbow, and he turned to her, muttered, "Sorry," and then gave his attention to Miss Magraw again.

She glanced at them and realized that they were no longer gay and animated, but appeared to be discussing something with deadly seriousness. Miss Magraw's painted mouth drooped a little, and Dick was talking in a low, rapid voice, with an occasional sharp gesture of his arm.

Anne stood up, said, "See you later," and made off. Dick half rose with a hand on the back of his chair, and Miss Magraw said abstractedly, "Be seein' ya."

Anne returned to her section where she sat quietly, with her head resting against the back of the seat, until her nausea had passed. She opened her eyes after a while and they fell on Miss Magraw's coat, which lay carelessly tumbled on the opposite seat. It was rather an odd coat, and Anne had noticed it with some attention when she had first seen it on Miss Magraw the previous night.

It was a black seal—genuine, but very old—and somehow vastly unsuited to Miss Magraw's rather cheap sophistication. It had leg-of-mutton sleeves and a tightly fitted waist which flared into fullness over the hips. As it happened, it was more or less in style again—and yet there was a difference, somewhere, which labeled it as being very old. There was a star with tiny bronze points attached to the shoulder. It had been a really beautiful coat in its day, Anne reflected, and probably Miss Magraw had pinched it from her mother, figuring that it would be better than anything she could afford to buy.

Anne sighed, stirred, and turned her head to look out of the window. They must be getting close to Philadelphia, and then only a couple of hours or so and she would be in New York. She took up her book and settled herself comfortably to read.

About five minutes later Miss Magraw returned and said, "Hi, Anne," in an absentminded sort of way. She did not sit down, but stood with one hand on the seat to balance herself, a faint frown wrinkling her forehead.

Anne closed her book and looked up. "Do you have a problem?"

Miss Magraw gave her a sudden grin and seated herself abruptly. "You going to New York?"

Anne nodded.

"Someone meeting you?"

"Yes."

Miss Magraw said, "Oh," and appeared to fall into deep thought. Anne fingered her book, and after a moment's silence said, "It's rather silly, really. I don't know the man who's meeting me, and he doesn't know me. I'm staying at the apartment of a friend, and since she is unable to meet me herself, she's sending this friend of hers. I told her it wasn't necessary, but she insisted."

Miss Magraw's eyes focused on her with sudden attention. "For corn's sake! How's this yap gonna know you?"

Anne smiled. "I have an artificial rose pinned on my coat, and he's supposed to look for that."

It appeared to amuse Miss Magraw, and she laughed for some little time. "This," she said presently, "I gotta see. You standin' around like a cluck with a shrub hangin' on you, waitin' to be picked up."

Anne laughed with her, and admitted, "I'll be glad when I can unpin that awful rose from my coat. It looks terrible."

Miss Magraw glanced at the coat—a new tweed, warm and conservative and eminently suitable for traveling. "Oh, I dunno," she said tolerantly. "The flower sorta dresses it up. Coat's kinda plain without it."

Anne shrugged, and Miss Magraw became abstracted again. She stared out of the window, but her thoughts seemed to be turned inward, and Anne presently picked up her book again.

There was a lengthy silence, and then Miss Magraw suddenly jumped to her feet.

"Come on, Anne, we gotta have one more celebration. We got interrupted tryin' to have the last one—but we got to drink to each other before this old crate gets to New York. Come on, will you!"

Anne looked up, laughing and shaking her head. "I couldn't possibly drink again before lunch."

Miss Magraw hesitated with puckered forehead. "Well, no— maybe I shouldn't either—drinkin' too much. But we can have a coke. Come on, we'll celebrate with a couple of cokes. What's the use wearin' out the plush on this crummy seat? We can't even smoke here. Come on, will you, and I'll buy you a coke."

"It isn't plush," Anne said mildly, but she laid her book aside. She hadn't thought of a cigarette until it was mentioned, but now she felt she wanted one.

They went along to the lounge car again, and Anne thought that Miss Magraw seemed nervous and jumpy. She almost fell as she went to sit down, and thudded heavily against one of the arms of the chair. She ordered two cokes, and then turned to Anne and asked directly, "What do you do for a living?"

Anne resented it, and allowed a moment to pass before she said coldly, "Commercial art."

"How's that?" Miss Magraw asked, looking puzzled.

Anne explained briefly, and then looked around as the train slowed.

"Hey! This must be Philadelphia," Miss Magraw yelled in sudden excitement. "You wait here, Anne, I'll be right back."

She fled, balancing perilously on her high heels, still clutching the coke in her hand. Anne watched her go, laughing a little, and wondering if the girl had had too much to drink. She was very young—not more than eighteen or nineteen to Anne's twenty-six. Her clothes were a bit extreme, and she had already bleached her hair, but she was very pretty, and Anne felt uneasily that someone should be looking after her better.

The train had stopped now, and she looked idly out at the station, but there was not much to see. She was conscious of an increase in her feeling of nervousness. New York was very close, now, and she was half eager and half afraid. She had wanted to come, even though several people had told her that she was dead wrong, because she'd been doing so well at home. But she'd always wanted to travel and see other places, and now that Mother was so nicely settled with Jim and Betty—Jim and Betty. They'd told her that she should give up her work and get married—and there'd been a couple of prospects for marriage. But Betty had three children, and appeared to work without ceasing for something like twenty-four hours a day, so she'd never been much impressed with that idea.

The train started slowly, with little jerking movements, and she looked out onto the station again. There was a girl walking along the platform with a coat very like her own—in fact, it was exactly the same. Anne moved her head quickly, her eyes widening, and just before she was swept from further sight of the girl she saw that there was a red rose pinned to the shoulder of the tweed coat.

CHAPTER TWO

ANNE SAT BACK in her seat, her puzzled eyes still on the window, although she could no longer see any part of the station. Surely that could not have been Miss Magraw wrapped up in her tweed coat. Why would the girl steal it? It was not the sort of thing she would choose for her blatant blond prettiness, and anyway, she had been going to New York. Or had she? Uneasy, now, Anne was unable to remember that she had mentioned her destination. In any case, she might as well return to her section. Probably the coat on the platform was just a coincidence, and she would find her own where she had left it.

As she entered her own car she saw at once that Miss Magraw's black seal was still tumbled on the seat, and she drew a little breath of relief. The girl would never go off and abandon a fur coat.

But her own gray tweed was missing. After a rather wild search for it, she hurried along to the ladies' room in a forlorn hope that Miss Magraw had taken it there for some reason of her own. It took her only a moment to discover that the swaying, rattling little compartment was empty, and she returned to her section and rang for the porter.

She asked if he had seen a gray tweed coat, and he looked at her as porters do who have had years of experience with crazy travelers. He said politely, "No, ma'am."

She asked about Miss Magraw, and he nodded at once. "Yes, ma'am, the lady got off at Philadelphia. Came rushin' back here at the last minute. She was goin' to New York, and changed her mind. I had trouble gettin' her off— yes, ma'am." Travelers, his look seemed to say, were all more or less crazy according to their lights—some more, some less, but all suffering from some form of insanity.

Anne confirmed this reflection by asking, "What sort of coat did she have on?"

He scratched his head for a moment, and then shook it. "I don't rightly know, ma'am," he said, still courteous.

Anne dismissed him and sank into her seat. What could she do now? Put in a complaint? Try to have the girl arrested? There was something wrong with that girl's background. She was too young to be bleaching her hair and picking up men on trains. Perhaps Dick had been getting off at Philadelphia, and the silly girl had decided to go along with him. Whoever her people were, they were not looking after her properly.

Anne sighed and pulled the black coat toward her. She'd have to wear the thing—it was too cold to go without a coat. She took it along to the ladies' room, put it on, and viewed herself in the mirror.

It was, she decided, quite a sight. The puffed sleeves looked far bigger on than off, the bronzed star was garish, and the flaring skirt was rather short.

Anne muttered, "I look like a lampshade," and was not comforted by the fact that, in a way, it suited her blond hair. Natural blond—no bleaching— and she thought of Miss Magraw again. Well, she simply didn't have the heart to accuse the girl of theft, so she might as well forget her tweed coat and wear this thing until she was able to get another.

She experimented with her hat, and decided that the coat looked better without. A hat merely added to its fussiness.

She went back to her section and jammed her hat into her suitcase, her thoughts busied irritably with Miss Magraw's flightiness. She tried to read for a while, unsuccessfully, and was vastly relieved when at last the train reached New York. She shrugged into the coat, realizing with fresh annoyance that she now had no rose, and so probably would never connect with Mary's friend. Well, she'd simply have to take a taxi to the apartment and try to straighten things out from there.

She had only one suitcase—the rest of her things were being sent by express—and she walked briskly from the platform to the station, carrying it herself. She had decided not to try to locate Mary's friend, but she had walked only a few steps when a man approached and took the suitcase from her hand. He said, "Hello, Anne, what's the rush?"

It was a relief to be relieved of the suitcase, for the coat was hot and heavy and dragged uncomfortably from her shoulders. She looked up at him, and supposed that Mary must have shown him her photograph. "I lost my rose," she smiled, "and I didn't think you'd—"

"Come on," he interrupted cheerfully. "We can get a cab over here."

He caught her arm and swung her and the suitcase through a confusing panorama of people, newsstands, ticket offices, lockers, and benches, and at last she was in a cab, relaxing gratefully on the leather seat. The man seated himself beside her and immediately pulled out a cigarette and lit it. She glanced at him shyly, and reflected that Mary must go in for good-looking men. He was dark—tall and good-looking and assured.

He exhaled smoke, and then observed conversationally, "You know, you really do look older than thirteen."

Anne stared at him, her lips parted. "But—why wouldn't I?"

"Well, dammit, you're supposed to be thirteen."

"Nonsense!" said Anne sharply. "I left thirteen long ago."

He looked her over carefully, apparently paying particular attention to the coat and its absurd star.

"This coat—" she began.

"Yes, it's the coat—no mistaking that at all. But I wish you'd fix yourself up to look a little younger before you see her."

Anne was held silent by astonishment for a moment, and before she could speak he went on, "I'm George Vaddison, your grandmother's nephew by marriage."

Anne came to the rather helpless conclusion that he was mentally unbalanced and edged away from him. She was silent for a while, and then asked feebly, "May I have a cigarette?"

"Certainly not," he said firmly. "At your age—or the age you're supposed to be—you can't go around smoking cigarettes."

She let it go at that because she was afraid to ruffle him for fear he might get violent.

He took another look at her and shook his head. "I can see that you're only young—it's the way you're trimmed that makes you look older. I don't know why you do it—childhood is such a lovely time, and you'll be sick of being an adult before you're through."

She merely eyed him warily, and he presently shrugged. "Anyway, when you get in, try to look a little younger. Let your hair down."

"It is down."

"Yes, but straighten it out a bit, and put a bow on it."

"No thirteen-year-old," said Anne, "would be caught dead in a ditch wearing a bow."

He looked at her with his brow wrinkled. "I don't believe you are Anne, but I'll go into that with you later. It's pressing just now that you see her. I'm glad that your hair isn't bleached, anyway." They drew up at a brownstone in a side street, and Anne had no idea of where she was. She hoped desperately that this was Mary's apartment, and that the man with her was merely trying to be funny. She knew that Mary lived in a brownstone on the third floor.

George paid off the taxi, took the suitcase in one hand and Anne's arm in the other, and ran her up the steps to the front door. They went through a hall and started up a narrow flight of stairs. Anne caught a glimpse of a large room with several people sitting around in it, and then had to watch the dark, narrow stairs so that she would not miss her footing.

On the second floor George led her to a room and said, "This is yours, but don't wait to unpack anything. Just smooth your hair and come over and see her."

Anne swallowed and said bravely, "What do you mean, 'Come over and see her'? I know perfectly well that Mary won't be home until this evening." She looked around the room. The door opened onto the main hall, and it was certainly no part of an apartment.

But George apparently had not listened to her. He relieved her of the sagging weight of the black coat and then divested her of her suit coat as well. He went to a washstand in a corner of the room, and moistened his handkerchief, and then returned to her.

"I hate to do this to my show handkerchief," he said, grinning at her, "but it seems the only course. I know you won't do it on your own steam."

He began to wipe the makeup off her face, and fear held her still. He must certainly be unbalanced—there seemed to be no doubt of it. She'd simply have to wait for the right opportunity to get away.

He stood back, looking from her to his smeared handkerchief, and said ruefully, "I can't seem to get it off."

Anne glanced into the mirror over the bureau, and then silently opened her suitcase, got out some cream, and cleaned all the red marks and streaks from her face. She smoothed her hair, tucked in her simple white blouse, and straightened her skirt.

George nodded and took her arm. "That's fine—you ought to pass now."

He led her across the hall and went into another room without waiting to knock. It was furnished in heavy old mahogany, with hard, dark, overall carpeting. There was an immense four-poster bed, and it took Anne a moment to locate the tiny old lady who lay against a mass of pillows along one edge of its vast area. The hands were like little claws, and the face wizened and negligible save for the lively dark eyes. There was a quantity of snow-white hair lying across her shoulders in two smooth braids.

"Here she is, Aunt Ellen," George said, and moved Anne up to the bed, where he placed her hand in one of the little claws.

The dark eyes snapped with eagerness, and the little claw fastened onto Anne's hand with surprising strength.

"Oh, child, this means so much to me. My dear, dear little Annie. And to think I never saw you grow up. That wasn't right of Missy, was it, George?"

Anne saw it all then. The coat—the black seal—was to identify the girl for George, and that little Magraw brat was the thirteen-year-old Anne. She could be—it was quite possible. But she'd have to be found, and these people must be told—

The old lady pulled her down, and Anne, in pity, kissed her gently. George had slipped out of the room, and after a moment's hesitation she sat down on a chair that stood beside the bed. There was no use in trying to explain anything to this poor little creature now—it was not in Anne to spoil her intense pleasure. It could be set right when they caught up with that other little devil.

"I'm going to tell you where it is," Aunt Ellen said suddenly. "I had to kill a man to get it."

CHAPTER THREE

ANNE FELT AN ODD prickling along her scalp, and glanced over her shoulder to see whether anyone were listening. But the room seemed to be empty. She felt the tiny hand relax its hold on hers, and a glance at the old lady showed that she had dropped off into a sudden sleep.

Anne waited for a moment, and then quietly got out of her chair and left the room. She found George just outside the door, and before she could say anything he announced abruptly, "Look here—I've got to have a talk with you."

He urged her toward her own room, and she said a little indignantly, "You want to have a talk with me! I simply must have a talk with you."

As usual he didn't listen to her. He closed the door of the room, and then turned around and faced her. "There's something wrong with all this—you can't be Anne."

"I am Anne," she said impatiently, "but I'm not your Anne. It's a pity you couldn't have found it out before you brought me here."

"Well"—he frowned—"I did notice something. You remember I told you I thought you were older than thirteen. But Aunt Ellen would have been bitterly disappointed—she's been waiting so long—"

Anne was annoyed. "I really tried to tell you, but you simply wouldn't listen—you insisted on rushing me in there. Your Anne is somewhere in Philadelphia, and I think you'd better have her traced immediately if she's only thirteen—although she looks older than that. I think she got off with a man she picked up on the train."

George was instantly concerned, and showed it by battering her with questions until she said rather irritably, "Don't start blaming me for things that are the fault of you and your Anne."

He was irritable too. "Don't call her my Anne—I can see that the little pest is going to give me plenty of trouble."

Anne shrugged. "I'm sorry, but that has nothing to do with me. I'll have to go now—I'm expected somewhere else, and they'll be getting the police out after me if I don't turn up pretty soon."

George ceased to be irritable at once and became charmingly persuasive instead. "Wait—please do. You could see for yourself that Aunt Ellen hasn't much longer—and how happy she was to have you there. She isn't very lucid at this point, and it was obvious that you satisfied her completely. We can easily switch when I catch up with that brat, but it may take some time. In the meantime, won't you stay here for a day or two? It will cost you nothing— this is a painfully refined private hotel owned by Aunt Ellen and now being run by her daughter-in-law. Your meals will be served to you here, and you can visit with your friends or relatives—and go to stay with them later. I know it's a lot to ask of you, but I'm hoping that it won't be for too long."

"But I think it's ridiculous," Anne said rather helplessly. "After all, if it's so vital, I could come around here and visit with her."

He made an impatient movement with his arm. "You must realize that that wouldn't do at all. She is not always in a condition to receive visitors, and it would mean everything to her for you to be here just when she wants you."

"Like in the middle of the night, perhaps," Anne said coldly.

"That's it," he agreed quite seriously. "She's often restless and frightened at night."

Anne gave in in the end, but more from pity for Aunt Ellen than because of anything George had said. She followed him rather sulkily to the phone in the lower hall and called Mary at her office. She tried to explain everything, but Mary, voluble and concerned, simply couldn't get it, and at last Anne said she'd come around to dinner that evening and try to make everything clear.

"Fine," Mary said, sounding relieved. "But what about Tim?"

"Who's Tim?"

"I sent him to the station to meet you. He's probably still there looking for a red rose."

"My red rose was pinched," Anne said.

"Then, darling, you'd better get another one and go on back to the station or Tim will be bringing home some strange female just because she happens to be wearing one. I'm devoted to Tim, but he really is a fool."

Anne said, "All right," sighed, and put down the phone. She wouldn't have believed, she thought dolefully, that New York could be so strenuous. She relayed her problem to George, and he said at once that she must leave everything to him. He went to Aunt Ellen's room, where he found an artificial red rose after a brief rummage in a drawer. He brought it triumphantly to Anne, who was waiting in the hall, and said, "Here you are. She's still asleep— and she's also still alone."

But he had no sooner finished speaking than a nurse appeared on the stairs, and presently came toward them with a beaming smile that appeared to be all for George. She wore the plain cap of a practical nurse, and was of uncertain age, with suspiciously black hair. She said brightly, "I was just washing out a few of Mother's things."

George frowned. "Surely there is someone else who could do that, Miss Kalms."

Miss Kalms smiled again—sweetly. "Mrs. Smith said she simply did not have time for anything of the sort, and I like to keep my patients clean."

George muttered under his breath, and at last became articulate enough to tell Anne to get her coat on.

She groaned as she assumed the bulky seal again, and George, who had followed her, pinned the rose to her shoulder. She looked in the glass and groaned again.

"My God! Look at me! Rose, bronze star, and Grandma's coat—all in perfect taste."

"Yes," George said absently, "It looks very nice. Let's go. I'll have to get down to the office some time today."

"For heaven's sake!" Anne snarled. "Go ahead. I can do the rest by myself."

"No, no. I must look after you and get you properly settled, since you are doing this for us."

They returned to the station, and Anne paraded around with her rose, feeling conspicuous and thoroughly self-conscious. George trailed her, smoking cigarettes and trying not to show his impatience. After a while he said, "Look—it's lunchtime. Let's have something to eat. Perhaps this Tim is stuffing his face somewhere."

Anne agreed at once. She was hot, tired, and out of sorts, and very hungry. George took her into what appeared to be a nice place, and after they were seated, ordered cocktails for both of them. She relaxed enough to smile at him, but he said abstractedly, "Excuse me for a minute, will you? I want to go and telephone. I'll have to get that kid traced, and I know of a man who I think can handle it."

He was back again before long, and proceeded to make himself very agreeable. He asked her all about herself, and said that he thought he might be able to help her to get a job.

After lunch they went back into the station for a last look around, and, unexpectedly, found Tim almost immediately. He was a beautifully dressed young man, with blue eyes and golden curls, and he said dramatically, "Ah! The rose! The red, red rose! You must be Mary's little Anne. But my dear girl! Where on earth have you been?"

Anne said, "Looking for you," and saw out of the corner of her eye that George's face was draped in a cold sneer.

Tim said, "We must have a drink or I shall collapse. I have been wander-

ing for hours in this jungle of plodding creatures. I simply cannot go on until
I have a drink."

Anne shrugged and glanced at George, who nodded briefly. "That'll be
all right. I'll get along to the office." He gave her the address of Mrs. Smith's
private guest house and also took down Mary's address on the back of an
envelope. "Just in case there should be a mix-up. But you will drop back
there this afternoon, won't you, and look in on Aunt Ellen? She'll be expecting you."

Anne nodded. "I'll do that, and then go to Mary's for dinner, and then go
back there again. But for heaven's sake try to find that girl so that I can settle
down."

"Yes, certainly," George said rather formally. "Good-by, and thank you."
He gave Tim the barest suggestion of a nod and took himself off.

Tim led Anne by the hand to the nearest bar, collapsed over a table, and
called loudly for two martinis.

"Oh no," Anne said instantly. "I don't like martinis."

"Of course you don't, my dear—nobody does in the beginning— they're
an acquired taste. But until you have acquired it, you are definitely missing
something. Now please explain everything—it's all been so confusing. That
rugged man, you know. Where on earth did you acquire him? I positively do
not trust rugged men who bring their Aunts Ellen into a conversation with a
pretty girl."

Anne tried patiently to explain the whole thing, but it soon became clear
that Tim was not the kind who listened to explanations. He kept interrupting,
and said at last, "Listen, honey—you don't have to explain anything to me.
But I do think it was mean of you to go horsing around with him, while I
wandered in limbo."

Anne couldn't help laughing, and he laughed with her. "My dear, I must
see a lot of you—I love you—actually. But you must learn to drink martinis
with me."

It presently developed that he had an appointment and had to fly. "But
I'll see you tonight, dear—definitely. Mary has a dinner planned—with two
men, you know—but I'm coming too. She'll be wild with me, but I don't
care—I'm coming anyway—because, as I said, I love you devotedly."

They went to get a taxi, and then found that they were going in different
directions and so had to take two cabs.

Anne leaned back against the seat and realized that she was exhausted. It
had all been so confusing and upsetting, but she'd stay in that room for a
while—at least until they got the girl back again. Perhaps it was just as well,
anyway—Mary's apartment was not large, and she had offered it as a temporary harbor until Anne could find somewhere to stay. Rooms were scarce,
and this was a nice room in an apparently decent place. Perhaps she could

keep it—only it might be too expensive, once she was required to pay for it.

The taxi stopped, and she got out and mounted the brownstone steps. As she went up the narrow stairs inside she realized that she was sleepy, and decided to take a nap before she unpacked completely. At the top of the stairs she remembered Aunt Ellen, and decided to look in on her first.

The nurse was not in the room, but the old lady was awake, and Anne went over to her. The dark eyes lighted up, and the feeble old voice said, "I've been waiting for you—I thought you'd never come. So long—it's been so long since I had my daughter with me. She ran away, and I wouldn't speak to her for all those years. She married that man, you see."

Anne, somewhat at a loss, nodded and smiled, and the clawlike little hand patted her own. The old lady continued to move her lips without actually saying anything more, and presently dropped off to sleep.

Anne removed herself quietly and headed for her room. "Now," she thought grimly, "I'm going to have a sleep—and to hell with unpacking anything first."

She walked into her room, and immediately a man emerged from the shadows against the wall. He moved around behind her, shut the door, and said, "Have you found out yet where it is?"

CHAPTER FOUR

THE MAN WAS small and dark, and his black patent-leather hair seemed to be lacquered to his scalp. A cigarette dangled from one corner of his mouth.

"Who are you?" Anne asked belligerently. "And what are you talking about?"

"Ahh, come on, Annie, don't waste my time. I'm Paul Depilriattia, and I'm in on this with you and Spike—as you know damn' good and well. I been in communication with Spike this morning, and he'll be here himself next week. I'm warnin' you, don't try to pull anything on your own, because I'll be right here beside you all the time. Now, have you found out where it is?"

Anne was frightened into silence for a moment, and then she said faintly, "No, I don't know what you're talking about. I'm not that girl—she—she ran off —"

Paul looked at her uncertainly for a moment, then said, "Ahh, nuts. Now, look, get going. The old dame is all set to tell you. For Crissake dig it out of her, and let's get the hell out of here." Anne nodded, unable to speak because her teeth were chattering. She opened the door for this Paul. He opened his mouth as if to say something more, then thought better of it and slid out.

She closed the door after him, and then dropped rather heavily into a chair. New York, she thought, was getting to be a bit too much for her. Evidently Anne Magraw was mixed up with a gang of crooks and had been sent up to act as the old lady's granddaughter—or perhaps she really was Aunt Ellen's granddaughter. At any rate, she was to discover the hiding place of some object of value, pick it up, and then make off in the company of Paul and Spike.

Anne stirred. She'd have to tell George as soon as possible. He was presumably at his office now, but she'd have to speak to him when he got back. She went to the bed and stretched out on it, but found that she was quite unable to sleep. She moved restlessly from side to side for a while, then got up and started to unpack her suitcase. She put her things away with a feeling that all this was only temporary—she couldn't stay here with a character like Paul living in the place. Well, George would know how to handle it, anyway.

She lay down on the bed again and lit a cigarette, trying to relax her tense nerves. She should never have involved herself in a situation like this, but after all, she had supposed, until the last minute, that George was the man Mary had sent to meet her.

She crushed out the cigarette, and after a few more restless turns went to sleep rather suddenly.

She woke up to find that it had grown dark outside and that her head was aching. She groped on the bedside table, where she eventually found a lamp, and switched it on. The face of the traveling clock, suddenly revealed in the light, sent her scrambling off the bed in a hurry. She was due at Mary's in ten minutes.

There was no connecting bath with her room, but she went to the washstand in the corner and was relieved to find that there was running hot and cold water. She dressed quickly, putting on a skirt and heavy jacket so that she would not need to wear the seal coat. The jacket would not be quite warm enough, but she was quite prepared to shiver, rather than wear that awful coat again.

She hurried out, and was dismayed to find that there was no way of locking her door. Probably no one locked his door in this cultured guest house—only, how did Paul get into such a place? She'd better see whether George had come home and tell him about Paul without delay.

She met a maid in the lower hall—uniformed and   untidy, who informed her that Mr. George was not expected home for dinner.

"He works too hard," the woman said mournfully, "but it just seems as though he won't give in. Something come up there at the office, and Mr. George, he'll stay there and see it through, if it's midnight. That's the way he is."

"Where is Mrs. Smith, Jr., then?"

"Eh?"

"Old Mrs. Smith's daughter-in-law."

"Ah, yes," said the maid. "We call her Mrs. J., that being her initial, and saving confusion with the old lady. Mrs. J. is in the kitchen doing something that she calls cooking, our cook having the night off, and no one brought in to take her place."

Anne held back a smile and said, "I'm sorry—then I won't bother her now." She turned and headed for the door, glancing into the large drawing room as she went, where a group of people appeared to be sitting around waiting for dinner.

She took a taxi to Mary's apartment, deciding uncomfortably that she would get in touch with George on her return.

Things were very gay and cheerful at Mary's apartment. Tim was there, and two other men whose last names she failed to get, but who answered readily to Ralph and Biffy. Mary was slim and smart in black, with carefully groomed hair and a touch of amethyst jewelry here and there.

Anne told them her story, raising her voice over Tim's many interruptions, and Mary said it was all very thrilling.

"It may sound that way," Anne demurred, "but I don't feel thrilled. In fact, I think I'm a bit scared."

"Oh, you mustn't be scared," Mary declared gaily. "Ralph will keep you out of trouble. If you land in jail, he'll get you out, won't you, Ralph?"

"Certainly will," Ralph agreed, grinning.

Anne laughed a little. "Let's forget it—I'd like to get it out of my mind for this evening at least."

"But the poor child is quite right," Tim cried. "There has been too much fuss and confusion. Come on, Precious, let's go into a dark corner and talk."

"Oh no, you don't," Mary said. "Ralph, Billy, and Anne are my guests, but you're merely a stray to whom I have kindly offered shelter. You're to keep in the background."

"But *darling*," Tim wailed, "wasn't I *trying* to get into the background? With Anne, of course."

There was a silver shaker of cocktails, and eventually dinner was served on a card table. Mary had done the cooking, but there was a maid to do the serving and the cleaning up afterward. Since the card table accommodated only four, Tim was made to eat at the coffee table.

"I don't know, Anne," Mary said after a while, "I think I'm a little uneasy about this thing, after all. Perhaps you'd better pack up and come over here. We can all go up and get your things, and bring them back. After all, we don't know anything about those people."

Anne glanced around the charming little room and realized that there was not much extra space. It had been kind of Mary to offer to share, but the chances were that they would both be uncomfortable.

She smiled and shook her head. "I'm all right, Mary. It's really a nice place, and you know how short rooms and apartments are. Probably I've been lucky enough to drop into a good thing— it's a private hotel. When the real granddaughter turns up, they can hardly refuse to give me a room, after all I've done for them, and, in the meantime, it's costing me nothing."

"Wonderful!" Tim observed from the coffee table. "I've been looking for a situation like that all my life."

"You'd run a mile if you ever found it," Mary declared. "I can hardly imagine you sitting with an invalid and holding her hand and smiling at the right times."

"It depends on the invalid," Tim said with dignity. "And I think it's simply *stinking* of you, Mary, to keep needling me."

"But the real granddaughter—" Ralph said doubtfully. "You said something about this fellow Paul, and Spike—and the girl seems to be in it—"

"Ralph's showing off," Tim said spitefully. "He's acting like a judge, just to prove that he's a lawyer."

"Perhaps that girl really is the granddaughter," Biffy suggested. "Might have got herself into the hands of crooks."

They had finished dinner, and Anne said, "I think I'd better phone George and tell him about this Paul fellow."

They had some trouble finding the number, but after going through a hundred Smiths in the telephone book they eventually located it and Anne put through her call. A woman answered—a hard nasal voice—and Anne asked for "George," because she could not remember his last name.

"Who?" the voice asked querulously.

"Well"—Anne hesitated—"this is Anne. I want the George who met me at the station this morning."

"Oh. Where are you?"

Anne explained where she was, and the woman then wanted to know when she was coming home.

"I really don't know," Anne said, beginning to be a bit annoyed.

"Does George know where you are?"

Anne reminded herself that the woman probably thought she was only thirteen and tried to control her annoyance.

"Yes," she said evenly, "I am with friends, and George knows all about it. May I speak to him, please?"

"Well, all right," the woman muttered reluctantly. "I'll see if I can find him."

Anne was presently relieved to hear George's voice against her ear, and she proceeded to tell him about Paul's visit to her room. She could not remember the man's last name, but said that it was something unpronounceable, and started with a D.

"Depilriattia?" George asked.

"Sounds like it."

"Repeat the whole thing and get it straight, will you?"

"I got it straight the first time," Anne said patiently, and went through it all again.

"I'll wait up for you," George decided. "Will you be home early?"

"You mean you hope I'll be home early."

"Well, answer anyway, will you? No matter what I mean."

"I don't expect to be late."

She put the phone down, and found Tim standing beside her.

"I'm frightfully jealous of George," he said darkly.

Anne swallowed a yawn. "George is jealous of you too."

"You're making fun of me," he said, looking sulky. "If that dour, rugged George has ever been jealous of anyone, he certainly never admitted it."

Mary was still a little doubtful about the whole situation and suggested again that they all go over and pick up Anne's things, but Anne brushed it aside.

Ralph proposed that they go somewhere and dance, but Mary decided against it. "Anne's had a long day, and she'd be too tired."

"Besides," Tim added, "I have to leave soon, and I couldn't come with you."

"We'd manage to bear up," Ralph said, and Biffy laughed loud and long.

Tim shrugged and murmured, "Canaille."

They decided on some bridge, and allowed Tim in first because he had to leave early. He became very serious over the cards, and moaned softly and continually at the things his partners did. Even his opponents came in for some of it. "Such bad defense," he muttered. "It confuses me—I can't place any of the cards." At the end of the rubber he suddenly looked at his watch and was out in an instant.

Biffy took his place, and Mary gave a little sigh. "Now we can enjoy the game, and have a little peace."

They played two more rubbers, and then Mary called a halt. "Anne must go to bed—I know she's tired, and I have to get up early myself."

The two men took Anne home in a cab, and Ralph saw her to the door. She had no key, but tried the door before ringing and found that it was open. She went in, wondering if they ever locked it, and found George sitting on a chair at the foot of the stairs. He was sound asleep.

Anne closed the door firmly, and he woke up with a start. He went over, and locked the door, and then handed her a key.

"Front door—for when you come in late. Now come in here, and tell me again what's been going on."

He led her into a small office that opened off the hall, and questioned her closely about the man Paul, and then about Miss Magraw. Anne answered patiently, and after a while he told her that she'd better go to bed, but asked her if she would look in on Aunt Ellen first.

He went upstairs with her and went into Aunt Ellen's room first to see if she were awake. She was, and smiled happily and eagerly at Anne. "You're just like Missy, child."

Anne murmured to her and kissed her, then said good night to Miss Kalms, who had gone to bed in a cot at one side of the room.

George had disappeared, and the hall was deserted and only dimly lighted. Anne went into her room, which was in complete darkness, and began to grope for a switch. She could not find one, and remembered at last that there was a lamp on the bedside table and a ceiling light with a dangling cord.

She moved into the center of the room and raised her arm, feeling for the cord, and touched instead a cold, inert hand.

CHAPTER FIVE

ANNE LEAPED BACK, stumbled over something, and scrambled frantically toward the door. She wrenched it open, and in the dimly lighted hall stood panting for a moment while her heart thudded uncomfortably. Once she called "George," in a thin quaver, and wondered why she was unable to yell it at the top of her lungs.

She presently thought of Miss Kalms, and after a moment's indecision went into Aunt Ellen's room without waiting to knock. Miss Kalms was in a peaceful sleep, and was very unwilling to be aroused out of it.

"Oh, Lord," she moaned, "isn't it enough that I'm up half the night for my patient, without people trying to make an information booth out of me? George's room is on the next floor, first to the right. I should think you'd be ashamed to ask me, anyway. If he'd wanted you to come, he'd have told you where it was himself."

"Please!" Anne said desperately. "You don't understand—it's not that at all. There's some awful thing in my room—"

But Miss Kalms evidently had her own ideas and intended to stick to them, and Anne left her without any further explanation. She hurried up to the next floor and knocked on the first door to the right, at the same time calling George's name softly.

There was no response, and she knocked again more loudly. She thought she heard some sort of movement inside and waited, biting a few nails indiscriminately. Then the door was flung open, and it was not George. She was confronted by an elderly man with gray hair and a gray mustache, who stared at her in astonishment.

"Where's George?" Anne asked helplessly. "I—there's some trouble downstairs. I thought this was his room."

"What is it?" the man asked. "What's the trouble?"

A woman's voice from the dark room behind him called, "What is it, Roger?"

"Please!" Anne whispered. "I must get George."

Roger did not bother to answer the woman, but came out into the hall and banged on the next door. "George!" he called. "You're wanted out here." He turned, then, and looked at Anne. "Why George, young lady? Wouldn't I do?" After which he roared with laughter, and someone across the hall opened the door a crack and peered out.

George emerged, wearing a pale yellow dressing robe trimmed in cerise, and Anne thought vaguely that it would be a perfect garment for Tim. But she brushed the thought away immediately and said, "You must come downstairs—quickly. There's something hanging from the chandelier in my room."

George gave her a puzzled frown, and Roger murmured, "Maybe it's the light."

They went down with her—George going first, and Roger close behind him—and two women in dressing gowns and slippers came to the landing and looked curiously down over the railing. One had come from Roger's room and was presumably his wife. The other one was the one who had peered out of her door. They appeared to be pleasantly excited.

At the door of her room Anne hung back, and said nervously, "You go in—I went to pull the light cord, and I—I touched a cold hand instead."

Both George and Roger looked at her oddly and then turned and entered the room together. The next moment it was flooded with light, and Anne moved forward and looked in fearfully. The two men stood in the center, under the light. The chandelier was where she had thought it was, with a dangling cord, but there was no hand attached to it. The room seemed to be perfectly normal in every respect. She went in, and while they watched her, she made a thorough search, under the bed, in the closet, and even in the various drawers. She opened the window and looked out, but there was no fire escape—nothing close by.

She closed the window and faced them a little defiantly.

"I suppose someone was playing a practical joke on me—but when I reached up to pull the light on, I touched a cold hand instead."

Roger fingered his gray mustache and continued to regard her in silence, while George shook his head. "Too much party, I'm afraid."

"If you call a few rubbers of bridge too much party, then that was it," Anne said furiously. "Look, I want a key for this room. Every time I go out of it, someone comes in."

Roger laughed and poked George in the ribs, and George showed very plainly that he did not like being poked in the ribs.

Roger didn't notice it. "Get the young lady a key, George," he boomed.

George nodded. "I'll get one for you tomorrow. In the meantime, you can bolt the door on the inside, can't you?" He went over to examine it without waiting for an answer, and presently nodded his head. "Yes, it's working all right."

"Never needed one myself," Roger observed. "Lived in the house here for twenty years, and not once did I lock m' door."

"Will you be all right now?" George asked.

Anne nodded. "I'll be all right. I'll bolt the door."

Roger bowed and said a flowery good night. When they had gone, Anne bolted the door behind them. She switched on the bedside lamp and turned off the chandelier, then stood for a while with her head thrown back, looking up at it. It was, in keeping with the past splendors of the room, rather an ornate affair. The ceiling was patterned with scrollwork, but the design was off center, and she realized, after a moment, that the room had originally been much larger and had since been partitioned. Probably it had been a drawing room—they used sometimes to have drawing rooms on the second floor.

She got into bed, but her eyes returned to the chandelier. The cord was an exceptionally heavy one, capable she thought, of supporting a body. The idea made her shudder, and she closed her eyes for a moment. She had felt that hand—there was no mistake about it. A big hand—a man's hand—and it was about where it would be if a man were hanging from the chandelier, because the ceiling was high. A dead man hanging from the chandelier—it had been a dead hand.

She got quickly out of bed and began to move restlessly around the room, until fatigue sent her back to bed once more. Then she lit a cigarette, and stared at the chandelier again. There was a curving bracket with several sockets, but there were only two bulbs—the usual private hotel economy. Above the bracket she could see a bar—a strong-looking bar. A man could hang from that bar and it would support his weight.

She shivered, although the room was warm—too warm, even with the window open. A hotel like this would be full of elderly people, and they always liked a lot of heat. They wouldn't stay if you didn't keep them warm.

She put out her cigarette, switched off the light, and settled onto her pillow. She must get her mind off the chandelier and put it on trifles—and keep it there.

She did sleep, although she dreamed wildly and awoke several times. As soon as dawn broke, she went into a deep sleep, and was only dragged out of it at eight o'clock by a persistent knocking on her door. It was Miss Kalms, and, apologetically, she wanted Anne to come to her patient.

"She's been hollering all morning for you, but I waited until now so you could get a little sleep."

Anne groaned and struggled into a rope and slippers. She washed her face with cold water, ran a comb through her hair, and sleepily followed Miss Kalms across the hall. Just outside Aunt Ellen's door Miss Kalms stopped and faced her.

"Say, listen, would you mind staying with her while I have a decent breakfast in peace for once?"

Anne shrugged. "All right, but is anything likely to happen? I wouldn't know what to do."

"Oh, nothing will happen," Miss Kalms assured her. "You can always call me if she turns blue around the gills. Gee, thanks. I'll bring you up a nice breakfast when I come. See, breakfast'll be over by then."

She hurried off downstairs, and Anne went into Aunt Ellen's room.

The old lady was sitting up against her pillows looking brushed and clean, but the lively dark eyes snapped angrily as Anne approached. "I don't want any."

Anne took the little hand and sat on a chair beside the bed. "What don't you want, Grandma?"

"It's no use," Grandma said in a warning voice, "because I can't eat it." She closed her mouth tightly.

Anne smiled at her. "All right, you don't have to eat it, Granny."

Grandma turned her little head and gave Anne a piercing look through narrowed eyes. "You get out of here," she said, "and send my little granddaughter in, little Annie."

Anne sighed, got up, and left the room. In the hall outside she pulled her hair around her face and turned her robe inside out, so that it was pink satin, instead of a dark wine color. She then went back into the room, over to the bed, and leaned down and kissed Mrs. Smith on her dry old forehead. "Hello, Grandma. I'm your little Annie."

For a moment Grandma remained quiet, her dark eyes still full of suspicion, and then, suddenly, she raised her arms to Anne, her mouth making little kissing sounds.

Anne sat beside her and tried to talk, but the old lady didn't listen much. She did most of the talking herself, and a great deal of it was an unintelligible mumble, although occasionally she became quite clear. Once she said, "I would tell you, but not with him standing there."

Anne looked over her shoulder, but there was no one in the room, although Grandma was shaking her fist.

"I don't want him to hear," she said querulously. "He's always poking in here."

"I'll send him out," Anne said soothingly.

"Don't bother—he'll only come back. But lean close, and I'll whisper."

Anne rested an arm on the bed, lowered her head, and Grandma whispered vigorously for some time, while Anne nodded wisely, although she could not understand a word.

Grandma settled back into her pillows and said in a slightly louder whisper, "You'll have to go up for it, of course." She glanced over Anne's shoulder, and her eyes snapped with sudden fury. "Get out!" she cried shrilly.

Anne turned around and drew in her breath sharply. There was a man standing behind her—short, gray-haired, and dour.

He said quietly, "Where's Paul?"

CHAPTER SIX

ANNE GOT SLOWLY to her feet. Grandma was mumbling excitedly, and the man stood silent, his hands in the pockets of his coat. He must be another crook—mixed up in some way with the unpleasant Paul person. He moved closer, and Anne found that she was shaking a little.

"I don't know where he is," she said clearly. "I saw him only once."

The gray-haired man said, "He's missing. I spoke to him on the phone yesterday and then I came on by plane. What sort of a deal did you make with Anne Magraw?"

"Don't go away," Grandma cried fretfully. "I want to talk to you. Don't go. Missy was like that—always running away."

The man stepped back and made a sign to Anne to sit down by the bed again, but she did not move.

"Look," she said quietly, "I made no deal with that girl. But she stole my coat, and I should like to have it back. And I'd like to know who you are."

There was no change in the expression of his face. His eyes still held the faint annoyance which had been there when she first looked at him, but there was nothing more. He said, "You don't know me, so there's no necessity for you to have my name. What happened to Paul? I know he contacted you."

Anne gave him a level look. "Yes, he did, and I gather that the two of you are after something belonging to the old lady."

The old lady gave voice at this point and said quite clearly, "Come closer, dear, while I tell you."

The man withdrew farther and urgently motioned Anne toward the bed. She turned around, patted one of the thin little hands, and said, "I have to go now, darling, but I'll be back soon."

She left the bed and went to the door—only to discover that the man had moved over so that he stood between it and herself.

"Where's Anne? What happened to her?"

Anne, a little frightened again, wished that Miss Kalms would come back.

"I don't know," she said, frowning at him. "She left her coat and took mine, and got off at Philadelphia with some man. Owing to the switch of coats, I landed up here by mistake. But I wish you'd find her, that is, if she really is old Mrs. Smith's granddaughter."

The man nodded. "She is, and I'll find her as soon as I can. Now, where's Paul?"

"I have already told you that I don't know, and as a matter of fact I don't care, either. Will you let me get to the door, please?"

The man was silent for a moment, and when he spoke there was a slightly easier note in his voice. "I'm Spike Magraw, Anne's uncle, and of course I'll have to find her. But we want a little miniature of Anne's mother, Missy. Anne's father is very ill, and he's set his heart on having it. Old Mrs. Smith promised to tell Anne where it was, and to let her have it. But, as you could see, the kid is flighty, and Paul was supposed to look after her while she was here. If the old lady happened to tell you where it is, or to give it to you, we'd be grateful if you'd keep it for Anne, so that she can take it back to her father. It's in a small bag."

Anne said, "Of course," and started to walk around him, but he laid a hand on her arm.

"I'll be around," he said softly, "waiting for it. So be sure and keep it for me until I contact you again."

"I've said I would, but don't you want to speak to George?"

"No," he said, with a completely expressionless face, "I don't want to speak to George."

"I think George would like to speak to you."

"Life," he said, "is full of disappointments, and George will have to take his share."

He turned abruptly and left the room, and by the time Anne had followed him into the hall, he was nowhere in sight.

"Probably sitting in my room," she muttered impatiently, and went across to see. But Spike was not there, and since Miss Kalms had left her in charge of Grandma, she decided that she'd better go back.

Grandma was talking in a lively fashion although there was no one else in the room, and as Anne approached the bed she said, "I told him—I said, 'Shut up, or get out.' Always talking, you know—never gives anyone else a chance—listening at doors—always knows everything that is going on. I'll tell him again, next time he comes in here."

Anne sat down by the bed, and Grandma went off into a low mumble which, though unintelligible, was still a little indignant. Anne thought of Spike, and wondered uneasily whether she should have tried to follow him—only he had disappeared so quickly. She must tell George about it without delay, but she wasn't dressed, and, anyway, it was probable that George had already left for his office.

Grandma drifted off to sleep after a while, and she took the opportunity to hurry over to her room and get dressed. It did not take her long, and Grandma was still asleep when she got back, but Miss Kalms had returned.

She gave Anne a look of reproach. "I thought you said you'd stay with her."

"I did, until she fell asleep, and then I went over to get dressed. Where's that breakfast you promised me?"

"They're going to serve you downstairs—said it would be easier than lugging up a tray. The dining room is closed, but just go in, anyway."

"Where is the dining room?"

"First floor, straight down the hall at the back."

Anne went down and found the daughter-in-law, Mrs. J. V. Smith, waiting for her at the foot of the stairs. She looked neat and tidy, but a bit overdone. Each permanented and blended curl was in its right place and the makeup had been carefully applied, but with too lavish a hand. She was dressed plainly, with a suggestion of smartness.

She smiled at Anne and said, "I'm sorry I couldn't greet you yesterday, but I was busy as the devil. Since Granny's been ill I haven't had a minute for anything. But come and have some breakfast. George told me all about you this morning and, my dear, I think it's just lovely of you to do this for us."

Anne smiled and murmured, and then asked if the real Anne had been located yet.

Mrs. Smith frowned and shook her head in a bothered way. "George got in touch with the police, and they're supposed to be trying to trace her. I expect she'll turn up sometime, but I think it was real mean of her. It meant everything to Granny to see her—and she knew it. Honestly—these young things!"

They went back to the dining room, which was small and gloomy, not nearly so light or cheerful as the drawing room, or lounge, at the front of the house. It was necessary to have the lights on even at this time in the morning, and the half-dozen small tables were so close together that they had a crowded look. A man was seated at one of the tables, reading a newspaper, but he did not look up or take any notice of them as they came in.

Anne sat down, and Mrs. Smith went to the swinging door and called for Ginny, who proved to be the untidy maid to whom Anne had spoken on the previous evening. She had a big nose and straight bobbed hair that had a way of straying across her face. She gave Anne a cheerful grin and said, "Good morning, miss. What would you like to have, in case we got it, which I doubt?"

Anne gave a modest order and Mrs. Smith, who had sat down beside her, frowned at Ginny and said, "Hurry it up. Miss Hillyer must be hungry."

Ginny departed, and Mrs. Smith sighed. "She's good, as a matter of fact. But you wouldn't know it, the way she looks. And she talks too much."

Anne nodded absently and, after a moment, said, "I'm a little confused—naturally enough, I suppose. Now, that Paul, whatever his name is—"

"Oh, him." Mrs. Smith shrugged. "That was sort of peculiar. George told me about it. Looks fishy, don't it? But, see, we don't know the Magraws at all and George thinks maybe this Anne who got off at Philadelphia was an impostor. It's like this—Granny's daughter, Missy, ran away and married this Magraw that Granny never liked for a cent. Granny's a tough old bird, and she never spoke to Missy again. But now, since she was ill, she got this idea that she wanted to see Missy and forgive her. It wasn't easy to track her down, but, finally, we found out that Missy was dead and had left this daughter and that Magraw was still alive. But he was an invalid in some sort of home. When we told Granny nothing would do but we must get hold of the daughter and bring her here. That wasn't so easy, either, because she'd been living around with Magraw relatives. But George handled it—all by long distance—and we sent money for the girl's trip here. Another thing—Granny insisted that the girl must wear her old sealskin coat. The coat really belonged to Granny, but Missy took it when she ran away. It wasn't even in style then, but Granny told her she could have it. Only, if you ask me, I think Missy simply wanted something warm—and that was the warmest coat in the house. Granny, you know, is as tight as the paper on the wall, and always has been."

Mrs. Smith laughed and then shook her head. "Anyway, the coat turned out convenient, after all, because it was the only way we had to identify the girl."

Anne, eating her breakfast, and listening to Mrs. Smith, suddenly found that her attention had wandered. She had cast an absent eye on the man across the room from time to time, but as Mrs. Smith's narrative neared its end her gaze fastened on him and stayed there.

She had been so sure about that hand last night—a man's hand—cold and dead—and this morning she had almost succeeded in convincing herself that it was all imagination. But that man over there—still reading his paper and sipping coffee—that man had only one hand. The other was a hook.

CHAPTER SEVEN

IT WAS WONDERFUL, Anne thought, how well he managed the hook. There was no fumbling or hesitation in his movements as he read his paper and sipped his coffee. She watched him in fascination until Mrs. Smith, suddenly conscious of her abstraction, lowered her voice and said, "Don't let him see you looking at it—he's very sensitive about it."

Anne turned her eyes away at once, and Mrs. Smith went on, "He's always been very vain about his appearance, and when he lost his hand in an accident, he had one made—paid a fortune for it—and you honestly couldn't tell the difference from a real one. You could even shake it and you wouldn't know. But it was sort of more ornamental than useful, I guess, so now he only uses it for his professional appearances. See, he's an actor."

Anne nodded, and felt comprehension and relief seeping through her. Some practical joker had tied that artificial hand to her chandelier, then removed it before there could be any trouble. It must have been that way.

"Well—" Mrs. Smith sighed, and touched her curls with a careful hand. "I'd better get started. There's always so much to do in a place like this."

"Wait," Anne said quickly, and added, "That Paul man. Has George spoken to him yet?"

Mrs. Smith frowned and shook her head. "He wasn't around this morning. George went to his room quite early, but he wasn't there, so of course George has to take it out on me. Wants to know why I rented the room to such a character, especially now, when you can take your pick of guests instead of them taking their pick of hotels. George finally got it out of me—and he was furious—that the creature paid double in advance for the room. It meant a little extra money for me and God knows I need it. But of course that didn't cut any ice with George."

Anne thought of Spike and wondered whether she ought to mention him. In the end she went at it obliquely. "Who's the short man with a lot of gray hair and a sort of sinister expression?"

Mrs. Smith gave her a blank look. "Nobody like that around. Old Roger has a bit of gray hair left—some of it on his upper lip—but he's a big man, and you couldn't call him sinister any more than a babe in arms." She indicated the man who still sat reading the paper and lowered her voice. "Mr. Courtney there has plenty of gray hair—or maybe even white—but he keeps it dyed, so you'd never know it."

Anne stood up, lit a cigarette, and they began to move toward the hall. "I thought the dining room was closed," she whispered.

Mrs. Smith nodded. "So it is, but he likes to sit there and drink extra coffee and read every word in the paper. We're used to him now, and Ginny just clears up all around him." She began to move more rapidly as they approached the front hall and said, "Honest, I've got to go now—I'm late starting and I'll be flying all morning. Do whatever you want to, but please look in on Granny once in a while, she's so pleased with you, and it doesn't really matter that you're not her granddaughter, because she hasn't long to live, poor old thing."

She disappeared into the lounge, and Anne walked on to the foot of the stairs, where she came upon a man who held his expensive and tasteful hat in his hand while he surveyed his exquisitely dressed body in a mirror. He turned as she came up behind him, and she saw that it was Tim.

"Darling!" he exclaimed. "I was just wondering how on *earth* I could find you in this dismal place! I came to take you out to lunch."

Anne laughed. "I've just had breakfast."

"Well, naturally, you'd hardly have it any earlier. But you're so divinely slim that you can eat lunch as well. And of course we must have something to drink."

"All right," she agreed, in some amusement, "but I have some things to do first. I'll have to get around to some of these places and look for a job, and I want to send a telegram to say that I arrived safely. I must get a new coat too. I can't go around wearing that awful thing."

"Wonderful!" Tim cried. "I shall go with you, and we'll get the coat first. I'd love to help you buy a coat. Let's see, I should think a long, dark green—"

"Oh no," Anne said firmly. "Green won't do because it won't go with things, and it can't be too long or I'll be tripping over it."

"My dear, we can argue all that out later. Go and get some sort of a wrap—it's cold today—but do avoid the black seal, that fatal coat."

"I'll have to wear it," she said, starting up the stairs. "It's all I have. I can't simply freeze."

"Ah well," he called after her, "I suppose worse things have happened. But we shall buy the coat first."

Anne looked in on Grandma before she left and found her peacefully sleeping. There was an elderly woman sitting beside the bed—a rather horse-faced individual—and Miss Kalms introduced her casually, "Anne, this is Miss Burreton."

Anne thought her status as Miss Hillyer had been dropped rather abruptly, but she nodded amiably, and Miss Burreton gave her a pleasant smile. "You don't look much like Missy."

Anne murmured politely, and wondered whether she ought to tell why it was that she didn't look like Missy. Apparently the situation had not been generally explained, and it bothered her a little. She decided to let it go for the present and talk it over with George later, since she had to see him about Spike in any case. She was decidedly troubled about Spike.

She shrugged into the black coat and went downstairs to where Tim waited, his eyes once more on the mirror. He grinned at her, unabashed, and said, "There was simply nothing else to do, so I was making a critical survey."

It developed that he had a car outside—a long, shining thing that made Anne draw in her breath.

"Rich father?" she asked, raising her eyebrows.

Tim looked stunned for a moment. Then he tossed his head. "My father was a butcher," he said defiantly. "He wanted me to follow in his footsteps actually, and if you think I verge a little on the flossy at this point in my life, you must realize that it is reaction from the brutality of the butcher shop."

Anne laughed, but as the car swung away from the curb under Tim's skillful guidance he remained deadly serious. "My father lost two fingers and all his hair in the line of duty, but he claimed that his career had been worth it." He shuddered, and managed to insert a cigarette into a long holder and light it, without disturbing his driving in any way.

He took her to one of the best shops for the coat, but as soon as the elegant attendant could be induced to mention anything so crass as a price, Anne realized that she was in the wrong place. She told Tim so quite frankly.

"You'll have to take me to a basement somewhere. I'm just starting out, you know."

Tim sighed. "Yes, my dear, although I've always found that it was better to start at the top and work down. However—"

He took her to a popular-priced place and worked long and hard before he selected a coat that he thought would do.

"Of course you realize, dear, that it's just a pinch hit until you're on your feet."

Anne bought it. She liked it after she had put it on, although she would never have picked it out in the first place. She wanted to wear it and leave the black coat to be sent, but Tim wouldn't hear of it. There were a few alterations that were absolutely necessary, he insisted, although neither Anne nor the saleswoman could see it. However, Tim was adamant, and had his way in the end.

Anne resumed the black seal rather sulkily, and complained of both its looks and its weight on her slim shoulders.

"Far better to put up with it for a day or so," Tim said firmly, "and have the new one right. Good God!" he added petulantly. "People walk out of shops in garments fitting like gunny sacks, and then wonder why chic is an elusive quality. But don't get me started. Now, we must have some lunch and a martini or two."

"I don't like martinis." Anne sighed.

"You must—you will—at this place."

He took her to a small—almost dainty—place, and in short order Anne found herself sipping a martini. She made a face after each sip and presently observed, "You're a stubborn mule."

"Yes, of course. But tell me, how are you doing in the role of grand-daughter? And what of the mysterious Paul? I was thinking about it last night."

"Well"—Anne shrugged—"Paul seems to have disappeared, but Spike has turned up just to keep things lively."

"Spike!" Tim exclaimed. "But this is thrilling! You must tell me every-thing—everything that has happened—including the smallest detail."

Anne was a bit bored, but she told him, although it took rather a long time, because he kept interrupting with exclamations and questions. When she had concluded, he sat staring at the opposite wall for so long that she finished her martini—making the usual face—and tackled a roll and butter that had appeared.

"The miniature," Tim said after a while. "That must be wrong. Can you imagine a venomous individual like Spike taking a plane simply to pick up a miniature for his sick brother?"

"Why not? And I don't remember calling him venomous."

"He sounds venomous—and don't try to confuse me. Oh no, those people are crooks, and if George, that sound and rugged businessman, had any sense, he'd get the police in."

"Give him a chance," Anne said tolerantly. "I haven't told him about Spike yet."

"Why not?"

"Because he left for his office before I could get to him."

"Of course. These conscientious business executives—a plague on them."

He retreated into deep thought again, and Anne started to eat her lunch with tranquil enjoyment.

Tim emerged to observe briefly, "Poor Paul."

"Why?"

"Disappeared into the unknown. Sinister."

"Off on business maybe," Anne suggested carelessly.

"Darling, do try not to be silly. Paul's business was to watch you. This Magraw child was not dependable, and so Spike sent one of his crooks to New York to see that she arrived and went about her business. No doubt Spike had duties that kept him at home—a bank to be robbed perhaps. In any case, Paul's job was to watch over the Magraw—and then you turn up, a self-proclaimed impostor. Paul telephoned the bad news, and Spike has to drop his bank robbery and come steaming down here, which is odd, because you wouldn't think it was that important. Although possibly he thought the plane ride would do him good. And then the girl—Ah yes, the girl—A relative perhaps. His daughter, not his girlfriend? Some child that he more or less brought up? So she is missing, and he is concerned and comes on to find her. More trouble—Paul is also missing. He comes across you in the sickroom, places you, in his clever way, and spins the yarn about the miniature. I do not swallow the miniature—I gag on it. There could hardly be room in it for anything valuable enough to draw both Spike and Paul away from important bank robberies."

"So?" Anne asked.

"So I shed a silent tear for poor Paul, lying dead in some dark corner."

CHAPTER EIGHT

ANNE MADE A STARTLED motion that almost tipped over Tim's martini. The natural reaction was irritation, and she asked crossly, "What nonsense are you drooling about now?"

He finished the endangered martini in a hurry and gave her an odd smile. "Nothing, my dear, nothing. No doubt Grandma is without valuables of any sort and merely hints at their existence to give herself prestige. It has been done before."

"Sounds more like it," Anne agreed.

"Yes. And that hand hanging in your room was a practical joke. Spike is really Anne Magraw's uncle, and Anne Magraw is really Grandma's long-lost relative. Spike is a little shady—early childhood association, no doubt—and does not entirely trust his niece. So he sent Paul on to watch her, thinking that there might be something in it. But Paul, the rotter, has gone off on a bender and is not doing his duty."

"Well, what's wrong with that?" Anne asked warily.

Tim gave her another odd look. "Why was an obvious mug like Paul allowed into the refined doss house?"

"Mrs. Smith did it, and George has already spoken severely to her about it."

"Oh." Tim devoted himself to his lunch for a while before asking, "How is it that George cracks the whip about the running of the place? Isn't that entirely up to Mrs. Smith now that Granny is bedridden?"

"Well"—Anne shrugged—"I understand that George is a lawyer and handles the financial affairs of the house."

Tim nodded. "And under the heading of financial oversight he tells them all what to do, pointing out cobwebs and dust behind the radiators, etcetera."

"Don't be catty," Anne said amiably.

"I must. It seems incredible that you could fall for a man whose shirt is stuffed with prunes and ethics—but you just might."

Anne picked up the menu and ran her eyes over it in search of a dessert. "You ought to be a bit more careful. You're implying that you want me all to yourself, and I'm only an innocent girl from a small town. I might take you seriously."

Tim smiled delightedly. "Darling, I know—I never would have believed it of myself. That I should be absolutely enchanted with a rustic from the sticks! Impossible, surely."

"Absurd," agreed Anne, who was slightly offended. "Who are you anyway?"

"The butcher's son," Tim said, and chuckled.

The afternoon was gone before Anne could get anything done. Tim insisted upon taking her to a couple of places, one of which proved to be an art exhibition. Anne looked carefully at the paintings, but found she couldn't understand any of them.

"Do you think I could run up one of those things and get away with it?" she asked in an undertone.

"Don't be ridiculous, darling," Tim said, looking deadly serious. "This sort of thing takes years of study—and, even more important, complete understanding."

"Oh? Understanding of what?"

"Just understanding," Tim said airily.

They had to have more martinis after that, and then Tim drove her back to the brownstone, expressing the deepest regrets that he would be unable to dine with her.

"Quite all right," Anne said. "I really should keep George company in the hotel dining room tonight."

Tim shut his eyes for a moment of pain. "Precious, how can you call this mournful place a hotel?"

"Who says it isn't?"

"I say it isn't, and, darling, I am so right about so many things."

He escorted her up the front steps, then went inside with her, although Anne told him that he'd better hurry away since he was parked beside a hydrant.

"It's the only place you can park these days, dear," Tim explained. "And anyway, I must speak to Mrs. Smith."

"Here I am," Mrs. Smith called graciously, and emerged from the back hall.

"How nice," Tim said, "that I no sooner speak of my need for you than here you are. Now, I understand that you have a vacant room which I would like to rent."

Anne looked at him in astonishment, and Mrs. Smith said regretfully, "Why, no, I really haven't. I wish I had—I can see you and Anne are good friends."

"But you have," Tim insisted. "That Paul—nobody seems to know his last name, which is perhaps just as well—he has left."

"Well," Mrs. Smith said doubtfully, "he's away, but he'll surely return."

Tim shook his head. "I think not, and I should like to have this room."

Anne shivered, and Mrs. Smith asked, "Do you know where he is, by any chance?"

"Not exactly," Tim admitted, "but I do know that he's not coming back. In any case, you have my solemn promise that I shall leave immediately should he ever return."

Mrs. Smith needed a little more coaxing, and Tim gave it to her deftly. Finally she agreed to store Paul's things and have the room ready for Tim later that night. Even after that, she was inclined to murmur doubtfully, "It's very irregular, but since you say you know him, and he won't be back—"

When she had left, Anne turned on Tim at once.

"Are you quite mad? What on earth do you want that room for?"

"So that I shall be here, on the premises, and can keep my end up against that earthy brute, George."

Anne laughed grimly. "You'll have to think of a better one than that."

"My dear, I can't—and, anyway, I think that's a very good one."

He went off, laughing, and Anne watched him, shaking her head a little. As a matter of fact, she thought, he really was a lot of fun—but she couldn't quite make out what he was up to. She didn't believe in his declared infatuation for her—he was not that susceptible, she felt sure. Perhaps, since he seemed to work at odd hours, he merely wanted some company during the day.

She turned to find George beside her, watching Tim's departing car.

"Nice job," he murmured.

"Tim or the car?"

"Strictly the car," said George. "What does that lace valentine do that he can run such a luxury item?"

Anne shrugged and said that she had no idea.

"But he seems to be a close friend of yours."

"Oh no, my friend Mary knows him, but I never saw him before yesterday. He hints that I have ensnared him."

"Very natural," George said politely.

Anne grinned at him. "Have they found Anne Magraw yet?"

George shook his head. "So far they haven't been able to trace her. Why? Are you getting tired of staying here?"

"Oh no," Anne said hastily. "In fact, when you no longer need me for Mrs. Smith, I'd like to rent a room and stay on. It's just that I don't like being mixed up with Paul and Spike."

"You haven't seen Paul again?"

"No, but Spike dropped in this morning, and he's even more sinister than Paul."

"You'd better tell me all about it," George said, and led her into the small office.

Anne told him the whole story, and after he had questioned her for a while he sat back and rumpled his hair abstractedly.

"I don't get it," he muttered. "I never heard of any miniature, and certainly I never heard of Magraw having a brother by the name of Spike."

"Spike may be just a nickname," Anne suggested. "Perhaps his real name is something ordinary, like George, or—"

"I have never," said George rather coldly, "heard of Magraw having any sort of a brother." He stood up abruptly. "Well, it looks as though a bunch of crooks has moved in on us. I don't know whether to go to the police or not, although there isn't much that I could tell them at this stage—particularly since neither one of them seems to be around. I think I'll go upstairs and see whether Paul has returned."

Anne followed him up and went into her own room as he walked down the hall toward Paul's room. She paused, with her door half open, and watched him. She saw him start talking to someone within the room in an angry manner and decided that he had found Mrs. Smith and Ginny in there, cleaning up for Tim. Certainly, she thought, they were being a bit precipitate, since Paul had been missing for only a day. She wondered whether he had taken his things or had left them there.

She removed the black coat, which was so heavy that it made her shoulders ache, and hung it away. It was a gruesome garment, she thought wryly, but at least it was warm. She combed her hair and washed her hands, then went in to see Grandma. In the doorway she almost collided with Miss Burreton, who was also going in. Miss Burreton gave her an indignant look, and Anne murmured, "Excuse me."

They stumbled into the room together, and Miss Kalms said cheerily to Anne, "Oh, there you are." She ignored Miss Burreton, who scuttled around to the bedside and sat down.

Miss Kalms gave Anne a brilliant smile. "My dear, I wonder if you'd keep an eye on things here while I go down and have my dinner. Of course I could bring it up here, as usual, if you're going to be busy with something else."

Anne was irritated, but could not smother a feeling of pity for Miss Kalms. She sighed inwardly, put on a false smile, and said, "Certainly."

Miss Kalms flew off at once, and Anne turned to find Miss Burreton regarding her with deadly intensity.

"I think you should know that she's just had her usual four hours off duty. She always tries to make it sound as though she were cooped up here all day."

"Oh well"—Anne shrugged—"I don't mind."

Miss Burreton compressed her lips and observed that the days of real conscientious nursing had passed.

Grandma said, "Burry, I don't like it when night comes, because I'm all alone. I'm all alone, you know, and I'm frightened." She began to cry quietly, the tears slipping over her wrinkled old cheeks.

Miss Burreton patted her hand and said soothingly, "We'll see that she stays with you—we won't let her leave you alone like that. It's downright wicked of her."

Anne moved over to the bed and asked gently, "Can't you sleep at night, Grandma?"

Grandma caught her hand and fondled it. After a moment she looked up and said, "I'm afraid of him. He's a ghost, and he searches through all my drawers."

CHAPTER NINE

ANNE CAUGHT HER BREATH and looked quickly at Miss Burreton, but Miss Burreton remained calm. She said soothingly, "Come now, Ellen, you've been imagining things. There's no one like that around here.'

"You're not alone, Grandma," Anne reminded her. "Miss Kalms is with you all night."

Grandma gave a snort, and in a voice of utter scorn said, "That one! Runs off as soon as it's dark." She muttered for a moments and then added, "You get out, Burry. I want to talk to my granddaughter."

Miss Burreton settled herself more comfortably into her chair and observed serenely, "I just came."

"Well, you come too often."

Miss Burreton chewed her cud peacefully. "I don't either come too often. I know my duty, and I do it."

"You talk to your friend, Grandma," Anne said. "I'm going to be here for quite a while, you know, and you can see me any time you like."

Grandma looked stubborn. She said, "I don't much want to talk now," and closed her eyes to prove it.

Miss Burreton hitched her chair a little closer to the bed. "Did you know that Liz Sampson is after a new man?"

Grandma's eyes flew open. "That one!"

Miss Burreton nodded. "It's Roger now—she doesn't give the man a minute's peace—and of course Roger's wife might as well be invisible. You know how Liz is. Remember when she took Dick right out from under your nose?"

Grandma didn't seem to notice this last remark. She muttered, "Liz Sampson, Liz Sampson, Liz Sampson."

Anne went out quietly and slipped across to her own room. She washed, changed her dress, and freshened up her appearance, then sat down for a hasty cigarette.

When she returned to Grandma's room she found that Miss Burreton had departed and the old lady was asleep. George stood by the bed looking down, but he glanced around as Anne came in.

"She looks better today, don't you think?"

Anne nodded with reserve, since she was convinced that Grandma would never be well again.

George sighed, then turned away from the bed abruptly. "I can't find the slightest trace of that man Spike. He doesn't live here, and no one seems to have seen him but you."

"I suppose you think I just imagined him," Anne said resentfully.

"Not at all. I merely say that it's puzzling."

Grandma, who had appeared to be asleep, opened her eyes, gave George a sweet smile, and closed them again.

Mrs. Smith, standing outside in the hall with her ear against the door, decided that there was nothing worth listening to and moved away. She glanced at her watch and realized that it was time to go downstairs and herd the hungry into the dining room. As she descended she crossed her fingers in the hope that Paul would not show up again. George intended to put him out, anyway, but it would be an unpleasant fuss, and she'd have to refund him some money. This Tim, now, had slipped her a twenty and looked as though he might be good for more from time to time. She thought of George with an accustomed flare of anger. Grandma had given him power of attorney some time ago—entirely overlooking herself, who did all the work around the place. It wasn't fair, and it had cut into her income drastically. Grandma had never given her a salary, but she'd been able to make plenty. Now, George insisted on a regular inspection of the books and had put her on a salary. She hadn't been able to make half as much—only things like Paul paying double for his room and the twenty from Tim. Liz Sampson had been helpful—she was the generous type—but Liz was broke these days. She'd slipped her a five now and then, when she got behind with the rent, but then George had to step in, of course. He'd given Liz's room to this Anne and moved Liz to a tiny sewing room at the back. Liz was so furious that it was doubtful whether she'd come across with any more fives. Perhaps she'd get over it, though, and George couldn't put her out entirely—she was too old a friend of Grandma.

Mrs. Smith reached the foot of the stairs, heaved a weighty sigh, and headed toward the back of the hall to ring the gong. She pounded on it absently, while her thoughts turned in another direction. Miss Kalms had a nerve, sneaking out at night the way she did, although she always insisted that Grandma didn't need much attention at night. But then—the fives that Miss Kalms slipped her were useful.

Mrs. Smith left the gong, heaved another sigh, and went out to the kitchen. The cook raised a hot, perspiring face and said, "Now you get outa here, Miz Smith."

Mrs. Smith nodded absently and got out. She went to the dining room where the old crumbs were assembling. Mr. and Mrs. Roger Crimple; Liz Sampson, spraying Roger with laughter and gay remarks; and Roger's wife, Pet, being coldly refined about it all; Miss Burreton, with her quivering nose pointed first this way, then that; and old Mr. Alrian, his bald head shining brightly, paying no attention to anyone. He was merely waiting for his dinner, which he loved, and then he would go to his room and get back to his radio, unless Liz trapped him into a detour to the lounge, to offset the preponderance of women there.

Mrs. Smith tapped her foot and frowned toward the door. Where was Monty? What was he doing? She hardly ever saw him these days—her own son. Well, no use waiting for him. No telling when he would come, or whether he would come, even. She sat down, but could not keep her eyes from straying toward the door.

Monty, she thought, would show them all someday. She was convinced that he would land on his feet eventually. He hadn't finished school, and he couldn't seem to get a job—but that was just because ordinary people didn't understand him. He'd be all right—it was just a matter of time.

Anne and George approached her table, and she put on a bright smile for them. George, seating Anne, reflected that there was one nice thing about Min—she was always cheerful.

He returned the smile and asked, "Where's Monty tonight?"

Min Smith's cheerfulness faltered, although she tried to maintain it. George knew very well that she couldn't answer for Monty, he came and went as he pleased. After all, he was no sissy to be tied to his mother's apron strings. She knew that George disapproved of the poor boy, although he'd never said so. But it was his attitude—she could tell.

She said shortly, "He'll be in later," and had no sooner finished speaking than Monty appeared in the doorway and moved over to their table with his own peculiar slouch. He sat down without saying anything to anyone, although he gave Anne an appraising look from under half-closed lids.

Mrs. Smith assumed an animation that was faintly feverish. She put a caressing hand on his arm and exclaimed, "Why, dear, I'm so glad you were able to get here in time for dinner—it's nice to see you. Did you have a good day?"

Monty did not trouble himself to answer, and George said in a flat voice, "Anne, this is Mrs. Smith's son, Monty—Aunt Ellen's other grandchild."

Anne nodded coolly, and Monty gave her a half-smile, after which he turned and called loudly for Ginny.

Ginny, rushing around wildly with loaded plates, gave him an abstracted nod, and Mrs. Smith said uneasily, "Now, don't rush her, Monty, or she'll get all mixed up—you know how she is. She's supposed to serve people in the order they come in."

Monty said, "Nuts. Those scarecrows have nothing to do but eat and sleep. I'm in a hurry."

"What are you doing these days, Monty ?" George asked.

Monty gave him a slit-eyed look and said, "Playin' pool. Howdya like that?"

"Very much," George replied equably. "I wish I had time to play with you."

"Yeah," said Monty, "me too. Playin' with you would earn me some real dough."

"Oh no," George murmured, "you'd merely be owed some real dough."

Mrs. Smith interposed nervously, "I wonder where in the world Mr. Courtney is? He's late tonight."

"Puttin' on a benefit show of *Hamlet* at the Cat and Dog Hospital," Monty said. He turned in his chair and yelled, "Hey! Ginny!"

Ginny came flying over with two plates of soup splashing around her thumbs. She panted, "Sorry I couldn't get here sooner, but you got to feed them when they come in or they'll holler." She placed one of the soup plates in front of George, and after a moment's hesitation set the other before Anne. Monty picked up his spoon, but before he could use it, George reached over, lifted the plate, and put it down in front of Mrs. Smith.

"Ginny," he said easily, "is not thoroughly trained."

Monty gave him a furious glare, and Mrs. Smith said hastily, "I don't believe I want any tonight, George."

"Eat it anyway." George sounded almost sleepy. "You're getting quite thin—you really should make an effort. Don't you agree with me, Monty?"

"Aw, shut up."

Mrs. Smith dangled her spoon unhappily and murmured, "Now, dear."

George said, "Go ahead, girls—don't let it get cold."

Ginny appeared with two more plates of soup, and, at the same time, Mr. Courtney came in and made his way toward his table.

He seated himself without looking at anyone, and Liz Sampson immediately leaned over and trilled, "Good evening, Mr. Courtney."

Mr. Courtney gave her a stiff bow and unfolded his evening paper.

There was not much talking during the meal, and when it was over, there was a rather speedy exodus. Anne, following along to the lounge, found that coffee was being served there and realized that the rush had been to get good chairs. The stragglers had to perch on small, straight chairs which seemed to have been designed to stimulate backache.

Mr. Courtney, one of the last to appear, seated himself carefully on a straight chair, accepted coffee, and then began to talk—deliberately, and with perfect diction. His subject was the affairs of today versus the affairs of yesterday.

Monty took some coffee, gulped it hastily, and then started out of the room. His mother stopped him before he had reached the door and drew him into a corner, where she talked to him in a low voice.

Liz was giving Mr. Courtney competition in the holding of the floor, displaying perfect diction herself. George told Anne quietly that she had been on the stage, too, but was a good deal older than Mr. Courtney. Roger tried to put a word in now and then, but it was uphill work.

Presently Liz was forced to stop and cough, and Mr. Courtney took the opportunity to speak.

"Somebody," he said clearly, "has attempted a particularly childish and annoying practical joke. You all know that I have a very expensive artificial hand which I use for my professional appearances. This prankster has tried to put nail polish on the fingernails—so inexpertly that the hand has the appearance of having been dipped in blood."

CHAPTER TEN

EVERYBODY HEARD Mr. Courtney's complaint—even Liz, who was still trying to get her breath—but no one appeared to be disposed to comment.

Mr. Courtney allowed several moments to pass, by way of emphasis, and then resumed. "Now I hope I am not deficient in humor, but I have always deplored practical joking, and, in my case, this is very serious for me. You all know that my hand is necessary for my professional appearances."

Roger's wife Pet was the first to find her voice. She said indignantly, "Why, that's an awful thing. It's mean and vicious, and whoever did it ought to be punished."

"Are you sure it's nail polish?" someone asked from the doorway, and Anne saw it was Tim.

Mrs. Smith hurried over to him, while Mr. Courtney stood up and said formally, "I don't believe I've had the pleasure, sir."

Tim evaded Mrs. Smith, after according her a brief nod, and advanced toward Mr. Courtney. He bowed from the waist and murmured, "Timothy Capri, sir, at your service."

Mr. Courtney, rightly suspicious of mockery, stiffened and murmured, "Really!"

Tim, accepting coffee from Mrs. Smith, said, "Yes, sir, really. Registered at the American Kennel Club. But as I grew to manhood, that was discovered to have been a mistake." He sat down between Liz and Mr. Courtney, and Liz was delighted to the point of being feverishly animated.

George murmured to Anne, "He didn't even say hello to you, did he?"

Anne shrugged. "It's this dazzling company. He has Liz now, so I suppose he'll cast me off like an old shoe."

"What's he doing here, anyway?" George asked. "Do you have a date with him?"

"No. He lives here—moved in today."

George spilled coffee into his saucer and put it down on the table with a bang. He got up, muttering, "That woman!" and began to make his way purposefully toward Mrs. Smith. She saw him coming and disappeared into the hall like a streak, but George followed her, gathering speed.

Tim immediately shifted to the vacant seat beside Anne but kept a polite smile going for Liz. At the first opportunity—which was created by Liz being obliged to pause for breath or strangle—he whispered to Anne, "Darling, must you sit around and allow that big brute to murmur into your ear?"

"I don't know why not," Anne said tolerantly. "He doesn't spit when he murmurs."

"Precious!" Tim cried. "Don't be crude!"

Mr. Courtney threw a quieting glance around the room and announced, "I am waiting for someone to confess."

Everyone fell silent—even including Liz.

After a moment Tim said, "I didn't do it, Mr. Courtney—but I think I might repair the damage for you. Nail-polish remover should do it, and I always carry some with me, because it will take practically anything off anywhere. I'll be glad to try it for you—and I think I'm pretty expert."

Mr. Courtney swung around on him. "That's uncommonly kind of you, my dear sir. Thank you very much indeed. If you will follow me—"

Tim stood up, and the two moved toward the door. Liz batted her eyes a few times and then followed them. "I simply must watch," she cried brightly. "I do love to see men fixing things." This made Roger a little jealous and he boomed, "That one isn't a man—he's a pantywaist."

Tim, already at the door, turned around at once, came back to face Roger, and said sternly, "Take that back, sir."

Roger was somewhat abashed. The boom had gone out of his voice when he said, "No need to get huffy, boy—no offense meant. Just joking, just joking."

Tim bowed and left the room, and Roger sank back into his chair, fingering his mustache. Pet made a few remarks, but they were delivered in too low a voice for any ear but his.

Anne glanced around the room and saw that Miss Burreton was sitting on the edge of her chair, with her head thrust forward and her mouth slightly open. Well, she thought, lighting a cigarette, there wasn't much diversion in a life like Miss Burreton's. She saw Mr. Alrian silently steal away, and then Miss Burreton padded across the room and sat down beside her.

"I can't keep up with their jabber," she observed, settling a lavender crocheted scarf across her shoulders. "Such a lot of noise, and so pointless."

Anne tried to be agreeable, because she felt a little sorry for Miss Burreton. The others were younger—in their fifties, perhaps—but Miss Burreton was of Grandma's generation—late sixties or seventies.

"I knew your mother," Miss Burreton said, her hands still busy with the scarf. "Such a dear, charming girl."

Anne flushed and dropped her eyes. What could she say? Apparently her identity was being kept secret, and it made her uncomfortable.

"Such a pity," Miss Burreton sighed, "that she went off with the Magraw man." She paused, and when Anne nodded absently, she gave a self-conscious little laugh. "My dear, I shouldn't have said that—so thoughtless of me. Of course if she hadn't married him, she wouldn't have had you—such a lovely daughter."

Anne laughed. "I never thought of that angle."

"Ah well," Miss Burreton sighed, "it's all over now."

Anne put out her cigarette. "I think I'll go up and see Grandma again."

Miss Burreton stood up and said promptly, "Fine. I'll come too."

As they went out into the hall the front door opened, and a young woman walked in. She was a slim brunette, with an ivory skin and eyes like deep brown pansies. She wore an expensive looking gray fur coat, with a matching hat, and a bunch of crisp, fresh violets was pinned to her lapel. She brought a faint, delicate perfume into the hall with her.

Anne and Miss Burreton stopped together and fastened their eyes on her.

The vision said, "Burry, you old darling, how are you?" She swished over and kissed Miss Burreton on the cheek and seemed unaware that the old lady backed away sharply. She looked into the darkness at the end of the hall and suddenly screamed, "George! My dear, is that you?"

George emerged into the light and opened his mouth to speak, but the vision forestalled him by flinging her arms around his neck and kissing him. He appeared to respond with a certain amount of enthusiasm, but presently held her off and looked at her. "You get more beautiful all the time," he observed.

"Beauty," said Miss Burreton clearly, "is as beauty does."

George and the vision laughed, and George turned around. "Anne, may I present Miss Lillian Devray?"

"Why not?" said Anne composedly. "How do you do, Miss Devray."

"What do you mean, 'Why not?'?" George asked.

"How are you, dear little Anne?" Miss Devray laughed. "But Anne what? George is very bad at introductions."

Apparently George had no intention of having Anne's last name mentioned before Miss Burreton, for he said hastily and firmly, "Just Anne."

"But that's impossible," Miss Devray protested prettily.

"Lily," said George, "don't be difficult."

Miss Burreton cleared her throat. "Your mother, Lily, God rest her soul, would never have allowed you to smear all that paint on your face."

Lily blew her a little kiss. "I know, honey dear, I'm just going to wipe it off. George! For heaven's sake—I'm expiring. Have you—"

George nodded. "Go on up, you know where I keep it."

Lily tripped up the stairs, and Miss Burreton followed more slowly. George put a hand on Anne's arm, and nodded upward. "We're having a couple of drinks in my room," he said in a low voice. "Get your boy friend and join the party."

"All right," Anne agreed, and went up to her room feeling a bit flat. A drink sounded all right—although she'd never been used to drinking at all times of the day—but George had disappointed her. She wanted George to be Tim's idea of him. And now he had produced a girl friend who dripped glamour and personality—and had money enough to drape them appropriately.

She combed her hair and applied makeup to her face, but she couldn't look as fancy as Lily no matter what she did. She sighed, shrugged, and left the room.

She went in search of Mr. Courtney's room, and found Tim just emerging. He called back, "I'm sure you'll find that stuff useful to you."

Mr. Courtney said, "I'm sure I shall, sir, and I am very grateful to you. You have restored my property to its former usefulness."

They bowed to each other with a good deal of elegance, and Anne sternly swallowed a laugh that had bubbled into her throat. She extended George's invitation, and Tim took her arm with enthusiasm. "Petite, a drink is *exactly* what I need—even one mixed by staid and stolid old George."

Anne had supposed that Lily and Tim would be kindred souls, and she was really astonished, as the evening progressed, to find that they were barely civil to each other. She began to realize, after a while, that they knew each other, and she supposed there must have been a quarrel.

George was obviously puzzled, too, and at last he asked peevishly, "What the devil is the matter with you two? This is supposed to be some sort of a party, and you sit there like a pair of ice cubes and leave everything to Anne and me."

"But, darling," Lily wailed, "this little Anne is much too pretty—I'm terrified—I don't want to lose you."

George frowned and looked a bit embarrassed. "Damn it, Lily, have some reticence," he muttered.

Tim looked full at her and said nastily, "I'll take care of Anne, dear—don't worry about your fine big man."

Lily shivered, and Anne glanced at her curiously. George said, "Oh, for God's sake have another drink, Tim."

Tim took the drink in silence, and when he had disposed of half of it in one gulp, he asked Anne in an aside, "Does she live here?"

"Not as far as I know."

Tim said, "Good!" and finished his drink. He handed the empty glass to George. "Just one more, please. I must be able to think clearly tonight."

"Why?" George asked, rattling bottles.

"That artificial hand of Mr. Courtney's—there was no nail polish on it—it was blood."

CHAPTER ELEVEN

"Blood," George said flatly, and Tim nodded.

"I knew there was something odd here, when Anne told me her intriguing little tale, and that's why I came."

"Are you a detective?"

"No," Tim said regretfully. "It's simply that I never have been able to get over the adolescent idea of wanting to be one."

George muttered, "I don't know what's going on myself. I think I ought to phone the police."

"Oh, darling, no," Lily protested. "Not tonight. We can't be grim tonight. We must go out somewhere and have fun."

"You really haven't much that would interest the police," Tim said, ignoring Lily. "What would you tell them? They're so brutally factual, you know."

"I'd tell them everything. The blood you were just talking about—"

"I washed it away myself—and I did not tell Mr. Courtney that it was blood."

George frowned down at the carpet and realized that there wasn't very much that he could tell the police. Paul seemed to have disappeared, but he was merely a boarder and, quite possibly, had gone about some private business of his own. He hadn't been missing long, in any case.

"Darling!" Lily cried petulantly. "Must you be so moody?"

George took a long, slow breath and straightened up. "All right, Lily, we'll go out if you want to. Where are you staying? I hope you had sense enough to check in somewhere. It isn't easy to get accommodations, and if I have to squeeze you in here, I want to know about it now, so that I can make arrangements to sleep in the bathtub."

Lily trilled pretty laughter and said, "Don't be silly, pet, of course I have checked in. I'm Lily Devray, George dear, and I *never* want for a place to lay my head."

Tim, though he said nothing, managed to convey by his silence a very sneering insinuation, and Anne got up and said hastily, "If you people are going out, I think I'll look in on Grandma."

Lily stretched her long, slim legs and smiled lazily. "Oh, my dear, there's no hurry. Have another drink first—do."

Anne shook her head. "My alcohol intake has been well above average today, and I think I'll leave it at that. I didn't have much sleep last night, and I want to go to bed early."

Tim moved over beside her. "Your behavior is always so correct and sweet, and even noble, as to be a little bourgeois, precious. But it stimulates me, and I think I'll go and see Grandma along with you."

They thanked George for the drinks and departed, while Lily hummed a gay tune to prove that Tim did not exist—at least for her.

"Miss Kalms may not let you in," Anne said as they made their way to Grandma's room.

Miss Kalms met them at the door, and after flicking a glance or two at Tim said hurriedly, "My dear, would it be too much to ask you to stay with Grandma while I take a bath?"

Anne gave a vexed little sigh, but said resignedly, "All right," and Miss Kalms fled down the hall, with a coat over her arm.

Tim looked after her with a faint smile. "Evidently going to take a cold bath—else why the coat?"

"Oh—bath!" Anne said impatiently. "She's going out to meet her boy-friend, or something."

Tim shrugged. "You can't blame anybody for trying—and their hours are preposterous. As for the work they do—I think nursing must be utterly gruesome."

Grandma was plucking at her blanket, but her eyes lit up as Anne stooped to kiss her.

"How are you feeling, Granny?"

The old lady caught sight of Tim and asked in a loud whisper, "Who's he?"

Tim moved closer to the bed and said, "I am Anne's friend—and I might be able to help you."

Grandma nodded her head up and down several times. "About time too. What good does that fool of a doctor do me? He gives me pills and they don't

help me. I won't take any more. I give them to Min and she uses them to
make her geraniums grow."

Tim grinned. "I'm sure your doctor is a very good man, but possibly I
have something for you too."

Grandma looked at him rather blankly and then gave her attention to
Anne. "I want to give it to you," she whispered. "It's a lot of money, and I
want you to have it. Missy, now—I gave it to her, but she didn't take it. I
know she didn't, because I didn't hear from her. But she should have written
to me. I knew she was going to run away—I'm no fool—but I never heard
from her. She never wrote to me at all—so she didn't get the money. Serve
her right, anyway, she didn't deserve it—not when she wouldn't write to me.
I wrote to her, and she didn't answer. Anyway, when I get a little better, I'll
tell you where it is. They're all looking for it—all of them. They come in
here, and sneak and search through my drawers, and I look at them, but they
don't find it. That man—he's a funny one—he gets hopping mad. The other
one doesn't get mad—he just looks and looks, and I know what he's looking
for, but I pretend to be asleep. He'd be cruel to me—he'd twist my arm—so I
have to pretend I'm very ill and don't know what he's talking about. I'm all
alone here, and I'm afraid of him. That hussy of a nurse shouldn't go off and
leave me alone. Every night when she goes, he comes in."

"What kind of a man?" Anne asked quietly. "Is he tall?"

"Tall? Tall—yes, tall—a tall woman." Grandma closed her eyes, and
Anne decided that her mind had drifted to Miss Kalms again—who must
appear tall to her.

She glanced at Tim and murmured, "She's gone off to sleep."

He nodded abstractedly. "The nurse is in the habit of slipping out at night
and leaving her alone—and then the vultures gather and start sniffing around
for the money."

Anne got up and stretched her tired body. "I wish that nurse would come
back, so that I could go to bed."

Tim came out of his abstraction and protested. "But, darling, I wanted
you to help me find Paul."

Anne shivered. "I wish you'd stop making Paul sound like a corpse. I
think you're being theatrical."

"But of *course*—I love being theatrical—it's so much more fun than plodding through life with your feet on the ground. Only I'm right about this. Paul
should be the only one searching through drawers for this money—but, you
see, there was someone else too. I assume that Paul was the one who got
hopping mad—the other is the methodical fellow. I suppose he found Paul
searching—and eliminated him. So—Paul must be found."

"Where does that artificial hand come in?" Anne asked.

"Well, it appears to be simply an effort to get rid of you by scaring you off."

"Then I think it was a pretty feeble effort. I took it to be simply a practical joke."

"Nevertheless, I think that was the idea. Whoever it was slipped into your room while you were upstairs getting George and removed the thing."

"All right, and so when did it get the blood on it?"

"Darling, you are so downright—almost earthy at times. You cannot always expect to follow an imagination of quicksilver like mine. While you wait for the laggard nurse, I shall go to my room and prepare some martinis for us. After we have refreshed ourselves, we shall find Paul—and then we'll keep watch during the night and catch that other one who slips in and searches for the money. It will be most exhilarating."

Anne shook her head at him. "For heaven's sake, Tim! You don't really believe all this, do you? And how are you going to make martinis without ice?"

"You will trust me more fully when you know me better, my sweet. Of course I believe all this—and undoubtedly there will be ice in the kitchen."

Anne settled back beside Grandma, who was still sleeping, and wished irritably that Miss Kalms would hurry up with her false bath. She was tired, and she wondered whether she could shake Tim and his martinis and go to bed instead.

The door opened quietly, and she started up, her breath coming faster. When she saw that it was only the pool-playing Monty, she sank back again, annoyed with herself for being so jumpy. After all, she didn't really believe Tim's fantastic story.

Monty looked at her and said, "Sorry. Did I startle you?"

"No, not really. I think I must be sleepy."

He advanced to the bed and looked down at the wizened little face on the pillow.

"The old bitch," he observed conversationally.

Anne gave a shocked little exclamation, and he grinned at her.

"You don't know her—and I do. My father died early, and we've had to live with her ever since. I don't know how Mother puts up with it—or maybe I do, in a way. Mother doesn't take anything seriously—not even me."

Anne looked at him curiously and asked, "What did Grandma do to make you hate her so much?"

"It isn't what she did—it's what she tried to do. Mother always got around it somehow. I did have birthday and Christmas celebrations—but only because Mother did them in secret. Granny didn't hold with that sort of foolishness—in fact she didn't hold with anything that might cost her a penny. She hated me and I hated her. Only now does she seem to like me, and I'm damned if I know why. I was a nice little boy, but I have grown up to be a no-good loafer whose mother supports him."

"You'll work it out," Anne said, feeling embarrassed. "Sometimes it takes a while."

Monty's face relaxed, and she realized that his smile had a great deal of charm.

"I only come to see the old devil because of the rumors about her having money hidden somewhere. I don't think I actually believe it—but Mother does, and most of the boarders, as well. If you run across any of them searching around the place, you'll know that they're merely looking for Granny's hoard. I think the whole house has been gone over with a fine-tooth comb, with panels pried loose, in case they might conceal secret compartments. Personally, I'm hoping that Granny will save me the trouble by telling me."

"She promised to tell me," Anne said mildly, "but she never has."

"And she never will. She won't tell me, either—not while she has breath in her body. It's just an idle hope that she'll get confused enough to drop a hint without intending to."

"I see." Anne was conscious of a sudden distaste for him. "So you spend a certain amount of your time away from the pool table sitting with Grandma in the hope of picking up a hint."

He looked at her, and said equably, "You're just like George—stuffy. Do you know that I never played pool in my life? Know what I do? I paint, and I study painting, and I go to the museums. I know that Mother supports me, and I know that I'm a big boy now and should be supporting her. So I'm a bum—but I do spend a lot of time in here waiting for hints so that I can get the money, give it to Mother, and go on with my painting."

He spoke lightly, and Anne laughed. "Does George disapprove of your painting?"

"Sure. Good old George—that solid citizen. He's offered me a job time and time again, and can't understand why I won't accept. He thinks business is simply fascinating."

"Maybe he disapproves of me too," Anne said. "I'm in the art field myself—commercial art."

Monty made a face and started to say something, but Anne interrupted. "It's no use telling me I'm prostituting my art. I love it—and I like the money I get for it too."

"All right," he said amiably. "I'm just not that worthwhile." He glanced at his watch, and added, "Even now I have a date at a party—a drinking party."

He left as quietly as he had come, and Anne yawned and mentally cursed Miss Kalms. She glanced at Grandma and saw that the old lady was awake again. She gave Anne a sly look and whispered, "Has he gone?"

Anne nodded, smiled, and patted the little hands.

"The money," Grandma said excitedly. "I had such trouble to sew it back again. He kept coming, and I told him it was just torn." The old voice ceased abruptly, and Grandma stared at the door.

Anne was conscious of a curious, frightened chill. She turned to look at the door, and at the same time it swung slowly inward to reveal the doorway—shadowed and empty.

CHAPTER TWELVE

GRANDMA'S VOICE was a hollow whisper in her throat. She quavered, "Who's there?"

Anne got up on unsteady legs and forced herself to walk straight to the door and look out. There was no one there—the hall was empty, dimly lighted, with closed doors. She advanced to the stairs, but could not see anyone, and, presently, she returned to Grandma's room and closed the door with a little bang.

The old lady was mumbling excitedly. She muttered, "That nurse—she goes away at night—" She moved her mouth for a while without producing any sound until she suddenly fell asleep.

Anne watched her uneasily for some time, and then fell to pacing the room restlessly. She saw, without much interest, that it was snowing outside.

Miss Kalms and Tim arrived at the door together about ten minutes later, and Tim gave Miss Kalms a charming smile. "So relieved to see you, dear, I was beginning to fear you might have drowned in that bath."

Miss Kalms was undisturbed. She said airily, "Oh no, not at all. I often take baths, and I've learned not to drown in them."

Tim flashed her another smile and turned to Anne. "Come, dear, my preparations are complete. Good-by for now, Miss Kalms—we shall surely see you again."

Miss Kalms said, "Adios—I'll count the minutes."

Tim gave her a third smile which appeared to be a trifle forced, and herded Anne out of the room. He took her to his own room where the martinis were neatly set out, and Anne surprised herself by drinking one rather quickly.

She set down the empty glass, feeling dizzy, and said wonderingly, "Now why did I drink that stuff ? I don't know what's the matter with me—I'm nervous for some reason."

Tim refilled her glass. "But that's understandable, pet. We are going to find Paul tonight."

"Oh, nonsense!" Anne shook her head in an effort to clear it. "We might see Paul tonight, at that, when he walks in here and asks what we're doing in his room."

"Darling, you really must trust me. Now what did Granny tell you?"

"She practically told me where the money is. She sewed it back, which gave her a lot of trouble, and he kept coming and looking over her shoulder, and she told him it was just torn."

Tim was very much interested in this bit, and flung questions at her for some time before going off into a thoughtful silence. Anne took a sip of the second martini and shuddered at the taste.

Tim had just observed that they must go and look in the linings of all the drapes when there was a knock on the door, and George walked in without waiting to be asked.

"Good heavens!" Tim exclaimed, staring at him. "You go out for a night of revelry with an attractive woman—and here you are back already. What happened? Did she slap your face?"

George shrugged. "I'm uneasy about what's been going on here, and I'm bothered about Anne too. I brought her here, and now we can't locate that other girl—"

"All right," Tim said kindly. "You needn't struggle with it any further. It's quite simple—you find yourself preferring the honest little Anne to the gilded Lily."

Anne blushed and tried to bury her face in her glass, and George said coldly, "Why are you going to look in the linings of the drapes? Mrs. Smith isn't going to like that much."

"I shall leave them," Tim replied, "in more artistic folds than Mrs. Smith could ever achieve. We are looking for the money, of course."

George groaned. "You too? Look—there isn't any money. The old lady is entirely dependent upon this establishment. She has no money—if she'd had any, she'd have put in improvements here some years ago. She tried to borrow for it, but the house is so old that she couldn't get a loan."

"Oh well"—Tim waved a hand—"that's not an uncommon thing. People put away a wad of money in an old sock, and won't touch a penny of it to keep from starving."

George shrugged, and Tim handed him a martini. He took a couple of sips and said, "Just the same, I know the old lady better than you do. She was a bit tight, undoubtedly, but she was what you'd call sensible with her money. She wouldn't buy Monty a bicycle, but she had the plumbing fixed and the roof properly repaired. She was practical."

Tim frowned into the flare of the flame of his lighter, then snapped it shut, and blew smoke toward the ceiling. "You try to ruin all my theories," he said crossly.

"You *are* a private detective, aren't you?" George asked curiously. "Who hired you?"

"I am not a private detective. I simply haven't outgrown Deadeye Dick—

and this thing is mysterious and therefore thrilling."

"You know," Anne said thoughtfully, "Grandma told me that she had killed a man for this money, and that she was going to tell me where it is. She said she'd given it to Missy, but that Missy hadn't used it."

"She's raving," George declared. "Missy often wrote asking for money, and she always refused because she was afraid Magraw might benefit."

Tim considered it. "She's bothered at having refused to help her daughter, so now she tells people that she did give her money."

George nodded. "That sounds more like it."

"Ah well—" Tim heaved a sigh. "Have another martini, George, at least you appreciate them. Anne is nearly hopeless—perhaps I can educate her. I really do make the best martini I ever tasted."

George accepted the drink in silence, and Tim said, "You might as well wipe the worthy scorn off your face. Why shouldn't I educate her to appreciate my martinis? Actually, I really like you, George, although you are interested in my girl and might even nose me out before the race is run."

"Your girl?" George said mystified. "Who?"

"Don't be naive. This little Anne, of course."

George colored and muttered, "What are you talking about now? You've only just met her."

"Certainly. But I think twice as fast as you do. You're slow, but you're heading in the same direction as I am, I'm afraid."

"These may be good martinis," Anne said, "but they seem to have got into your head."

"It's odd." Tim gazed at the ceiling. "Astonishing, really. I believe it's your true, solid worth that attracts me—since I never had any myself. But why should it attract George? He, too, is worthy. And why should worth attract worth? It usually doesn't."

"Are you telling our fortunes?" George asked.

Tim gave him an odd smile. "You know, I believe I am. I don't suppose either of you is in love with the other yet, so why not give me a chance to sweep Anne off her feet first? Anne, my sweet, I do want you. Won't you view me with favor?"

Anne rubbed the back of her hand across her sleepy eyes and said, "I'm the slow type, like George."

George coughed. "This is all very entertaining, but what do you intend to do next? In the role of Deadeye Dick, I mean."

"I don't think you should brush love aside so lightly. It is one of the most interesting and colorful things that we have to amuse us in this silly business of living. In any case, I have a certain peculiar honor and I was exhibiting it. I was simply giving you fair warning about Anne."

"Yes, yes," George said. "Thanks. But about this mysterious business—"

"Ah yes." Tim stood up. "The mystery. I've reached the boring part of it now. I love to do the thinking, but unfortunately I have no one for the hack work. I must do it myself."

"May I help?" George asked politely.

"I was about to suggest it." Tim caught at Anne's hand and pulled her to her feet. "Come along, precious, you must help too."

They went out into the hall, and as they passed Grandma's room, Tim speeded up a little. "Mustn't linger here," he murmured, "or Miss Kalms may appear with a frenzied desire to take a shower, and you would be stuck again, darling."

"Listen," George said from behind. "For God's sake, don't start insulting Miss Kalms. She's the best one we've had, so far, and we don't want to lose her."

They went up to the third floor, and Tim hesitated. "Is there an attic up above?"

George nodded. "Storage space and two bedrooms. Mrs. Smith and Monty have the two rooms."

"You seem to have been favored," Tim murmured. "Your room is so much better."

"I pay full rent and always have. In lean times I rent the most expensive rooms, and when the house is full, I'm shoved around from here to there."

Tim mounted the stairs to the fourth floor and stopped to look about him. "Where's the storage space?" he whispered.

"You needn't be so quiet," George told him. "Both Mrs. Smith and Monty are out."

"Monty, of course. Where did Mrs. Smith go?"

"She's out with a friend," George said rather stiffly, and proceeded to open a door at the end of the hall. "This is the storage space."

"Male or female?" Tim asked, and when George merely looked puzzled, added impatiently, "Mrs. Smith's friend."

"Oh—Min. It's a man—an old friend of hers."

George turned away as he spoke and snapped on the light in a small wall fixture that was near the door in the storage room. Tim walked in sniffing, and George said to Anne, "What does he want to know a thing like that for?"

Anne giggled. "Detectives must be in possession of all the facts, and it's not for the dullards to know which are important."

Tim, poking around among dusty old boxes and trunks, raised his head and called, "Come on, I need your help."

They advanced into the dusty litter, and George asked, "What are we looking for?"

"A corpse," Anne told him, and giggled again. "You know—that Paul."

"You don't say!" George looked amused. "Is he dead?"

"Tim thinks so."

"Look at the size of this trunk," George said, slapping at the lid with his open hand. "Made them big in those days, didn't they?"

Tim moved over and said, "Open it. Everything must be opened."

"I can't. It's locked, and I don't know where the keys are for any of this stuff."

"I came prepared for that, naturally." Tim drew a jingling key ring from his pocket. "Try these."

George knelt down in front of the trunk, and Tim wandered away again, but Anne stayed, watching, and wondering why the palms of her hands were suddenly damp.

George worked for a while in silence and presently said abruptly, "This one fits."

He turned the key in the lock and threw back the lid. Anne retreated a step and gave a gasping little cry.

A skeleton grinned up at them from a rubble of yellowed old rags.

CHAPTER THIRTEEN

TIM BOUNDED over, peered into the box, and murmured, "Ah."

"Oh, God!" Anne moaned. "That must be the man."

George glanced up at her. "What man?"

"The man Grandma said she had killed. She told me—she said she had killed a man for it—the money, I mean—"

Tim and George both spoke together, and for several minutes they bombarded her with questions. But there was nothing more that she could tell them, so that they presently turned back to the skeleton.

It was not clean, Anne thought confusedly—not the kind that they use in colleges. There were bits of dark stuff sticking to it, and Tim, leaning closer, said in an absorbed voice, "She couldn't just have killed him and left him up here in the trunk. Odor, you see—too much of it to be explained away by bad drains or dead rats."

"Well—" George mopped his forehead and bunched the handkerchief back into his pocket. "This place wasn't always a hotel—the attic might have been far enough away from the rest of the house—"

Anne shook her head. "Oh no, they'd have had servants, and the servants would have been sleeping up here."

Tim straightened up suddenly and dusted his hands. "There are those bits of dirt still clinging to it, but the lining of the trunk is fairly clean. I think it has been moved up here recently."

George was silent for a while, frowning, and then he said abruptly, "I don't think you've any right to assume that Aunt Ellen killed this—this thing. Her mind is very much impaired just now, and the things she says should not be taken seriously. I'm perfectly certain that she wouldn't have killed anybody. She was always a very honest and moral sort of person."

Tim nodded. "But very fond of money. A practical soul who refused Monty a bicycle when he was a little boy."

George made an impatient movement and said stubbornly, "You've no right to accuse her when she isn't in a position to defend herself."

"That's noble of you, George," Tim observed.

George murmured, "Who asked you to call me by my first name?"

"George is right," Anne declared emphatically. "Grandma says all sorts of odd things, and maybe this was just a released inhibition that floated to the surface. Lots of people would like to kill a man at one time or another."

Tim carefully closed the trunk and held out his hand for the key that had opened it. George handed it over in silence, and Tim turned the lock, then stood up and carefully dusted off his clothes.

"Now," he said, "we'll go out and see if it was ever buried in the yard. Perhaps we'll be able to clear your Aunt Ellen, George, and then you can stop agitating and get your mind back on business, where it feels most comfortable."

"I don't see the connection," George said, his troubled eyes still on the trunk. "How do you intend to clear her?"

Tim smoothed his hair back with a sweeping gesture of his hand and made for the stairs. He called back, "Follow me, fellers." They followed him, and George muttered, "I think I'll call the police in. I don't like having unknown skeletons in the attic."

Tim stopped on the stairs and turned around. "Please, George, don't do anything so stupid. Do you want the whole thing mishandled? The police are outstanding bunglers—everybody knows that."

He went on down, and George continued to mutter. "I've never found that the police were outstanding bunglers—quite the reverse. Smart as a whip, most of them."

"They naturally appear to be bunglers," Anne explained, "to an outsize brain like Tim's."

Tim came to a halt on the second floor and turned to them. "Now wrap up warmly, because it's cold outside, and I don't know how long this will take."

"Why didn't you say so before?" George asked in an aggrieved voice. "I'll have to go back up to the third floor in order to wrap up warmly—that's where my room is."

Anne went to her room and put on two sweaters and tied a scarf over her head. When she came out again, Tim was impatiently pacing the hall, attired in a red-and-green lumber jacket with a matching cap. He looked her over critically and shook his head. "Darling, you must get a knitted cap to wear for this sort of thing—that scarf does not suit you. There are only a few women for whom the scarf over the head is suitable—and you are not one of them."

Anne said, "I'll rush out first thing in the morning and buy a knitted cap. Then, when another occasion like this comes up, I'll be ready for it."

"Good. Perhaps I shall come with you and help you choose it. Where on earth is George?"

George came down the stairs, wearing a fairly colorless golf jacket, and stopped on the last step while he looked them over. Of Tim's outfit he said briefly, "Where do you buy things like that? In the kitchenware?" And added to Anne, "You look very pretty with that scarf around your head."

"Good heavens, man!" Tim exclaimed. "Don't exhibit your taste in clothes—try to keep it hidden. Come on, let's go."

They went downstairs and started for the back hall, but were interrupted immediately. Roger appeared at the entrance to the lounge and hailed them cheerfully.

"Well, well, well, going out for a walk, I see. Now, if you'll wait just a minute, I'll come with you. Glad to. Always did enjoy a walk."

"Well—er—no, Roger," George said uncomfortably. "We—we're just going to post a letter."

Tim laughed shrilly. "Isn't George a scream?" he asked of no one in particular.

Roger laughed with him, and said, "Now just wait for me—won't be a minute."

He bounded up the stairs, and his wife Pet and Miss Burreton wandered out into the hall. Miss Burreton looked sour and disapproving, but Pet looked like a sweet, aging lady, as usual.

"I wish Roger wouldn't go running up the stairs like that," she said plaintively. "He's not so young, and I'm sure it isn't good for him, but he will do it. I guess he doesn't want you to go without him—he loves a walk."

"Glad to have him come along," Tim said courteously and gave Anne and George a look which seemed to indicate that Tim, the detective, was incognito as far as these people were concerned and must remain so at all cost. It appeared that their next step was simply to take a little walk with Roger, and Anne cast an appealing and desperate glance at George.

George rose to the occasion. When Roger came pounding down the stairs, bulky in overcoat and muffler, George firmly pushed him and Tim out the front door. "Have a good time, you two," he said with finality.

Roger looked crestfallen. "But aren't you coming? And the—er —young lady?"

George was removing his golf jacket. "No—we just came in. We've had our walk. But it's nice of you to keep Tim company."

Tim was trying to get back in, but Roger took him by the arm and marched him off.

Miss Burreton heaved a little sigh and asked, "Will you two play bridge with Mrs. Crimple and me?"

Anne gave George another stricken look, but this time he failed her.

"Oh yes—please," Pet said eagerly. "Just for a little while. You see, we have the table and cards all ready—we were playing three-handed with Roger."

Anne removed her sweaters and the scarf from her head and refused to look at George, because she felt that he could have saved her if he would. They sat down around the bridge table, with Pet and Miss Burreton partners, because they said they were used to each other and preferred it that way. But the game had no sooner started than they began to argue, loudly, and with active venom. It went on for some time, until Miss Burreton suddenly got up, announced that she was bored by such stupid bridge, and padded angrily out of the room.

Pet sighed. "If only she were not so temperamental, it delays things dreadfully."

Anne murmured something and started to get up, and Pet said hastily, "No, no, do wait. We might as well finish the rubber."

George stood up and took a few restless steps, and Anne asked, "But how can we, when Miss Burreton has gone?"

"Oh, she'll be back right away," Pet said. "So tiresome."

Even as she spoke, Miss Burreton reappeared and seated herself quietly in her chair.

When the rubber was finished, George stood up at once and said firmly, "I'm afraid that will have to be all. I've had a hard day at the office and need sleep."

"Sleep!" said Miss Burreton contemptuously. "That's all you ever think of—that and work. And Ellen was the same."

"I don't think that's quite fair, Burry," Pet protested. "Ellen was energetic and interested in a lot of things when she had her health. Where's Liz, George? Maybe she'll play when Roger comes back. Or perhaps that new man—whatever his name is."

"Don't ask Tim," Anne said quickly. "He's a very serious player and gets nasty at a bridge table."

"What were you two taking a walk together for?" Miss Burreton asked suddenly. "You going together? You don't really know each other well enough for that."

Anne felt herself blushing, but George said easily, "Oh yes, we're keeping steady company."

"But you're cousins," Miss Burreton pointed out. "Cousins shouldn't marry. You ought to know that."

Pet said, "Burry! For mercy's sake! Hush!"

"Well—" George appeared to consider it—"we don't need to have any children. I think that would make it all right."

Miss Burreton murmured something about vulgarity and turned away, looking offended, and George took Anne's arm and urged her out into the hall. They went upstairs, and on the second floor Anne broke away and steered a determined course toward her room.

"I have to go out and look for a job tomorrow, and I'm tired, and I'm going to bed. Whatever tonight's work is, Tim can finish it up by himself."

"Good idea," George agreed heartily. "I'm going to bed too."

Anne undressed quickly, opened a window, and slipped into bed. But although she was very tired, she could not sleep. She kept thinking of the skeleton—and of how Grandma had sewed something, while some man kept interrupting her. The bedroom door had opened, Anne remembered, when Grandma was telling about that sewing, and it seemed likely that someone had heard it—only probably it didn't mean anything.

Suddenly Anne's eyes opened wide in the darkness. Missy had had the money and had never used it. The coat. That awful black coat that was so heavy—because it had money sewed into the lining. Probably Grandma had never told Missy that the money was there. But she had insisted that her granddaughter must wear it when she came home and had pretended that it was merely a means of identification.

Anne switched on the lamp and flew to the large, old-fashioned closet. She pulled open the door, and then stood staring in baffled disappointment and dismay.

The black coat had disappeared.

CHAPTER FOURTEEN

ANNE CLOSED THE DOOR of the closet and stood for a moment with her forehead wrinkled into a frown. Someone had been listening at Grandma's door when the old lady talked about sewing up a lining—someone who was smart enough to know what she meant, who had taken the coat without delay and, presumably, extracted the money. Spike, perhaps. But Anne had a confused feeling by this time that she had dreamed Spike, and Paul as well. They seemed shadowy and unreal. Where were they, anyway? She wished fretfully that she could be sure they'd never turn up again—she was comfortable here, and she'd like to stay. But now she had to go out and tell someone that the coat had disappeared, and the money with it.

She put on a robe and went slowly out into the hall. It was still dimly lighted, but silent and empty, and she had a moment of nervous indecision before she forced herself toward the stairs. Better tell George, she thought—Tim wasn't in, anyway—and there was something solidly comforting about George.

She had to knock several times before she was able to rouse him, and when he finally pulled the door open his hair was tousled, and he was still struggling to pull his robe around him. Beneath the robe she caught glimpses of a riot of yellow pajamas.

She giggled, and he said defensively, "I didn't expect it to be you, or I could have done better. I thought it was that daft martini fancier."

"Well"—Anne glanced down at her slippered feet, conscious of a faint sense of embarrassment—"I thought I ought to tell you. The coat has disappeared."

George looked at her with sleep-drugged eyes, and repeated, "The coat has disappeared. Why?"

"What do you mean, 'why'?"

"I guess I mean what," George muttered. "What coat?"

"That old black seal, the one I've been wearing."

"Oh."

"It wouldn't matter, except I've just figured out that the money is sewed into the lining."

George rumpled his hair, then suddenly took her hand and drew her into the room. "Just sit down a minute, will you, and explain it to me slowly. I was asleep, and I can't seem to collect my thoughts."

He led her to a chair and gave her a cigarette, but as he turned to close the door, he found that it was stuck against something. He peered around and discovered that it was Tim, still arrayed in lumber jacket and cap.

Tim looked stricken and advanced into the room with a low moan. "Darling, I know you're innocent, but you should never go into a man's bedroom, men are such beasts."

Anne flicked ash from her cigarette and observed, "I was in yours tonight."

"But not undressed, darling—and anyway—" He faced George and said bitterly, "You're a much faster worker than I gave you credit for, I must say. I no sooner turn my back than you inveigle her into your bedroom—and both of you in negligee, yet."

"What does he mean, 'yet'?" George asked helplessly.

"It's a leftover from my upbringing as a butcher's son," Tim said, still bitter.

"If you'll stop jabbering for a minute," Anne interrupted, "I'll explain that I came here simply to announce a new development in—in what's going on here."

Tim's expression changed at once and he said eagerly, "What is it? Tell me."

Anne told him of the loss of the coat and of her ideas concerning it.

Tim nodded rapidly several times and whispered, "That's what I thought—I knew it. Of course the crooks didn't know about the coat, or they wouldn't have bothered coming here at all—so it's one of the people in the house." He was silent for a moment, squinting at the light. "I wonder what he did with those two crooks. Remember Mr. Courtney's hand?"

Anne shuddered. "I still don't see why it was hung up in my room."

"I told you, precious, it was to scare you away. He didn't want you here. But that seems to let Roger out."

"Why?"

"Because you woke him up when you were trying to get George. And remember that the hand was gone when you got back downstairs."

"Why don't you come down to earth?" George asked peevishly. "That was done by a practical joker—we have practical jokers in the house."

"Name two."

"Well —" George kicked the leg of a chair, forgetting that he was wearing soft slippers. "Liz," he said, when he had recovered himself.

"Who?"

"Liz Sampson."

"All right. Who else?"

"Oh—I don't know—but there must be somebody."

"I'll have to talk with Liz Sampson tomorrow," Tim decided. "Just now we must find out where that skeleton came from.''

"Deal me out," Anne said, yawning. "I'm going to bed."

George nodded. "I, also, am going to bed."

Tim gave him a stricken look. "You're just trying to get rid of me—you have a secret date with her."

Anne yawned again. "You're jumping to silly conclusions. There are some people who really need to go to bed early. I happen to be one of them, and I presume George is another."

George agreed emphatically and Tim said, "That's a good name for him— he's just another. Do you mean to say you aren't even going to look for the coat?"

Anne shook her head. "Not tonight. They're all sleeping in their rooms now. But maybe I can search tomorrow, when I see them go out. Although I hate doing a thing like that. But if I don't get the coat back, I'll have nothing to wear outside until my new one comes."

Tim and George started to speak together, but Anne took the opportunity to say, "Good night, all," after which she fled.

She did not get as far as her room. Miss Kalms was waiting for her in the hall and said brightly, "Oh, here you are. Dear, your granny has been calling for you—do come and see her before you go to bed." She eyed Anne's dressing robe and then her eyes slid around to the stairs in obvious query as to whom Anne had been with.

Anne gave her a level look. "I went up there to the bathroom—the one on this floor was occupied."

"Oh, of course—of course, my dear. Look, I'll just run out and post a letter while you're talking to Grandma."

"All right," Anne sighed, "but please don't be long. I'm very tired, and I want to go to bed as soon as possible."

Miss Kalms nodded, smiled, and flew off. Anne sighed again and went into Grandma's room. The old lady was plucking at the bedclothes, but she gave Anne a wide, toothless smile. Her teeth were in a glass of water on a table beside the bed, and she looked somehow bereft and pathetic. She clung tightly to Anne's hand and spoke with a slight lisp. "I'm glad you've come." She peered nervously over the edge of the blanket and added, "Has he gone?"

Anne said, "Yes," automatically, and looked around the room, but it seemed to be empty. She wondered vaguely whether Paul or Spike had been there.

"He was here," Grandma went on, "he was right in here tonight, when that fool of a nurse was out. But he didn't get anything out of me. I'm not afraid of him."

"Of course you're not," Anne murmured soothingly.

The old lady smiled and said, "It's good to have you back, Missy."

Anne looked at her, a little startled, and she went on, "It's been so long." She closed her eyes for a moment. "You should have come home sooner—you should have come when my boy died."

Anne murmured, "Yes, I know—I'm sorry. But I'm here now."

Grandma closed her eyes again and seemed to go to sleep, but her hand still clung tightly to Anne's. Anne glanced around the room, the furniture looming heavily in the dim light, and the carpet iron-hard under her feet. After a while she felt Grandma's hold relax, and she withdrew her hand and massaged her stiff fingers.

When the door opened quietly she got to her feet with a stiffening of her whole body. But it was only Tim—still resplendent in the lumber jacket. He came in and shut the door behind him.

"Darling, I saw that resourceful nurse go out, so that I was sure I would find you here, holding the fort."

"She went to post a letter."

"No, precious. I followed her, because I like to turn stones over as I go along. She goes to the corner pub on these little excursions."

"Pub?" Anne said vaguely.

"A place where they dispense alcoholic beverages, dear. She needs a drink now and then—such a hideous job, nursing—lights, a few cheery souls, and a short snort—it isn't too unreasonable."

"Who said it was?" Anne asked sourly. "But this is her job—not mine—and I need my sleep. I have to go out and look for a job myself tomorrow."

"But you can't, my sweet, unless you find the black coat. It's frightfully cold outside."

"I'll borrow a coat," Anne said almost sulkily.

"Darling, you can't. You promised to search all their rooms tomorrow—and a promise is a promise. I must know in which room that coat is hidden. Besides, you would look forlorn in any coat you could borrow in this house."

"I don't see why you didn't go into the police force," Anne said crossly, "so that you could have had flatfeet to assist you instead of putting it all on to me."

"There's a very vast difference," he explained, "between work that must be done and work that is just a hobby. This work is my hobby, and I find it fascinating, and you are a fascinating helper. It makes all the difference. And please don't be difficult, pet."

Anne swallowed a yawn, and he said anxiously, "I could be more entertaining, but I don't want to wake the old trout."

Anne ended the yawn on a giggle and asked, "Did you find any dug-up places in the back yard?"

"My dear, the back yard is covered with snow—fairly smooth snow—so that if the skeleton came from there, it was not a recent job."

Anne moaned over another yawn, and he said, "If you find that coat tomorrow morning, you will surely bring it to my room, will you not?"

"Your room?" Anne said, with mock horror. "Certainly not. How dare you suggest such a thing!"

"Darling, you are being difficult. You know I was merely thoroughly jealous—and why not? You very meanly pushed me out to walk with that crashing bore, Roger, who cannot possibly have anything to do with all this."

"Why not? He walked right into my room last night. He could have pulled the hand down and stuffed it into the pocket of his robe before George switched on the light."

Before Tim could reply, Grandma's voice spoke up suddenly from the bed.

"I should have locked him up in that room, but I didn't like to with that other one there."

CHAPTER FIFTEEN

ANNE AND TIM to look at the old lady, but she had closed her eyes again and was plucking at the bedclothes. Her lips continued to move, but she said nothing more. Anne went over and took her hand, and she opened her eyes for a brief smile, then appeared to drift off to sleep.

Miss Kalms came in quietly, stopped in the middle of the floor, and gave a gasp, with one hand over her heart.

Anne looked up at her, and said, "It's all right—it isn't a stickup—only a gentleman in casual clothes."

Miss Kalms breathed again. "How silly of me—really very silly —but he gave me such a scare."

Tim looked thoroughly offended. "There's an ailment known, vulgarly, as d.t.s, Miss Kalms," he said coldly. "You want to be a little careful about that."

Miss Kalms widened her eyes innocently. "Really? What are the symptoms? Does it feel terrible?"

Tim took Anne's arm and urged her out of the room. He said, "Come, darling," in a slightly shaken voice.

"I'm going to bed," Anne said firmly.

"Of course—you must. You are tired out." He opened her door and she went in and said good night, but when he closed it after her, she found that he'd shut himself in with her.

"Tim!" Anne said in an exasperated voice. "I'll have to scream if you don't get out of here—you told me so yourself. You said that men were such beasts."

He ignored her and cast himself into an armchair, holding his head in his hands.

"It's there," he muttered. "It's all there for me to see—but I'm blind. She was going to lock him up in the room, but didn't, because that other one was there. It's just as though I knew it—all of it—but had forgotten it. I must think."

Anne gave a loud sigh. "Tim, for God's sake, go and sleep on it—and let me sleep too."

He looked up at her, then closed his eyes as if in pain. "It's dangerous— I know it's dangerous—and I don't know how to protect you. If I had only thought, we could have run around the corner today and gotten married. Then I could have slept in here with you. I don't like your being here alone—I do not like it."

"How many times have you been married, Tim?"

"Only three," he said absently.

Anne murmured, "Goodness!"

He looked at her. "Goodness is exactly what it was. I always marry—I'm not like the worthy George, who has never been married, but who certainly doesn't spend all his spare time picking daisies in the green fields."

"All right," Anne said wearily, "you're a good boy, and George is bad—but will you please go away and let me get some sleep? I'll lock the door and even put the bureau in front of it, if that will make you feel any better."

"Very well, dear." He got to his feet. "But I must search the room first. It would be hideous to lock yourself in with something."

Anne moaned, but he began to move swiftly around the room, and she presently dropped onto a straight chair and watched him. He did a thorough job, but when he began to go through the bureau drawers, she protested. "There's nothing there but my personal belongings."

"Of course, dear—but you're so innocent. Something might have been planted. For instance, what's this?"

Anne looked at it and explained through a yawn, "It's a sharp book knife that my uncle Percy brought me from India."

"Oh well, keep it hidden. Now I think that takes care of everything." He went to the door, locked and then tried it, and nodded his head. "It holds, you see—so now you should be quite safe."

"Except that you've locked yourself on the wrong side of the door."

"Don't be silly, pet, I'm going now. But I shall wait outside until I hear you lock the door, and then I shall try it." He opened the door and added, "Good night, my darling. Isn't sudden love like this wonderful?"

"How would I know?" Anne said, and banged the door behind him.

She could hear him giving instructions from outside for a while, but he presently went away, and she staggered over to her bed and fell into it. She went to sleep at once—possibly reassured by Tim's protective measures—and slept heavily.

When she awoke, she thought that it was dawn, but since the room was never very light during the daytime, because the adjoining building was so close, she rolled over and looked at her watch. It was eleven o'clock.

She groaned and got out of bed in a hurry. She dressed as quickly as possible, cursing Tim occasionally, and longing for coffee to drive away the blurry feeling in her head. She had gone all the way downstairs before she realized that the dining room would most certainly be closed. There was no one about, and after hesitating for a moment she advanced to the archway that led into the lounge. The place was deserted except for Mr. Courtney, who sat in an armchair, reading his morning paper. Probably, Anne thought, they had a deadline in the dining room, at which point even Mr. Courtney was put out into the lounge to finish his paper.

He looked up at her, and she said, "Good morning."

He stood up, bowed slightly, and replied, "Good morning, Miss Anne. How is your grandmother today?"

Anne, always uncomfortable about her false status, felt herself coloring as she said, "About the same, thank you."

She turned to go, but he called after her rather peremptorily. "Come and sit down for a moment, will you? I should like to talk to you."

Anne came back reluctantly, her longing for coffee beginning to sharpen into a headache.

"That friend of yours," said Mr. Courtney, "the one who did the little service for me. What is he?"

Anne looked blank. To tell Mr. Courtney that Tim was the butcher's son would certainly cause him to look down his nose—and what else did she know of Tim ?

"I mean," said Mr. Courtney, becoming more specific, "what does he do for a living?"

"Well, I really don't know. But he seems to have plenty of money."

Mr. Courtney frowned and muttered something about Mrs. Smith, Jr., becoming very careless about whom she admitted into the house.

Anne gave him a frown of her own and said stiffly, "Tim was introduced to me by a very good friend of mine."

"You are already calling him by his first name ?"

"Why not?"

"And I suppose he calls you 'Anne,' " Mr. Courtney said severely.

"Oh no—hardly ever. Mostly, it's 'darling' and 'precious' and things like that."

Mr. Courtney sniffed, and after the sniff, said in a distant voice, "I see."

Anne stood up. "See you again," she said lightly, and hurried from the room before he could think of anything else to detain her. She had decided that she'd better go out and find a restaurant where she could get some breakfast and went upstairs to get sweaters and the light jacket she had worn to Mary's.

Miss Kalms was waiting in the upstairs hall. She caught at Anne's arm and said breathlessly, "Just for a few minutes, dear, if you wouldn't mind? I'm out of chewing gum—and I have to have my gum while I'm on duty—it keeps me from getting nervous."

Anne said, "I haven't had my breakfast yet—I'll bring your gum back with me," but Miss Kalms was already scuttling down the stairs.

Anne ground her teeth in annoyance and went in to look at Grandma, who appeared to be sleeping peacefully. She wandered out into the hall again and saw Mr. and Mrs. Roger Crimple on the way to their room. They bowed politely and asked after her grandmother, and Roger boomed out the information that they had been for a walk.

Liz Sampson came down the stairs a few minutes later and waved gaily. "Lovely day, isn't it, dear?" she called cheerfully.

Anne said, "No," but Liz was the kind who never bothered to wait for answers. She went straight into Tim's room without knocking.

Anne stared at the closed door. So Tim was already working on Liz— or perhaps she had worked on him—and Anne was to be tossed aside. She had been feeling irritated and cross, but this thought lifted her face into a faint smile.

Miss Burreton came up the stairs, wearing an outdoor costume which looked a bit like an old skating print. Anne smiled and said, "Good morning." Miss Burreton cut her dead. Probably, Anne thought, her unseemly behavior of the previous evening had gotten about. It seemed likely that there was little Miss Burreton did not know about the clientele of the Smith menage.

She could hear Liz and Tim talking in his room, and, presently, Liz emerged, calling back over her shoulder. "Thanks a million, Tim, darling, I'll be ready at one." She closed the door before Anne could get so much as a glimpse of Tim.

She gave Anne a brilliant smile and trilled, "Still here? Now don't worry, dearie—I've no designs on your nice boy."

Anne said, "I was only waiting for—" and let the sentence die away, when she realized that Liz was already out of earshot. She wondered whether Liz liked martinis, and whether she was twenty years older than Tim, or more nearly thirty.

She glanced in at Grandma again, found her still sleeping peacefully, and went across to her own room to get her jacket, so that she would not be delayed when Miss Kalms returned. She put on two sweaters, then went to the closet for the jacket. She pulled the door open, then stood for a moment, looking at the clothes that hung inside. The black seal coat had been replaced.

Whoever had taken it, then, had brought it back. But when? While she was downstairs talking to Mr. Courtney, of course—it was the only possible time.

She pulled it out, and the hanger fell to the floor with a clatter. She kicked it away—too irritated to be bothered picking it up— and flung the coat onto the bed. She exposed the lining and felt her breath quicken. It had been ripped open, then pinned together again with small, straight pins. She pulled the pins out with frantic haste and rooted around energetically inside the lining— but there was nothing except dust and odd pieces of desiccated padding. She stood for a moment, tapping her lip with her forefinger, then she picked the coat up and draped it over her shoulders. She felt an odd sense of excitement rising in her when she thought that it was considerably lighter. There had been money in the lining, then—surely there was no doubt of it now.

She threw the coat onto the bed again and began to explore the lining slowly and methodically. If the thief had left just one bill there, then she could be sure. She was careful, this time, and patient—and, presently, her efforts were rewarded. Her exploring fingers closed over paper. She withdrew her dusty hand and saw that she held a twenty-dollar bill.

She sat down on the bed to think it over. It would take a great many twenty-dollar bills to make up the fortune that had seemed to be indicated—but of course there might have been bills of a larger denomination as well.

She stood up abruptly, hung the coat back in the closet, and put on the jacket. It seemed thin and inadequate for the weather outside, and she surveyed what she could see of herself in the bureau mirror and longed impatiently for a full-length one. The jacket really was not right for her costume, and, besides, she'd freeze in it. She cursed Anne Magraw for stealing her coat and Tim for insisting upon alterations on the new one.

She remembered Grandma at last and decided that she'd better have a look at her, in case Miss Kalms had not returned.

The door to Grandma's room was slightly open, as she had left it, and when she went in, she saw that Miss Kalms was not there. She thought that the old lady was awake, because her eyes were wide open, and she approached the bed hastily, with an uneasiness that she could not have explained.

Grandma's eyes were not only open, but bulging hideously—and her skin had changed from waxy paleness to a livid purple.

CHAPTER SIXTEEN

THE OLD LADY WAS DEAD, and Anne, through her shock and horror, realized that she, herself, had left her alone to die. But perhaps there was still some life—something that could be done. She must get a doctor at once. She ran to Tim's room and flung open the door.

He was sitting before a small portable typewriter, but when he saw her face, he pushed back from it and got to his feet with a look of alarm.

"Oh, Tim—quickly! We must get a doctor! The old lady—Mrs. Smith—I think she's dead."

Tim took her arm without any words, and they hurried out into the hall together. Miss Kalms had just reached the top of the stairs, and after one brief glance at them she began to run. She reached Grandma's room a few steps ahead of them and went over to the bed. The sound of her breath was audible as she drew it in sharply, and she turned away again almost immediately. She said flatly, "I'll get the doctor," and ran out again.

Anne stood in the middle of the room, her eyes on anything but the bed.

She wished despairingly that she had stayed with Grandma—she might have been able to help her somehow.

Tim was leaning over the still little figure, and presently he gave a low whistle. Anne turned her head sharply, and he said, "Darling, she's been murdered."

"Oh no!" Anne protested, sounding like a child. "She's been so ill—this—this wasn't unexpected."

"Come here."

Anne moved over beside him, and he carefully lifted the bedclothes a little from under the sharp old chin. She forced herself to look down, but it was some time before she saw it—a deep crease in the neck—so deep that the cord which made it was nearly invisible.

Anne gave a little cry and said frantically, "Oh, take it off—quickly—please take it off!"

Tim replaced the bedclothes and shook his head. "She's quite dead, dear."

Miss Kalms returned, followed by Mrs. Smith, who went quickly over to the bed, then turned away with her hands over her face. "Oh, dear," she sobbed, and repeated it desolately through her tears, "Oh, dear, oh, dear."

Anne put an arm across her shoulders. "You shouldn't cry for her, she—she's better off. She was ill and miserable, and there was no chance for her."

Mrs. Smith raised her face and brushed at her wet eyes with the back of her wrist. "She did, too, have a chance—the doctor said so only this morning when he was leaving. He said she was much better, and maybe, this time, she'd come out of it."

Tim said tensely, "The doctor said that? You are sure?"

Mrs. Smith looked at him as though she were wondering vaguely why he was there.

"The doctor said definitely that she had a chance to recover?" he repeated impatiently.

"Why, yes. It was this morning."

"Where was he when he said it?"

Mrs. Smith brushed at her eyes again and muttered, "What?"

"Where was he—where were you standing—when he said she might get better?"

"He told me this morning—he said she had a good chance."

"He said it here—in front of her?"

"Oh no," Mrs. Smith said. "It was down in the front hall—just before he left, you know. That's when he always talks to me about her condition."

Tim chewed his lip for a moment and then said abruptly, "We shall have to call the police."

Mrs. Smith stared at him, and, at the same time, Miss Kalms, who had gone to the bedside, let out a little shriek. "My God! I thought there was something wrong as soon as I looked at her—I couldn't make it out. Oh, Lord—this is a mess!"

Tim said, "I'll go and call them," but Mrs. Smith stopped him with a hand on his arm.

"What do you mean? What are you talking about? We don't want the police here."

"Let him go," Miss Kalms said quietly. "Come here, Mrs. Smith—I'll show you."

But Mrs. Smith covered her face once more and moaned, "I can't—I can't look at her again. What is it? Tell me."

Tim went off quickly, and Anne took a few uncertain steps after him. Mrs. Smith, fumbling unsuccessfully for a handkerchief, eventually took a tissue from a box on the table and said in a muffled voice, "Don't go—please. Stay and tell me what it is."

Anne glanced at Miss Kalms, who said directly, "I'm sorry, Mrs. Smith, but she's been strangled."

"What? Strangled? But—"

Miss Kalms explained about the cord, her voice professionally unemotional, and Mrs. Smith muttered stupidly, "You mean someone put a cord around her neck and—and killed her? But who did it?"

Miss Kalms was silent, and Mrs. Smith looked at Anne.

"I don't know," Anne said unhappily. "I was supposed to be looking after her, but she had gone to sleep, and I went to my room for a while. It—must have happened then."

"You mean she was alone?"

Miss Kalms colored and said quickly, "It was not for long. Her granddaughter was with her—you know I'd never leave her alone—I was just posting a letter."

Anne looked down at her feet and said nothing. Mrs. Smith threw the tissue into a wastebasket and took another one, and when she spoke, her voice was firmer and more normal. "You have four hours off in the afternoon when you could post letters and do things like that. I don't see why you have to post letters in the morning."

Miss Kalms fingered the fancy handkerchief that sprayed out of the pocket on her left shoulder and said readily, "Now, you know I've always stuck to business here, Mrs. Smith. I never left her alone—but when she had visitors I always thought it was better to slip out. A patient gets tired of her nurse being there all the time."

Mrs. Smith was silent for a while, and it began to appear that Miss Kalms had won her point and had the last word. When Mrs. Smith did at last give voice she changed the subject completely by going into hysterics.

Miss Kalms took charge competently and presently said to Anne, "I'll have to get her to bed. You stay here—you mustn't leave until the doctor comes."

Anne nodded miserably, feeling that she'd like to be put to bed herself. She watched the two women until they disappeared out the door, and then decided that at the first possible moment she'd return to Mary's apartment— where she should have stayed in the first place.

Tim came back after a while, looking grim and unhappy. He said bitterly, "What good am I? I should have foreseen all this—foreseen it and prevented it. I had no idea that her life was in danger, but I should have known it. As soon as the coat was stolen, I should have known. He'd naturally want to close Grandma's mouth at once. That coat—did you find it?"

Anne nodded and explained—a necessarily halting explanation, since he kept interrupting with questions. He considered it for a while and then said abstractedly, "He returned the coat while you were downstairs talking to Mr. Courtney. Unless, of course, it was Mr. Courtney himself. He could have slipped in and out again while you were with Grandma."

"There wouldn't be much time."

"No—it is not at all probable, but it is a possibility. I must overlook no angles this time—I cannot let anyone else get murdered because I am too slow in my thinking."

Anne gasped. "Who else?"

But Tim shook his head and muttered, "It's odd he didn't sew the lining up again."

"Perhaps he can't sew."

"Possibly. Most men assume they can't sew, and, therefore, they never try."

"You're sure it's a man, then?"

"No—not sure. But Grandma knew who it was, and she always said 'he.' "

Anne nodded soberly. "And now she's dead and can't tell us who it is."

"Darling, don't make me feel worse than I do. Come and show me the coat."

They went across to Anne's room, and she took the coat out of the closet and handed it to him. She had put the twenty-dollar bill into a drawer, and she showed him that too—although, as far as she could see, it was merely a twenty-dollar bill, without any distinguishing marks.

Tim examined the coat with the utmost care. He was absorbed in it for so long that Anne presently lit a cigarette and began to wander restlessly around the room. She looked at him several times with growing impatience and, at last, burst out crossly, "My God! I must have some coffee. I've given up any hope of breakfast—but if I don't get coffee, I'll collapse."

Tim looked up at once and threw the coat to one side. "You've had no coffee, dear? Then we shall get some at once."

The sound of a gong suddenly boomed up from the lower hall, and Tim opened the door and looked out.

"It's lunch, precious—the inmates are streaming out from their rooms like ants. You can get your coffee now—and it will be better than going out somewhere. I can be here when the police come.

He caught her hand and pulled her toward the stairs.

Grandma's door was slightly open as they passed it, and they could see that the doctor had arrived, but as they started down the stairs the door was closed firmly. The police came just as they got to the lower hall, and Tim deserted Anne promptly and went back upstairs with them, his face eager and alert.

Anne went on to the dining room. Liz Sampson was there, and the Crimples, Miss Burreton, and Mr. Courtney. It was at once obvious that they knew of Grandma's death—but evidently no one knew that it was a murder. They were discussing it in hushed, shocked voices. Miss Burreton listened and shook her head occasionally in a doleful manner.

Anne sat down just as Monty appeared at the door. He hesitated for a moment, then walked straight over and sat at her table. The rest of them stopped talking and watched him, as one person, while he settled himself. Monty looked up, swept a glance around the room, and observed rudely, "Rubbernecks!"

They all looked away at once, and Monty gave his attention to Anne. He said in a low voice, "You look more upset than I do—and yet she wasn't related to you at all."

"Well, I—I knew her—and she was fond of me, because she thought I was her granddaughter. You must feel it a little, don't you?"

"Maybe a little—but not much." He offered her a cigarette, but she shook her head.

"I'm just going to have lunch."

"That's what you think. But all the old mossbacks were here first, so they'll be served first."

Anne sighed, and accepted a cigarette.

Tim came in and sat down with them. "They wouldn't even let me open my mouth," he said bitterly. "They don't want to be told anything—they want to find out everything for themselves—so that they can get their stupid backs patted."

Monty said, "What in hell is he talking about?"

Tim seemed to notice him for the first time. He said in an aggrieved voice, "Darling, *must* I find you with a new man every time I turn my back for a moment?"

"I'm not a man," Monty told him carelessly. "I'm a wayward boy."

Tim shrugged him off and turned to Anne. "I did tell you, precious, that the police are blundering fools—and this proves it. They wouldn't listen to one thing that I thought it was my duty to tell them."

Monty dropped his cigarette and picked it up again with shaking fingers. He said thickly, "What are you talking about—the police? They're not here, are they?"

Tim looked at him, then spoke in a clear voice so that the rest of the room would have no trouble in hearing. "Of course the police are here. Grandma was murdered. Didn't you know?"

Monty didn't know. He left the room without another word—in a great hurry—and left uproar behind him. All eating was suspended, and the loudest voice in the babble came from Roger. Pet tried to quiet him in an agitated fashion. Liz was talking and crying at the same time, Mr. Courtney was talking, but could not be heard, and Miss Burreton kept repeating like a parrot, "What is it? What is it? What is it?"

Mr. Alrian, who had just come in, asked each one in turn what was wrong and received no answer.

A man appeared at the doorway, an impressive individual who appeared to be well over six feet tall, with a build to correspond with his height, and a flaming bush of bright red hair. He said, "Will everybody be quiet, please?" and the din subsided at once. Only Miss Burreton's thin pipe survived, and she changed over to, "Who's this? Who's this? Who's this?"

Tim said to Anne under his breath, "Typical superflatfoot."

The man said he was Vally, of the police, and if they didn't mind, he'd like a word with each one of them in turn. They were to continue eating their lunches and were not to allow him to disturb them.

Nobody said anything but Miss Burreton, who asked again, "Who's this?"

Vally gave her a glance and cleared his throat. He said, "Oh, by the way, I wonder whether any of you knows to whom this belongs?" He held up a cord, yellowish in color, that appeared to have come from a robe. Anne knew at once that it had been used to strangle Grandma.

Ginny, standing with two plates firmly clutched in her hands, said, "Oh, sure—that belongs to Mr. George."

CHAPTER SEVENTEEN

TIM SMIRKED, and Anne frowned at him, but Vally of the police remained imperturbable. He merely asked, "Which one of you gentlemen is Mr. George?"

Roger Crimple rose to his feet and began, "She means—"

But Vally had never been a man to waste time. He said, "You're Mr. George? I'd like to speak to you."

Roger swelled and crimsoned. He hated being interrupted, and his wife rarely irritated him in this fashion—as he sometimes admitted in his more genial moments. He said to Vally, "I am *not* Mr. George, sir, he is at his office, which is usual at this time on a weekday. I merely wished to give you some information that would save you time—but it will delay matters considerably if you keep interrupting me."

Vally shifted his weight from one of his flat feet to the other and removed a toothpick from his vest pocket. He had met nuts before, and he would meet them again. "I'm listening," he said briefly.

Roger, comforted by the thought that he had put a member of the police force in his place, cleared his throat and began. "In the first place, the gentleman's name is Mr. George Vaddison, and he is a nephew by marriage of the elder Mrs. Smith, who is now dead."

"When did she die?" Vally inquired courteously.

Roger flung his napkin down on the table, and a corner of it landed in his luncheon plate. Pet quietly removed it and brushed it off.

"I am referring to the Mrs. Smith who now lies dead upstairs," Roger said furiously. "Why do you keep interrupting me, sir? As I was saying—"

Vally, gauging the well out of his long experience, decided that it had run dry of anything pertinent, and shut it off.

"Thank you, sir—very much obliged." He widened his attention to include the rest of the room and added, "I presume Mr. Vaddison will be here this evening?"

One or two of them nodded, and Vally nodded back, then went to sit with Miss Burreton. While she stared at him with open mouth, he waved an arm around at the others and said, "Kindly go on with your lunches."

They shifted their eyes, and some even picked up forks, but they all listened carefully.

Vally gave his attention to Miss Burreton and asked politely, "May I have your name?"

Miss Burreton continued to stare at him, and Tim tried to lend a hand.

"Miss Burreton, Vally."

Vally, giving him a cold eye, said, "Thanks, but I'll get along without any help," and excluded him by turning a broad back.

"It really is casting pearls before swine," Tim observed, "and I should know better. Darling, have you had your coffee yet?"

Everyone, with the exception of Vally, said, "Shh!"

Tim lapsed into an injured silence, and Ginny hurried out to the kitchen to get coffee for Anne.

Miss Burreton was saying, "Yes, she was my very old friend—very old friend—but sometimes she wasn't very nice to me."

"How come?"

"Eh?" said Miss Burreton.

"What did she do to you that wasn't nice?" Vally asked more specifically.

Miss Burreton merely sniffed and continued to stare at him.

"Did you know that somebody murdered her this morning?"

Miss Burreton looked mildly puzzled and said, "She's dead, I know, because that nurse told me."

Vally shifted in his chair and asked patiently, "Where were you all the morning?"

She chewed on her gums, blinked a couple of times, and evidently decided not to struggle with it, for she remained silent.

"Did you take a walk?"

"Yes, yes, yes—of course."

"Do you always take a walk in the morning?"

"Yes. Certainly."

Someone snickered, and Miss Burreton added, "A lady should always take a walk for exercise, you know."

Vally said, "Yes, I know," and got to his feet rather heavily.

Mr. Alrian hailed him and said in his precise voice, "I must get back to my office, so that if you wish to question me, I should appreciate it if you would do it now."

Vally exchanged a few brief phrases with him which brought out the facts that he had been at his office all the morning, that he usually came home for lunch, and that he could not remember when he had last seen Grandma, since he never visited her in her room—he did not know her that well.

As Mr. Alrian departed, office bound, Liz and Mr. Courtney entered into a polite scuffle as to who should be next. Liz eventually won out, since she had the louder voice, and she started in on Vally before he could so much as open his mouth.

"This is an *awful* thing, and I don't know when I've been so shaken. You see, we had no idea that it was *murder*—positively no *idea*. We heard that the poor old soul had died just before lunch, and of course we were all very shocked, but then, she's been so ill, so that we really expected her to pass away at any time—but when this gentleman"—she gestured at Tim—"came in and told us it was *murder!* Well!"

Vally said desperately, "What is your name, madam?"

"I'm Liz Sampson—Mrs. Edwin Sampson—divorced, however. I'm an actress, but just now I'm in the middle of a long rest. Some of the shows I've appeared in—"

Vally tried to stop it, but his voice was drowned out and finally lost. Liz mentioned the parts she'd had and quoted the reviews—all good. In the end, she explained that she knew Vally was the thorough type and would want all details, no matter how seemingly unimportant.

She was eventually obliged to pause for breath, and Vally asked feverishly, "Have you enough money for this long rest you're taking?"

Liz was furious. She explained, haughtily, that she had enough money for the rest of her life—no matter how long—but she might go back to the stage, since that was her real interest. Furthermore, it was most impertinent of Vally to insinuate himself into her private and financial affairs.

Vally admitted it, but explained that he was the thorough kind, and then asked her how she had spent the morning.

Liz cheered up and took a long breath. Directly after breakfast she had gone back to bed for a nap. This was a fairly frequent practice of hers, since breakfast was served at such an absurdly early hour in this place—and she would prefer to skip breakfast entirely, rather than get up so early, except that her doctor forbade it. However, she was such an old friend of the Smiths that she feared they would be offended if she stayed at the Waldorf or any of those silly places—and, in any case, this house had an old world air that was quaintly appealing—even though it was inconvenient in so many ways.

Vally waited patiently, and when he found a spot to put a word in, did so promptly.

"How long did you nap?"

"Oh—well—not late. Until a little after ten."

"And then?"

"Well—if I must tell the truth like a good girl—then I went in and flirted with Timmy."

"Who's Timmy?" Vally asked, mopping his forehead.

Liz waggled her little finger at Tim and flashed him a brilliant smile at the same time.

Vally stuffed his handkerchief back into his pocket and said with faint contempt, "Oh, him."

"Yes." Liz shook her head a little. "I know I interrupted him in his work, but I'm sure he didn't mind."

"Not at all," Tim said with a slight bow.

Vally glanced at him. "You attend to your lunch—I'll be at your table soon. In the meantime, don't interrupt."

"I'll eat my lunch as soon as I get it," Tim said coldly. "Meanwhile I'll just listen."

Anne nudged him. "It's in front of you, Tim. Ginny just brought it."

Tim looked down, murmured, "Oh. So it is," and picked up a fork, but he made no real pretense of eating.

Liz patted her bosom and her back hair and went on: "As I was saying, Tim and I had quite a chat. After that I went to my room to freshen up, and met no one on the way except dear old Mrs. Smith's little granddaughter— she was standing in the hall just outside Grandma's room. We spoke briefly, and then I went on to my own bedroom, where I stayed until lunch was announced."

"It took you all that time to freshen up?"

"My dear man," she said airily, "of course. Don't you know *anything* about us foolish women?"

Vally sighed and got to his feet. He thanked Liz for being cooperative, and although she was still answering him, he turned away and sat down with Anne and Tim. He gave his attention entirely to Anne and half turned his back on Tim—since he had run into amateur detectives before.

"You are Mrs. Smith's granddaughter?"

Roger suddenly spoke up loudly. "This is most unfair. My wife and I were next."

"I beg your pardon," said Mr. Courtney. "I believe I—"

Vally silenced them both with a glance and turned back to Anne.

She was shaking her head. "I'm not Mrs. Smith's granddaughter."

"Oh? But I thought— Where is she?"

"In Philadelphia, I think."

Vally ran a hand through his red hair, and Tim said, "Let me explain."

"Let the lady tell it," Vally said coldly.

Anne told it—and included Spike and Paul as well—although she was conscious that Tim was trying to stop her from being so frank. Tim, she knew, figured that the police worked better if they were not confused by too much information at one time.

Vally was silent for a while after she had finished, but the others—who had been listening carefully—began an excited buzzing. Valley cast a glance around at them and discovered that Miss Burreton was at his elbow, chewing excitedly.

"What is it, Miss Burreton?"

"Eh?"

"Do you want anything?" Vally asked patiently.

"No." Miss Burreton continued to chew for a while and then explained simply, "I can't hear properly over there."

Vally got up. "Well, I'm through here anyway."

"What about me?" Tim asked indignantly.

Vally gave him a look in which dislike was becoming acute. "You come last—you're the least important."

Mr. Courtney said, "If you please, sir, I have an appointment very shortly."

Vally nodded. "Oh yes—it was your hand that—"

Roger boomed, "Devil take it, man, do you think we can sit here waiting all day?"

Vally dashed him completely by saying indifferently, "Leave if you wish, sir, and I'll question you later."

Roger settled back into his seat, unwilling to miss anything, and Vally turned to Mr. Courtney.

Mr. Courtney was disappointingly uninteresting. He had chatted with Anne in the lounge and then had gone up to his room. He actually blushed when Vally asked him about his hand, and tried to keep the hook hidden behind him. He explained that he used it because it was convenient, and that the artificial hand had been very expensive and was for his professional appearances. Vally asked when his last professional appearance had been and when his next was due to be, but Mr. Courtney merely said coolly, "That can hardly be of any interest to you, Mr. Vally. Good afternoon," and left forthwith.

Mr. and Mrs. Crimple were interviewed together, and Miss Burreton moved over to their table with Vally. He asked her, politely enough, to go back to her own seat, but she answered with equal courtesy, "Thank you, but I've finished." She sat down at the Dimples' table, and folded her arms over her stomach.

Roger said, "Miss Burreton, don't you think you should allow the detective to speak to us privately?" But she merely blinked at him, and he sat back again with an irritated gesture.

Vally turned to Pet and asked, "May I have your name, please?"

Pet smiled sweetly and said nothing, since she knew that Roger would answer—which he did immediately.

"We are Mr. and Mrs. Roger Crimple."

"You have been living here for some time?"

"Are you asking us or telling us?" Roger demanded.

Vally mentally reviewed a rude expression, but kept it off his tongue. He heard Tim giggle, and Miss Burreton said, "Yes indeed, indeed, indeed."

Vally, in a rather childish desire to get even with Roger, turned to Miss Burreton and asked, "Have they been here as long as you?"

Miss Burreton nodded several times, and Roger shouted,

"That's a lie! She lived here before it became a hotel, and we moved in as soon as they opened it up for paying guests."

"How long has it been a hotel?" Vally asked.

Roger screwed up his face to think, and Pet was able to get in her first words. "Twenty years, dear," she said gently to Roger.

Roger nodded. "Right—right. Ever since the old lady's son died, and the widow and child came here to live."

Vally nodded, and hurried on to prevent Roger from telling any more. "Now, may I ask what you people did during the morning?"

"You may ask," Roger said belligerently, "but I defy you to demand."

Pet put her hand on his arm. "Now, Roger—it was nothing. We had breakfast, and then we read the morning paper in the lounge. We went to our room and performed a few small duties and then went out for a walk. We had several errands, and when they were done, we came back and went to our room again. When we heard the gong, we came down right away."

Vally said, "Thank you, Mrs. Crimple," and at that moment George walked into the room.

He looked grim and forbidding, and he went straight to Vally. "You are the officer in charge, I believe?"

Vally stood up and nodded, his eyes showing a sudden spark of interest.

"Then I want you to put the works in motion at once to find my relative, Monty Smith."

CHAPTER EIGHTEEN

ROGER SWEPT HIS NAPKIN across his mustache and said in a voice muffled by a mouthful of food, "Nonsense, George. Monty is here—he was in this room not a moment since."

Vally silenced him with a wiggle of the eyebrows and asked George, "Who are you, sir?"

George told him and explained rather feverishly, "Miss Kalms phoned me, and I came back at once. Mrs. Smith, Jr., was hysterical, but she managed to tell me that Monty had come flying upstairs, packed a few things, and fled, after telling her not to try to find him. Now, he's young, and he's impetuous and foolish—he's probably dreamed up some sort of trouble for himself that doesn't exist. I want you to find him."

"Why should he think he's in trouble?" Vally asked quietly.

George frowned, but he said readily enough, "He and his grandmother never got on, but there was nothing more than that to it."

Tim was busily taking down notes on a small pad, and Vally, glancing at him in an abstracted moment, sighed deeply and turned back to George.

"May I speak to you privately, sir?"

George nodded, and they went off, leaving a flat silence behind them.

Roger presently broke it by saying with a shake of his head, "Monty's a fool."

Liz sighed loudly. "He was just plain scared, but then, see, everybody here knows how he treated poor old Grandma."

Miss Burreton accelerated her chewing and said excitedly, "Disgraceful. It was disgraceful."

"Well, you know," Pet said gently, "she wouldn't leave him alone. Young people are impatient of supervision—and you really can't blame them."

Roger gave Anne a rather severe look and observed, "My dear girl, that was a fantastic story you told." He thought about it for a moment and then decided that it was funny after all. "Are you sure you just didn't make it up to amuse the redheaded policeman?" he asked, and roared with laughter.

Pet looked properly shocked at once. "Hush, Roger, hush! This is a house of death."

Roger sobered immediately and followed the others to the lounge on tiptoe. Out in the hall he felt a hand on his arm and turned to find Ginny regarding him with a worried eye.

"Mr. Crimple, that man didn't ask me no questions."

"Well, don't worry, my girl, he'll get around to you."

Ginny narrowed her eyes and said thoughtfully, "I could tell him a few things, believe me—there being not so much else to do in a job like this but keep your eyes and ears open."

"Yes, yes—no doubt, no doubt," Roger muttered impatiently, and moved away.

But Tim had heard, and he stopped so suddenly that Anne, whose had he held, was jerked around and bumped into Miss Burreton. Miss Burreton gave her a fierce look and said, "Disgraceful!"

Anne had time to murmur breathlessly, "So sorry," before she was pulled to the back of the hall, where Tim immediately began a low-voiced conversation with Ginny.

Anne heard her say, "I get a rest in about half an hour, and I'll talk with you then."

"Right. Up in my room."

"Not up in your room," Ginny said firmly, "that being against the rules— and who am I to break a rule with the old lady lying dead in her bed?"

"I'll come to the kitchen, then," Tim agreed hastily, "in half an hour."

Ginny nodded and made off, and Anne said mildly, "Tim, don't you think you should let the police take over?"

"Good heavens, darling, this thing is becoming dangerous, and you want me to let the police take over—the *police!* There is somebody around here— somebody—and I must find out *today*—before anything more happens."

She tried to free her hand, but he clutched it more tightly, and led her up the stairs to his room, where he sat her down.

She looked up at him with an exasperated sigh that was nearly a laugh. "Look—don't you think you could get on with this sleuthing better if I left you alone?"

"Darling, *please.* I want you here beside me—I *need* you—while I think. You stimulate me."

Anne gave another sigh, in which there was no laughter at all, and reflected that it would be very boring indeed to sit around doing nothing while Tim thought. She wondered, in a confused fashion, why she didn't simply say so and go.

Tim was making martinis with some ice which he unwrapped from a piece of newspaper.

"Where did you get that?" Anne asked, staring at him.

"Out of the water glasses," he said absently. "Now the way I see it, precious, Monty would not have fled simply because he didn't get on with his grandmother—there must have been some other reason."

"A couple of them, probably. Listen, Tim, I think I should move out of here and go and stay with Mary."

George walked into the room—without having knocked—and, picking up Anne's martini, drained it at one gulp.

Tim was furious. "Look what you've done! That's all the ice I have, and I can't make her another."

George dropped rather heavily into a chair and rubbed his closed fist across his forehead. "If you want ice, stick a glass of water out on the ruddy windowsill—it's as cold as hell out there. Anyway, my need is greater than hers. Tim, if you have any way of getting Monty back, for God's sake get him—it's most important. He's made a lousy mess of things—running off this way."

"Why did you run straight to the police about it?" Tim asked, forgetting Anne's martini.

"Miss Kalms saw him rush off and heard what he said to his mother. Naturally she'd have told about it sooner or later, so that I thought the best thing would be to make out that he's a scared kid and try to get him back."

Tim nodded. "Something to that. Why *did* he run off?"

George hesitated while he ran a hand through his already disordered hair. He said at last, "Because he *is* a scared kid. He never got on with his grandmother, and everybody knew it—and he's been hanging around here depending on his mother for support. He was afraid they'd accuse him of the murder."

"Oh no." Tim shook his head. "There are several things you could call Monty—and I've been tempted more than once—but he is not a scared kid."

George stared down at the carpet in silence, and Tim watched him alertly. Anne moved restlessly in her chair and said—as much to herself as to them—"I feel wretched about the whole thing. I was supposed to be watching Grandma—but she was asleep, so I went to my room for a while."

George looked up and said quickly, "You must not let that worry you. Miss Kalms should not have left her—but, in any case, she could hardly have been watched every minute." He stood up abruptly and began to pace the floor. "Who could have done a thing like that? And why?"

"The 'why' is quite simple," Tim said carelessly. "She was beginning to talk, and someone had to stop it."

George stopped and looked at him. "What do you mean?"

"The money in the coat—she practically told Anne about that—and this character was outside the door and understood immediately. Anne got it eventually—but, in the meantime the coat had been taken, ripped open, and returned."

"What money in what coat?" George asked, clutching at his hair again.

"Remember Anne's deduction of last night? And then she found that coat gone? It turned up again this morning—with no money in it, of course."

"Are you saying there actually was money in the lining of that coat?"

"There had been," Anne assured him eagerly. "I found one twenty-dollar bill away down inside."

"Why would he leave a twenty?"

"Overlooked," Anne said reasonably.

But Tim murmured, "I doubt it," and though they both looked at him expectantly, he refused to say more.

George muttered, "Oh, for God's sake, why don't you tell us what you mean? Things are bad enough without you sitting like a Buddha, bulging with secrets."

Tim jammed his hands into his pockets and said stubbornly, "I'll tell you—but not unless you tell me first about the cord."

"What cord, dammit?"

Tim groaned. "The cord that was used to strangle the old lady—they said it was yours. Surely Vally questioned you about it?"

"Oh, that." George dismissed it with an impatient gesture. "It was one of a set that was used to tie back the window drapes in my room. They made the place dark, so I had them tied back."

"Who tied them back?"

"Oh, my God!" George said. "I don't know. Mrs. Smith—or Ginny. How would I remember?"

Tim shrugged. "Keep your shirt on. You'll need it when the police really get to work on you."

"Well"—George made a halfhearted effort to smooth his wildly disordered hair—"I've plenty to do. Min—Mrs. Smith—has more or less collapsed since Monty ran out on us. But you promised to tell me what you meant about doubting that the money was in the coat."

"Oh yes—the coat. I can't actually believe that it was lined with money—there's something wrong with that—and I have an idea that the twenty was planted. I think perhaps there was something else there "

"What?" George asked, and at the same time Anne protested, "But Grandma said she'd sewed it into the lining—"

Tim held up a hand and stopped them both. "I think she sewed something into the coat—possibly something that contained money. A sop to her conscience, maybe—since Missy might eventually find it—"

"I have to go," George said abruptly. "You can stay here and go on dreaming."

"No." Tim stood up and reached for Anne's hand. "We must go too."

"I ought to be out looking for a job," Anne began helplessly.

"Dear"—Tim pressed her hand against his side—"you must not leave me—I cannot do it without you."

George looked back at them and said nastily, "The great love affair."

Tim raised his shoulders. "You are too coarse to understand. Come along, darling."

He made for the stairs, pulling Anne along with him. She gave a backward glance to George, who was watching them, but he merely raised his eyebrows at her.

They went down the back stairs and found themselves in a dark little hall with an open stairway to the cellar on one side. Tim looked downward into darkness and nodded. "We must go down there next and find that room. Darling, may I kiss you? We are so absolutely alone in this dim little place."

"No," said Anne. "What room?"

"The one Granny should have locked him in—except that that other was there."

"Who was the other?"

"The skeleton, of course."

"God almighty," said Anne, "what ideas you do get!"

They went through a large, old-fashioned pantry and from there to the kitchen. Ginny was seated with another woman at a table in the center of the room. She nodded to them, but the other woman said sharply, "Well! What is it?"

"This is our cook, Mrs. Johnson," Ginny explained. "The gentleman wants to ask me some questions, Mrs. Johnson."

Mrs. Johnson was old—probably as old as Grandma, Anne thought—but the small gray eyes in the seamed face were alert and watchful. She said abruptly, "We haven't much time to give you, young man—the police are coming down to talk to us in a minute."

"I shan't need more than a minute," Tim said, putting on his most charming manner. He sat down beside her, and Anne slumped into a fourth chair and groped for a cigarette.

"You have been here a long time," Tim was saying to Mrs. Johnson, "and you know everybody. Isn't that true?"

He was guessing, and Anne saw him draw a long breath when the old woman nodded and said, "That's right."

He was silent for a moment, then he said quietly, "You know all about this. You know who killed her."

Mrs. Johnson gazed out of the window, her lined old face set and hard. Then, suddenly, it crumpled, and she was crying.

Tim was an expert at this sort of thing. He consoled gently and unobtrusively and produced his own immaculate handkerchief to dry away the tears. "I know how you feel," he murmured. "I understand your grief—but she was very ill, and now she won't suffer any more."

The old lady said, "I know," on a long breath. "But if anyone deserved to suffer, she did—I've known her so long. Many's the time I was packed up ready to leave—but I never did. I'm used to it here, and I don't want to change now. I never let her come meddling in here, though—not but what she didn't want to—but she needed me, and she knew it."

"Did she treat everybody badly?" Tim asked.

"Ah, she was one of the meanest women I've ever known. She could let her own daughter starve—" She broke off, and turned her sharp old eyes on Anne. "Are you the granddaughter, or not?"

Anne shook her head. "I'm not."

"Well—if you came to get anything out of her, you've wasted your time. Nobody ever did—and now she's dead, nobody ever will. She hid her money where no one will ever find it."

"Perhaps she told her grandson," Tim suggested. "He might have found it."

"Oh no," said Mrs. Johnson decidedly. "She'd never tell him. No—she was determined to take it to the grave with her."

"But she was going to give it to her granddaughter," Tim said. "She thought Miss Anne was her granddaughter, and she said she was going to tell her where it was."

The old lady folded her hands in her lap and leaned back in her chair. "She never got around to telling her, though, did she?"

Anne said, "Not actually—but she dropped a lot of hints."

"See what I mean?" Mrs. Johnson said simply. She was silent for a moment, and then her hands began to twist together in her lap. "Oh, I don't know what's got into me, to be talking this way—I should let the dead rest in peace."

Tim patted the restless hands until they were still. "But you're only doing it to help find her murderer so that her death will be avenged."

"Oh no." The old lady's jaw snapped. "Nothing of the kind. I know who killed her—but I'm not telling."

CHAPTER NINETEEN

THERE WAS A BLANK SILENCE after Mrs. Johnson's statement, and then Tim said carefully, "Won't you tell us—just quietly here?"

The old lady said, "No," and closed her mouth firmly.

There was another silence broken by a loud snicker from Ginny.

Mrs. Johnson glanced at her and said grimly, "You get on about your work, girl."

Ginny shook back her short, straight hair and said with some spirit, "This is my rest period, and, anyway, the gentleman wants to ask me some questions—that being what he came here for." Tim looked at her vaguely and asked, "Do you know who killed Mrs. Smith?"

Ginny shook her head until her hair flopped back over her eyes again, and Tim returned his attention to Mrs. Johnson. "If you tell the police what you have just said, they'll take you in and beat the truth out of you."

"No policeman is going to beat anything out of me." But she looked a bit disturbed and turned an uneasy eye on Ginny. "You keep your mouth shut, you hear? Or you'll have all the cooking to do with only Mrs. Smith to help you. Remember when I had the influenza?"

Ginny shuddered and said a little indignantly, "I ain't one to say more than my prayers—nor I ever was."

Mrs. Johnson shifted her gaze to Anne and Tim. "You two can forget about it as well."

"Of course, of course," Tim assured her hastily. "But I do think you might tell us. This person should be put where he can't do any more murders."

"Oh no." The old lady shook her head. "This has been coming on for a long time—but it won't happen again."

"Do you know who I think done it?" Ginny said brightly.

Mrs. Johnson fixed her with a pair of cold gray eyes. "No, we don't—and we don't want to know."

"I think you should let her express her theory," Tim suggested, elaborately casual. "It might have some value—you never can tell."

But Ginny had already backed away. She mumbled, "Oh well—I don't really know anything about it—except they all hate each other—that being one of their indoor sports when the weather is too cold for them to go out and fight with their relatives."

Mrs. Johnson sniped and said curtly, "Nonsense."

Tim stood up abruptly. "We'll have another chat together soon, shall we?"

Ginny murmured, "Sure," and Mrs. Johnson said, "That's as may be."

Tim took Anne's arm and urged her out into the hall.

"I'm frightfully sorry, darling, but I'll have to go out on some business now. I shan't be long, so wait for me—and we'll have martinis when I get back."

Anne heaved a sigh. "Fine. I'll see you later." She started to say something more and then saw that Tim's attention had wandered. He was looking at a letter that lay on the hall table, and she peered around his shoulder and saw that it was addressed to Min Smith. The name of a bank was printed in the upper left-hand corner.

"I'd like to read this," Tim said, "but I dare not just now. I must go."

He detached a coat from the old-fashioned hat rack and pulled it on.

"Is that yours?" Anne asked.

"It positively is, my darling—I left it here this morning." He dropped a light kiss on her cheek and flew off.

Anne, looking after him, shook her head a little. What was she doing, anyway? If she didn't watch her step, she'd find herself winding up as Tim's fifth or sixth wife. She ought to avoid him. Only how did you avoid Tim? Well, she could leave—it would be the best thing, anyway. This ugly mess was none of her doing, and if she stayed around here, she might get tangled up in it. If she could not find another place, she'd go to Mary's.

She heard footsteps descending the stairs and hastily backed into the lounge, where she hid behind one of the dusty old velvet drapes that hung in the archway.

Vally and George came down to the hall, accompanied by another man, whose hat was on the back of his head and who chewed a toothpick in silence.

George seemed to be talking about Monty.

"He's very fond of his mother, and I'm sure that if you could find him, she'd be able to reason him out of his panic."

"We'll produce him, all right," Vally said unemotionally. "You have no idea where he might have gone?"

"Certainly not—or I needn't have asked you to find him. I know nothing of his regular hangouts. I do know that he's interested in art—and that's about all."

Vally nodded. "All right. We'll pick him up."

"You'll let me know as soon as you get him?"

Vally nodded again, with reserve, and George said slowly, "I didn't exactly want to tell you, but I suppose I should. There seemed to be some indication in what he said to his mother that he might take his own life, and that's why I've been anxious for you to pick him up quickly."

Vally had his hand on the knob of the front door, but he dropped it and turned around. "You should have told me this earlier."

"Well"—George looked down at his clenched fist, and slowly relaxed it—"his mother didn't want it mentioned—but I—well, I thought you should be told."

Vally stood thinking for a moment, then he made an abrupt gesture to the silent toothpick-chewing individual, and they both went out.

George remained where he was with his head lowered, apparently looking at the carpet. He put his foot absently into a small rent, then suddenly wheeled around and made for the phone. Anne could hear him talking to someone at his office.

She punched aimlessly at a fold of the velvet drape and wondered what to do next. She ought to leave—she ought to go straight upstairs now and pack.

George finished with his office and put up the phone. She saw him hesitate beside the hall table and then, to her surprise, he gave a quick look over his shoulder and slipped the letter from the bank into his pocket. He was almost running as he went up the stairs.

Anne followed—not too closely. As she got to her floor she heard him close his door on the floor above—and Min Smith's room was still another flight up. Of course Min was supposed to be in a state of collapse—and perhaps George was merely holding her mail.

Anne moved along to Grandma's room and put her ear against the door. She could hear Miss Kalms talking and laughing and the occasional lower tones of a man's voice. He sounded pretty lively too, and Anne shrugged. A policeman of some sort, probably.

She went to her own room and found herself thinking about George again and Min's letter. She knew that George had charge of the household's finances—probably because Grandma had not trusted Min. So why was Min receiving a communication from the bank? Her own private account, perhaps. But if so, why had George taken it? What was really bothering her, Anne decided, was the quick look he had cast over his shoulder before picking up the letter.

Anne sneered at herself in the mirror. She was getting just like Tim—amateur-detective stuff. It was a silly hobby. She pulled out her suitcase and put it determinedly on the bed. She'd have to get out of this place, or she'd never get a job. There simply wasn't time for job hunting here.

She heard George come down the stairs and hurried over to open her door a crack and peer out. She saw him descend to the lower hall, and without waiting to hear from her conscience she sped upstairs and went straight to his room. He might have left Min's letter lying around, and she wanted to see it. It did pass fleetingly across her mind that New York had done something to her code of ethics, but when she found George's door open she went in without more than a momentary hesitation.

The letter was not in sight, but she found it lying carelessly in the first drawer she opened. The flap had been unsealed, but it was not torn, and she supposed that George intended to seal it again. She drew out the letter and found that it was merely a bank statement—but it interested her more than she had expected. Min had started off the month with several hundred dollars—and her final balance was one dollar and forty-nine cents. Anne riffled through the canceled checks and found that they were mostly for food and Monty. Monty, she saw, had cost more than the food.

"Tim's little handmaiden doing her work well," George's voice said nastily from behind her.

Anne started, and blushed to the roots of her hair. The canceled checks sprayed out from her hand and fluttered to the floor. George walked over and picked them up, then took the envelope from her hand. "I just went down to put this on the hall table again," he said stiffly, "but when I got there, I found I didn't have it with me."

"Look," Anne said uncomfortably, "you must not blame Tim for this— he's gone out. I—I just happened to see you pick it up— and I'm very ashamed—"

George's eyes were still cold and unfriendly. "Don't apologize —and don't bother to try to shield your boyfriend, Tim. I've no doubt he told you to keep your eyes open and do his spying for him when he wasn't around."

Anne shook her head. "No—that isn't right. He merely said he'd be back soon to make some martinis."

"I don't know why he dug himself in here," George said irritably. "I think he belongs in a home of some sort."

"He was attracted by the mystery," Anne explained, glad to shift the conversation from herself to Tim.

"What mystery? When he came here it was simply that Anne Magraw had found something to entertain her in Philadelphia, and so you very kindly took her place. Someone played a practical joke on you by hanging Mr. Courtney's hand up in your room—and that was all."

"But what about Paul and Spike?"

George dismissed them with an impatient movement of his arm. "Look here—you don't want to stick around any longer, now that Aunt Ellen is dead, do you?"

"Certainly not," Anne said, feeling a little offended. "In fact, I had already started to pack."

"Good. Perhaps I can help you, and then I'll call a cab."

Anne went to her room immediately, conscious of an unpleasant impression that she was being thrown out. George followed her and helped her to pack with more vigor than skill. The suitcase overflowed untidily, but he jammed the loose ends in and managed to close it by putting one foot on it. He carried it downstairs, and Anne followed, wearing the heavy old seal coat. It was much too cold to go out without it, but she determined to send it back at once, as soon as she got her new one.

When they got down to the front hall George seemed to have recovered his temper. He said quite pleasantly, "Before you go I'd like to show you something at the back of the house—it's quite a curiosity, really."

He led her to the little square of dark back hall where Tim earlier had asked permission to kiss her. George put the suitcase down and said, "Actually, it's a small, secret room—I ran across it when I was a boy. Wait a minute."

He ran his hand over the bare surface of the well and Anne stood quietly, thrilling with an inner excitement. She knew that this must be the room Tim had wanted to find—the one which had concealed the skeleton. George, she decided, had not yet put two and two together—but, then, it was Tim's hobby to be nosy.

The wall slid out of sight, and they were confronted by a door, but it was too dark to see very much. George muttered, "It was always locked from the outside with the key left in it—yes, here it is."

He turned the key and pushed the door open, and they looked into absolute blackness. She felt George's hand on her arm, and he said, "Come on—just step over the baseboard."

She stepped over and was conscious at once of a bleak, musty cold. George's voice said, "Hold on—I'll get a flashlight so that you can see it."

"I'll come with you," Anne said. "It's too cold to stay here."

"No, no—you wait. I shan't be a minute."

Anne began, "But I don't want—" and got no further when George suddenly took her into his arms and kissed her. "I've wanted to do that for some time," he said in the darkness. "If that monkey Tim can do it, I can too."

"I think I'll go now," Anne said coldly.

"No, not now." He moved away from her and she heard him fumbling with her suitcase. The next moment the door was shut firmly, she heard the key turn in the lock, and then the rumble of the wall as it slid across—and knew that he was outside.

CHAPTER TWENTY

ANNE'S FIRST COHERENT thought was that she was glad she was wearing the fur coat, since it was so cold there. These old houses often had a cold room where they used to keep food when there was no other refrigeration. Grandma had made this particular one in the form of a secret room—and then had killed a man and hidden him here until he became a skeleton.

Her throat contracted, and a chill shivered along her spine. She called, "George," and the sound came out in a hoarse whisper. She cleared her throat and called again, this time so loudly that she felt a bit self-conscious. After all, he had merely gone to get a flashlight—he'd said so, hadn't he?

She waited for what seemed a long time, clutching her purse tightly and not moving. She could not see anything—but George would certainly be back in a moment with a flashlight. Only, why had he locked the door and then slid the wall across if he intended to come back ?

He wasn't coming back—no use fooling herself—he had locked her in here, and he was going to leave her—perhaps because he had caught her in his room, looking through his things. She screamed sharply, moved a step forward, and found the door. She pounded frantically on it and screamed again. She listened then, sweating even in the cold, but there was no sound, and nobody came.

She moved again and stumbled over something—her suitcase, of course. Now there was no trace of her left in the house. She sat down on the suitcase, close to the door, and put out her hand now and then to feel its solid surface. Once she got up and turned the knob, pulling and shaking with all her strength, but she could not move the door, and there was no sound from outside. She sat down on the suitcase again.

George had not lingered outside that cold, dark little room—he was in the lounge, standing at the front bay window, seeing nothing. He took out his handkerchief and mopped perspiration from his forehead. Vally was coming back soon—he'd said so—ought to be here any minute. George swung away from the window and took a turn about the room. This damnable waiting—and Vally wouldn't be back any minute—after all, he'd just left—going down to headquarters, wherever that was—it would take some time. Oh, to hell with it. He'd go to the kitchen and see Mrs. Johnson—and he hoped Ginny wouldn't be there.

He avoided the dining room and went through the back hall instead. He paused outside the secret room and listened, absently mopping his damp forehead again. There was no sound—maybe she was quiet in there. The room was supposed to be more or less soundproof, but he didn't really know about that—if she started screaming—Oh well, he'd be close by, for a while, anyway.

He went on into the kitchen and found Mrs. Johnson alone, dozing in her rocking chair. She opened her eyes, smiled at him, and said, "Sit down."

George swung a chair close to hers with one hand and sat on it without appearing to be in any way comfortable or relaxed. He asked abruptly, "Where's Ginny?"

"Who wants to know?"

"Oh, come off it," George said impatiently. "You know I never tried to pick up any of the girls around here."

The old lady set her rocker into motion and said tartly, "Not good enough for you, eh? Well, let me tell you they're worth more than that painted hussy you've been gallivanting with so long—that Lily. Where's she? I heard she came in last night."

"She did, but she isn't staying in town long, and she has other beaux—plenty of them. Furthermore, she's a nice girl, and I'll thank you not to call her a hussy."

"I can get along without your thanks," Mrs. Johnson said placidly. "She is a hussy."

George changed the subject. "Has Monty been buying the groceries lately?"

"Mercy on us!" exclaimed the old lady. "What an idea! Of course not."

"Are you paying cash?"

"No—we're charging again. Mrs. Smith says she's running a little behind in cash."

George muttered something, and Mrs. Johnson shrugged. "It's your own fault—you shouldn't have given her a lump sum like that. You know she's a flibbertigibbet with money—gives most of it to young Monty. That's what she did, isn't it?"

George said, "Yes," and was silent.

They heard someone come in the front door, and George got up and went quietly through the dining room to the hall. He was back again in a moment and said briefly, "Mr. Courtney. Where are the others?"

"In their rooms gathering mold, as far as I know," the old lady said contemptuously. "Except Mr. Alrian—he goes to his office every day, and at five o'clock they wake him up and put him out."

George nodded abstractedly and took out a cigarette. As he lit it, Mrs. Johnson's wise old eyes noticed that his hand was shaking. She said comfortably, "Don't be a sissy. It will come out all right."

"What do you mean? How can it?"

The old lady sniped. "He's a veteran, isn't he? He was wounded, wasn't he? He's a bit wrong in the head, but they're not going to do anything to him."

George blinked through a mist of tobacco smoke and shook his head in a bothered way. "Well—he wasn't actually wounded, he was hospitalized because he was emotionally unstable—couldn't take it. I saw a lot of them that way—it doesn't mean that they're really wrong in the head, as you put it. And I could have sworn that Monty was all right after he got back."

"She left him everything, didn't she?" Mrs. Johnson asked. George nodded.

"Why did you go and tell them right away that he'd run off? Why didn't you give him a chance to get away?"

"Oh"—George rubbed his clenched fist across his forehead— "they'd have got him eventually, anyway—and, in the meantime, God only knows what trouble he'd have got into. That being pursued all the time would certainly have put him back in the emotionally unstable class—and in a hurry. I thought it was far better to have him picked up at once."

"Stop fooling yourself," the old lady said quietly. "He's back in that class already, and you know it. Mad as a hatter."

George stood up and began to pace the kitchen restlessly.

She watched him for a while and then said peremptorily, "Sit down. You're making me nervous—and I'm nervous enough, anyway. I think I'm going to spoil the dinner."

George sat down. "If you spoil the dinner, you'll be doing it out of plain damn contrariness. I don't believe you've ever been nervous in your life."

Mrs. Johnson stopped rocking, sat up straight, and said sharply, "What was that?"

George stood up again, his hands jammed into his pockets. He knew what it was all right—she was calling out, or shouting, or screaming, from that little room. The soundproofing was good, though—the voice was so muffled as to be unrecognizable. He wondered, in a vague, feverish way, why Aunt Ellen's husband had built that little room in the first place. What did he use it for? Nothing, probably. He had been interested in building things around the house, and when they got refrigeration there was no more use for the cold room, so he'd made a secret room out of it. It was typical of the old boy—and the chances were he'd never used it after all the work he'd put in on it.

But Aunt Ellen may have used it. Could she really have killed a man to get money? She loved money, God knows. That skeleton—was that the man she'd killed? And why had she taken the thing up to the attic? Of course she'd been babbling about someone she should have locked up, except that that other one was there—and the "other one" could have been the skeleton. Was it Monty she had wanted to lock up? Somehow, he couldn't believe it. She'd been strict with Monty and fought with him as he grew older—but she'd been fond of him, nevertheless. Then who else could it be? Who else could have killed her? But Monty had seemed so much better lately—quite normal, in fact.

"Sit down, or get out of my kitchen," Mrs. Johnson said curtly.

He said, "I have to go," rather vaguely, and went out through the back hall. He paused to listen outside the secret room, but she seemed to be quiet now, and he went on to the lounge, conscious that his hands were cold and clammy.

Vally came in the front door within a few minutes, and he hurried into the hall to meet him. "Have you found him? Monty Smith, I mean."

Vally looked him up and down and then nodded briefly. "He's on a train bound for Arizona. He'll be picked up."

George took a long breath. "Glad to hear it. He's young. His grandmother was strict with him, and sometimes he'd argue with her—so I suppose he was frightened. As a matter of fact, they were quite fond of each other."

Vally gave him a bored look and said, "Where's the mother? I'd like to see her again."

"She's in her room—I'll show you."

George led the way up the three flights and was pleased to see that Vally was badly puffed by the time they arrived at Min's door. George knocked and, after a slight delay, Liz Sampson opened the door and peered out.

She said crossly, "Now what is it?"

"I am very sorry to trouble you," Vally murmured, using what charm he had, "but may I see Mrs. Smith again?"

Liz backed up a little, looking undecided, and Vally swept past her at once and went to the bed where Min lay. Her eyes and nose were red and puffy, but Liz had combed her hair neatly and arrayed her in a pink bed jacket. She held a crumpled tissue in her hand and blinked up at Vally through a mist of fresh tears.

"Sorry to disturb you, Mrs. Smith," he said courteously, "but I think you should know that we have found your son and are bringing him back."

Min sat up, and her tears overflowed. "Oh, that's wonderful. I'm so glad," she sobbed. "He certainly never did that awful thing—and now you'll see for yourself—"

"Yes, Mrs. Smith," Vally interrupted smoothly. "He served in the war?"

"Yes—yes, he did."

"He had a little trouble?"

George, in the background, found that he was kneading his hands together and forced himself to relax them.

"Trouble?" Min repeated innocently.

"He was in the hospital for some time before he was discharged, I believe?"

"Oh. Well—yes."

"What was his trouble?"

Min looked helpless, and George said casually, "Some sort of nervous upset. He's always been high-strung—and a lot of the boys needed disciplined rest after it was all over."

Vally nodded and said, "Thank you, Mrs. Smith—I'll be on my way."

He left, and as George turned to follow him, he glanced at Liz, who had been strangely quiet. She looked flushed and uncomfortable, and George realized that she must have told Vally about Monty's sojourn in the hospital. Not that it mattered, he thought, since Vally must certainly have found it out for himself sooner or later.

At the bottom of the stairs Vally asked for the name of Monty's hospital, and George gave it without comment. Vally wrote something in a small notebook, closed it, and said, "All right. Now, where's the girl?"

"What girl?" George asked, and hoped he looked less self-conscious than he felt.

"The one that was mixed up with the crook."

George shrugged. "In her room, I suppose."

"Show me."

George walked woodenly to Anne's room, and Vally knocked on the door. He knocked once more and waited briefly before he turned the knob and walked in. He gave the room a brief, comprehensive search, then asked abruptly, "When did she leave?"

"How should I know?" George said irritably. "We don't ask the inmates to punch a time clock."

"She won't get far," Vally observed grimly. He considered for a moment and then said, "I'd like to look at Depilriattia's things. I understand you have them stored."

George nodded. "As a matter of fact, I don't know where Mrs. Smith put them—but I think they'd know downstairs. I'll ask the cook."

"Find out for me, will you? I've one or two things to do, and I'll be back in an hour or so."

They went down to the front door, and George let Vally out and then stood looking after him. He's going to check with the hospital, he thought—find out just how bad Monty was.

Anne, still locked in cold darkness, felt herself getting a little light-headed. There seemed to be some difficulty with her breathing—and that was odd, when it was so cold. But she could not even scream any more—she did not have breath enough. She got up off the suitcase and felt her head spinning, so that she stumbled, and stretched her hand to the wall to steady herself. She began to move slowly along the wall, thinking of George, and wondering confusedly when he was coming back. Was he going to kill her? Would he bring that cord with him—the same cord?

The wall was rough under her groping hands—brick or stone. Once she stumbled and fell on one knee, and she thought her hand touched another cold hand. She shrank back with a little whimper. Mr. Courtney's hand couldn't be here—that was impossible. She felt her way back to the door again and then, quite distinctly, she heard it opening. There was a flow of warm air against her face, and the sound of someone's breath—slow and labored.

It was not George.

CHAPTER TWENTY-ONE

ANNE FLATTENED herself against the wall as the slow, labored breathing passed by. In a panic of fear she felt for the open door and eventually, stumbled over the sill and out into the small, dark hall. She looked back and saw the wall sliding quietly into place again and stared at it, her mouth hanging open a little. Then, suddenly, she turned and ran through to the front hall—her one idea to get out and away as quickly as possible. But George was standing just outside the front door, peering down the street, and she stopped abruptly and backed toward the stairs, her hand held against her mouth. He had not seen her, and she turned and stumbled frantically up the stairs, her breath coming short and hard. She flung into her own room and slammed the door behind her, but her desperate fingers could not push the bolt. It had jammed, and she could not budge it. She looked wildly around the room for some sort of barricade. The bureau was too far away and too heavy, and at last she wedged a chair under the knob and stood looking at it, wondering whether it would hold. She became calmer after a while and realized that she was uncomfortably warm. She removed the seal coat and flung it over the bed, wondering how she could ever have thought it was lighter after it was returned to her—the thing was so heavy that her shoulders were aching. She wanted a cigarette badly, but there was none left in her purse, and she realized that she had left her suitcase in the secret room.

Downstairs, George had retreated into the warmth of the hall and closed the front door. He was cursing quietly but steadily. There was no knowing when Tim would appear—he would have liked to kill two birds with one stone—but he couldn't keep her there any longer.

The door opened as he stood there, and Tim walked in. He brought a blast of cold air with him and asked cheerfully, "How are things going?"

George shrugged and waited on a held breath for Tim to ask where she was.

Tim obliged immediately. "Where's our darling?" he asked, hanging up his hat and coat.

"She's either your darling or she's mine," George said with sudden heat. "What do you mean, 'our darling'?"

"Yours," observed Tim, "is such a pedestrian imagination—fit for planning into which corner of the attic the winter woolens should be stored. Where is she? I want to see her face even before I have my martini."

George dropped ash onto the carpet and carefully rubbed it in with his toe. "You'll have to wait for your martini then. She's gone."

Tim swung around from the hatrack. "What are you saying? She wouldn't do a thing like that."

"Why not? There's no reason for her to stay on, and God knows it isn't very cheerful around here."

"But she promised to wait for me—we were going to have martinis."
George dropped more ash onto the carpet but forgot to rub it in.

"I suppose she went to Mary's?" Tim asked.

"I suppose so. Look—er—I presume you'll want to go too. I—have someone waiting for the room."

"Who?"

"What does it matter who?" George exploded irritably. "Mrs. Smith isn't
well, and I'm handling things for her until she's on her feet. After all, it's her
living."

"Certainly—and that of her son as well. Have they caught him?"

George nodded. "Now, about your room—"

"Forget my room. I'm staying in it. Where did they catch him?"

"Why are you staying? You won't be anywhere near the girl."

Tim looked directly at him and asked, "Are you tired of her already?"

George gave a moan of utter exasperation and wished that he might tie
Tim up and drop him down a well.

"I don't know," Tim was saying, "why you want me out of the house, but
I'm not going, and that's flat. Just now I intend to look in Anne's room—she
probably left a note for me."

"She didn't," George said quickly. "The room is quite bare."

"Did she say good-by to you?"

"No."

"Then how do you know she has gone?"

George took a deep breath and expelled it slowly. "When Vally went to
her room to talk to her, she wasn't there, and her things were gone."

Tim looked at him for a moment, then turned away and walked up the
stairs. George followed, mopping abstractedly at his forehead with a bunched
handkerchief.

Tim went straight to Anne's room. "I know she left a note for me," he
muttered. "She's not a ruthless type—she has a gentleness about her. She will
certainly have told me where she is going—and I shall persuade her to come
back."

He had a little trouble with the door, but eventually there was the sound
of a chair falling and, at the same time, the knob came off in his hand. He
pushed the door and walked in, still carrying the knob.

Anne was standing on the far side of the room against the wall—her eyes
huge and terrified in her white face.

"Darling!" Tim exclaimed. "What is the matter?"

As soon as she saw him, Anne stumbled forward and dropped onto the
side of the bed.

"Oh, Tim, I'm so glad it's you. I thought it was that other—that—"

Tim flew to her side and put his arm around her. "My poor darling. What on earth— Who frightened you, sweet? Tell me all about it. I shall kill him for you."

Anne, who had been about to burst into tears, was able to swallow them and grin feebly, but there was a note of desperation in her voice as she said, "Tim, I've got to get out of here. The place is haunted—all over. That George— he locked me up in a secret room—" The words died away as she caught sight of George, standing just inside the door, with his back against it, holding it shut.

"How did you get out?" he asked quietly.

Tim swung around to look at him. "A secret room? But of course—that must be—"

George interrupted him, without so much as a glance at him. He said to Anne urgently, "How did you get out? Tell me quickly. Did you find another way, or did someone let you out?"

"Tim," she said, "will you see me safely out of this hideous place? That man locked me up—"

George interrupted again. "Go if you want—you probably won't get as far as the corner. The police are looking for you, because they don't believe there was an Anne Magraw who got off at Philadelphia. They quite naturally link you with Paul, who, it appears, has a police record."

"Is that why you locked me up?"

George gazed out of the window. "Well—yes. I had reason to believe that someone else would be picked up shortly—and the case closed. I didn't suppose you'd care about a trip to the police station."

"Who?" Tim asked eagerly. "Who did you think would be picked up shortly?"

George said, "You'll find out soon enough."

"Why didn't you tell me?" Anne asked helplessly. "Instead of scaring me into a fit."

"I didn't have time. It would have meant a lot of argument and explanation. And anyway, I dislike snoops who go sneaking through other people's rooms to find out things which are none of their business."

"Children," Tim said plaintively, "I am lost. Please come again."

"I wasn't poking through your damned things," Anne declared in a fury. "I was merely curious as to why you should steal other people's letters."

"So, having watched with disapproval while I stole a letter, you proceeded to steal it yourself."

"Stop it!" Tim cried. "For heaven's sake, stop it. You must explain everything to me. It is vitally important to keep Anne from being picked up, and I must be abreast of all the facts."

"How did you get out?" George asked.

Anne gave him a sulky frown and muttered reluctantly, "Someone else came in."

George gave her a silent, steady scrutiny. Was she lying? There was no one else who knew about that room—it was one of Aunt Ellen's deepest secrets. Even Mrs. Johnson didn't know of it—and it was about the only thing she didn't know. He still remembered quite clearly the time he himself had found it. He had been playing some game and had run his fingers over the wall and had come in contact with the button. You could not distinguish it from the wall itself—it was fairly high up—and it was the merest chance that he had happened on it. Aunt Ellen had been furious and had made him promise on solemn oath that he would never tell. He never had, either. But, of course, he'd found it by accident himself, so it was possible that someone else had done the same thing.

Tim was saying, "Anne, precious, you tell me—please do. I really must know these things."

"Wait a minute," George broke in harshly. "Who was it, Anne, who let you out?"

"I don't know, and even if I did, I wouldn't tell you. It's pitch black in that place, and I couldn't see anything."

"Whoever it was might still be there," Tim suggested. "Let's go down and see."

He was a little astonished and thoroughly pleased when George agreed to this plan. He might find out a few things now—no use trying to get anything out of them—they simply were not in the mood to concentrate.

Anne started to follow them, but George turned around and said, "Don't come out of your room at all. Vally has already looked here, and he probably won't come back."

"But I want my suitcase—it's still down there."

Tim, anxious to get started, said, "He's right, my sweet. You stay here, and I'll bring you your suitcase and a martini very soon."

They went off, paying no heed to her muttered remark that she did not want a martini—she loathed the things. She banged the door after them and then went and sat on the bed, feeling rather stunned. The police after her! And she'd never even had so much as a parking ticket! What an ugly mess it all was—and she had George to thank for it. He'd persuaded her to stay and play granddaughter—she hadn't wanted to do it. Perhaps that was why he had taken it upon himself to hide her from the police. Only what good would that do—since the police would surely find out? What was George up to, anyway? Demanding that Monty be found at once, and then hiding her and her suitcase away in a dark, cold room?

Her scalp began to prickle, and she realized that she was frightened again. What was George doing? He'd made it look as though she'd run away. She must get in touch with Vally—at once—and tell him the whole story. But she didn't move—she remained sitting on the bed with her cold hands clasped tightly together. Better, perhaps, to wait until Tim got back, and then he would go with her. Tears welled into her eyes, and she allowed one or two to spill over, wondering vaguely, at the same time, why she felt so sleepy.

Tim prattled in whispers as he and George went down the stairs, but George did not even hear him. He was trying to straighten things out in his mind. That black coat—it couldn't have been lined with money. Aunt Ellen would never have allowed precious currency to drift around in that haphazard manner. And yet there had been a twenty-dollar bill in the lining. George stopped suddenly on the landing, and Tim bumped into him. That was a large twenty—they made them smaller these days—then it must be an old bill. He started on again, as Tim urged him not to think about anything, as it wouldn't do any good. Well, probably it had been put there to make them think there had been money sewed into the lining, and that it was gone. Monty might do a thing like that. Perhaps he had found in the lining a map of where the money was hidden, and if that were so, it was likely that he had the money by now. Only, he had rifled his mother's purse before he left—took about fifty dollars out of it. He couldn't get to Arizona on fifty dollars. But of course she had given him money a few days ago—that last check—and anyway, Monty wasn't like that. He wouldn't take money from his mother if he had money of his own. Probably he hadn't had time to follow the map and get the money.

George halted on the bottom stair, his forehead wrinkled in thought. The money was probably hidden in the secret room—where else? And Monty hadn't had a chance to get it. But if Anne's story were correct, someone else was after it—someone who knew about the room—and perhaps this same person had the map that had been hidden in the coat. That would let Monty out. George clutched at the idea. One of these aging people who had known Aunt Ellen for many years and knew that she had money hidden somewhere. Tim had hinted at something of the sort, and George's lip curled unconsciously. But these people—the inmates of the house—couldn't get rid of a crook like Paul—or that other one, Spike. It didn't seem possible.

He was walking toward the back hall now with Tim treading on his heels. He thought of Mrs. Johnson—who had told this crazy Tim that she knew Aunt Ellen's murderer—and on an impulse he went through to the kitchen. Ginny was there, making tea, and she turned around as George came in.

"I'm trying to get this tea done all by myself. Mrs. Johnson has absolutely disappeared."

CHAPTER TWENTY-TWO

GEORGE HEARD Tim say, "Please! Why are you wasting time here?" but he did not bother to answer. He went through to Mrs. Johnson's bedroom, which adjoined the kitchen and in which she had slept for many years.

The room was empty. He even looked under the bed, and Tim, who had followed him to the doorway, nodded with sudden comprehension. "But of course you're afraid—naturally. She knows who did this thing. We must find her—at once."

George plunged out of the room without so much as a glance at Tim and took the narrow, steep back stairs two at a time. He went all the way to the attic, and Tim panted behind him, "This is silly. We should have gone to the secret room first."

George knocked on Min Smith's door and then walked in without waiting to be asked. She had been asleep, but she opened her eyes and looked up at him, blinking and confused.

"I'm sorry, Min—I'm looking for Mrs. Johnson—thought she might be up here."

"Why, she was here, George—a little while ago. But she said she had to go down to make the tea."

"Did Liz go down with her?"

Min shook her head. "Liz left some time ago. That one sure has ants in her pants—can't sit still a minute—and she's getting so old it's pathetic—not that she'll admit it." There was a moment of silence, and then Min dropped her arm across her eyes and whispered, "Oh, George! What am I going to do about Monty? Whatever am I going to do?"

"Look, Min"—George hesitated, his head bent, and his hands jammed into his pockets—"well—I've found out that Monty is—er—all right. He didn't—"

"Oh, George!" she cried out. "What—?"

"Not now," he said firmly. "Relax and go back to sleep. I'll come back later and tell you."

He went out, and Tim, who had been listening just outside the door, was nearly knocked on his face. George righted him and set him to one side, then passed on in an effort to ignore him, but Tim followed close behind.

"The secret room," he whispered urgently. "We must go there at once."

George looked into Monty's room, saw that it was empty, and made for the stairs. On the second floor Anne opened her door a crack and saw them pass, but they did not stop, so that she had no opportunity to ask them why they were going down, instead of coming up.

On the first floor in the hall Roger waylaid them and asked, "Is there any news?"

George said, "Not yet, Mr. Crimple," and added firmly, "You'll have to excuse me—I'm rather busy." He pushed on past, but Roger caught Tim by the arm.

"Perhaps you can tell me, sir—"

Tim wrenched his arm free, muttered, "I'm busy too," and flew after George, who was disappearing into the back hall.

Roger looked after them, chewing angrily on his mustache, and then decided to follow them. As he stepped into the dark little hallway at the back, George had his hand high up on the wall—but he dropped it and turned around with a blank look on his face.

"Oh—Mr. Crimple. I believe the—er—tea is ready. I'm trying to handle things until Mrs. Smith is on her feet again, but Mrs. Johnson is not well, and Ginny has it all to do, so if you could get them to have their tea at once, she won't be delayed in clearing it away. She'll have the dinner on her hands, you see."

"Nothing too unusual about that, old man," Roger observed. "She's accustomed to having the soup on her thumbs." He laughed heartily and then cut it short when he remembered that there had been a death in the house. "Sorry, old man—forgot for the moment. Inexcusable rudeness. I—er—I'll see that they lap their tea up in a hurry."

He departed, and George turned back to the wall, but he had no sooner raised his hand again than Tim hissed warningly, and a moment after Miss Burreton's voice spoke behind him.

"The tea is cold."

George turned around, his patience obviously wearing thin, and Tim said hastily, "Just take it to the kitchen and tell Ginny to warm it up."

"No," said Miss Burreton. "Roger said I must come to you and complain."

"All right," George said, through his teeth, "so you've come to me and complained. Now, if you'll just go to the kitchen—"

"No. We none of us should go to the kitchen—it's not our place. Disgraceful."

George, still speaking through his teeth, said, "Very well, then you must drink the tea cold."

She looked at him for a moment, chewing on her gums, and then turned and shuffled away.

George turned around to the wall again, and a moment later it slid away with a low rumble. He put his hand on the knob of the door and felt below it, muttering under his breath.

"What is it?" Tim asked anxiously.

"Damned key's gone."

There was a small space between the door and the sliding wall, and they searched there together, lighting matches so that they could see. But the key had disappeared.

"We'll have to dig the entire lock out," Tim said despairingly. "We can't get at the hinges this side, and that's not the sort of lock that any odd key will fit."

George straightened up, dusting the knees of his trousers. "I'll phone a locksmith."

"You can't—you must not," Tim cried excitedly. "That means that the police will be in on it, and they must not know about this room."

"Why not?"

"Let them find it out for themselves. Why should we hand them anything?"

"You are behaving," said George, "like a greedy little boy."

"George, I *beg* of you—"

But George was already striding through to the front hall, where Vally had just come in.

Vally nodded, said, "I'd like to have a word with you," and gave Tim a cold stare.

"Go ahead," Tim said carelessly. "I shan't interrupt."

George frowned. "There's something I want to tell you first. The cook—"

"I've found Depilriattia."

Tim cried, "What? No!" and received another cold stare.

"Come out to the kitchen, will you?" George suggested. "I want to see whether the cook has turned up—and you can talk to me there."

They moved toward the back hall, and Tim followed so closely behind them that Vally momentarily lost his urbanity. He turned around and announced that when he wanted his neck breathed on, like a lousy windowpane, he'd let him know.

Ginny was alone in the kitchen, sitting in Mrs. Johnson's rocking chair, her hands folded in her lap.

"Mrs. Johnson has not returned?" George asked.

Ginny shook her head. "I haven't an idea in the world where she could be, Mr. George. I looked all over."

"Perhaps she went to Mrs. Smith's room—old Mrs. Smith, I mean," George said, the idea having just occurred to him. "Sentiment, possibly— she'd known her a long time. Would you run up and have a look, Ginny?"

Ginny looked frightened, and George said reassuringly, "It's all right— the police have taken her away. Anyway, Miss Kalms is still there, and a policeman, as well."

Ginny nodded on a breath of relief and scuttled off, and Vally perched himself on a corner of the table.

"What kind of people do you have staying here that a seasoned crook like Depilriattia is scared off?"

"Scared off?" George repeated.

"Yes. He handed me a beautiful and uplifting story about how he wished to better himself and so bought some quiet clothes and went to live in a decent house. It had a pathetic angle—the other boarders did not want him. He claims he was able to take it when they started with practical jokes—like a ghost appearing at his door, and his light going on in the middle of the night. But his feelings were really hurt when he developed a continued sense of vagueness and floating and began to have hallucinations at night. What finally sent him off in dudgeon was when he awoke to see a dismembered hand floating above him, the fingers dripping with blood. After a struggle with himself, he managed to get the light on, and had a further shock. The hand had disappeared with the darkness, but the blood had apparently come from him. He had a fresh gash, still bleeding, on his arm. It seems that he can take a hint as well as anyone, because he got dressed and left then and there. He added that he didn't want what was left here, if it cost him an arm to get it."

Vally paused, fingered a toothpick in his pocket, rejected it, and glanced at Tim.

"Shut your mouth, son—you might get a fly in it."

Tim, considerably embarrassed, realized that his mouth had been hanging open and hastily closed it. He knew it was illogical, but he was bitterly annoyed with Paul for upsetting all his calculations.

"I suppose he'd been drinking?" George said slowly.

Vally shrugged. "Would the people in this place be likely to object to a man of that sort?"

"Oh yes, but they certainly wouldn't go to those fantastic lengths. They'd give him a cold shoulder, but that's about all."

"Where's the girl?" Vally asked abruptly.

"What girl?"

Vally drew a patient sigh. "She couldn't have left, you know— the place has been watched. She's still here."

"You'd better search for her then," George said indifferently. "The cook has disappeared too—Mrs. Johnson. She told Tim, here, that she knew who had murdered my aunt—and it has me worried."

Vally swung around on Tim and barked, "Who did she say it was?"

"She didn't say."

"Are you standing there and telling me that you couldn't get it out of her?"

"It seemed best to drop it at the moment," Tim replied, in a cold fury. "Naturally I was going back to her, but she has disappeared."

"Nice work," Vally said scornfully. "Excuse me while I go out and see if any of the boys noticed her going."

He stood up, and Tim asked sulkily, "What about that other one—that Spike?"

"Don't know who he is and can't locate him," Vally said briefly, and managed to convey that he did not believe there was any such person. He headed for the front hall, and Tim remained close at his elbow.

"Why would Miss Anne tells us about Paul, if she were associated with him?"

Vally looked scornful again. "She wanted him out so that she could make the entire haul herself."

He went out the front door, and George wandered up beside Tim.

"You'd better think fast, brother, or they'll have your darling in their clutches."

"I can always think faster than a policeman. We must get into that secret room."

"Go ahead," George said. "I'm going to search for Mrs. Johnson."

"But she might be in the room—it seems the most likely place."

George shook his head. "It's the most unlikely place. I'm going to the kitchen to see whether Ginny has found her. Probably she just decided to leave and walked out." But he didn't really believe it, and there was a cold feeling at the pit of his stomach. She'd been in the house for so long—and she was never afraid of things. He knew she had not left.

He went toward the kitchen, and Tim, after tapping his teeth thoughtfully for a moment, suddenly hurried up the stairs to Anne's room.

She was sitting on the bed, and she said at once, "I want to see that man Vally right away—I have no reason to run away from the police, and I want to tell him so."

"Darling, do wait a minute—there are so many things to think about. George mentioned someone who was about to be caught I but I can't get him to tell me who it is. Do you know?"

"No, I don't."

"Precious, please don't be difficult. Will you wait here, quietly, for just a few minutes?"

"Where's my suitcase?" Anne demanded querulously. "And I could even use that loathsome martini you promised me. Give me a cigarette."

He supplied her and then sped across the hall to Grandma's room. He listened at the door for a moment then went in quietly, his eyes seeking Miss Kalms. She was rummaging in a bureau drawer, and the man stood at the window, staring out, and just finishing a yawn. Miss Kalms glanced up, and Tim beckoned, and when she approached him, he drew her out into the hall.

"Listen, my dear, you must have heard poor Grandma talking a great deal. Who was the man she feared so much?"

"Oh, for heavens' sake—she was scared of all of them. Except Mrs. Smith, of course—and Monty—and the phony granddaughter. I hear she is a phony, all right."

"But she seemed afraid of one man in particular," Tim persisted.

"Oh no—she was scared if any one of them came in, and I had to watch. It wasn't only the men. You see, at the end, she'd started calling everybody 'he.'"

CHAPTER TWENTY-THREE

"DO YOU MEAN," Tim asked Miss Kalms, "that Grandma referred to women as 'he' as well as men?"

"Sure—she called 'em all 'he.' She wasn't right in her mind any more. For instance, can you imagine her being afraid of anyone before she was ill?"

"But I did not know her before she was ill."

"Well, I did—and believe me they were all afraid of her—including me. But after she got sick, she began to be afraid of them, and then she started calling them all 'he.' Sometimes she called them 'Dopey' behind their backs. She quarreled with them when they came to visit her, but only sort of vaguely."

Miss Kalms, apparently tired of the subject at this point, changed it, and informed Tim that she was certainly going to take it easy for a while—she'd earned a rest, and no kidding. She was going to step out a bit, and wished she had someone to step out with.

But Tim merely said, "I'm sure you'll find someone—an attractive person like yourself must have many admirers," and went back to Anne's room.

Anne was lying on the bed and appeared to be sleeping soundly. After a moment's indecision Tim closed the door quietly and ran downstairs. He found George and Vally in the hall and immediately insinuated himself between them.

"Listen," Vally was saying irritably, "I know you feel somewhat responsible for the girl, but I merely want to talk to her—so why not produce her, for God's sake? We've got Monty Smith—and, under the circumstances, it won't go badly with him. He's a veteran, and I know damn' well he's not responsible, but I want to button the thing up."

"She's around somewhere—she'll keep," George said. "But I want Mrs. Johnson found before anything else. I'm—worried about her."

"You're barking up the wrong tree," Vally said impatiently. "People disappear every day—family frantic—and then it turns out they went to the corner to post a letter. Young Smith is not here, remember."

George frowned down at the carpet, and after a moment, Vally inquired, "Where is she?"

"What the devil makes you think I'm hiding her?" George asked in complete exasperation.

"I've been in this business for a good many years."

"Oh, for God's sake! I think I saw her upstairs a while ago. Why don't you look in her room?"

Vally turned and started up the stairs without further comment, and Tim whispered, "George! You cad!"

"You get the hell into the lounge," George said fiercely, "and keep all those old fools amused—keep them in there. I've got to get that room open."

"I thought you were going to let Vally open it?"

"He'd have to send out for some red tape first," George said desperately. "I want it opened now. I've got to find the old lady."

Tim shrugged. "Very well—I shall entertain them."

He went into the lounge and, disregarding the rather heavy atmosphere, asked cheerfully, "Is there a spot of tea left?"

"It's cold," said Miss Burreton.

Pet gave him a tiny smile and murmured, "If you don't take milk with it, I think perhaps—"

"Quite all right—I shall have it neat." He watched while Pet poured the evil-looking liquid into one of the two remaining cups, and when she handed it to him, took a generous gulp in an excess of geniality. The stuff rolled down his throat, burning viciously all the way and seemed to pause in his stomach to add further burns there. He choked, coughed, and hastily set the cup down, wondering in honest amazement what sort of liquid fire they'd be willing to call hot tea.

They were all looking at him, and he had a moment of embarrassment. Pet and Roger sat side by side, looking depressed. Mr. Courtney was seated neatly on a straight chair, posed as he might have been on the stage. Miss Burreton sat in an armchair, surrounded by pillows, and gazed at him, her mouth hanging open a little. Liz Sampson, usually so lively and talkative, was slumped in another armchair, with the rouge oddly stark on her cheekbones.

Tim realized that they had been discussing something before he came in and had dropped it abruptly. They were obviously waiting for him to leave so that they could get on with it.

He swept a smile around at them, made a slight bow, and observed, "Very refreshing. I regret that I have no time to stay and chat. Good afternoon."

He retired to the hall, ran heavily up the first few step of the stairs and then crept quietly down again. George, watching from the back hall, with a screw driver in his hand, opened his mouth to ask him what the hell he thought he was doing, but Tim made frantic signs to him to be quiet, and he backed away in disgust.

Tim was feeling a delightful renewal of interest in the case. He had felt badly let down when Vally indicated that the capture of Monty would end it, but now his mind was alert and happily occupied once more. There was something more to this—and those people in the lounge knew secrets they were not telling. He drew close to the old velvet drape, his ears strained to catch every sound.

"I did not," Miss Burreton was saying crossly.

"Yes, you did," Roger declared, his voice a subdued rumble. "That's exactly what you did—only you've forgotten it. You're forgetting everything these days. Good God! It's something worse than forgetfulness when you go to bed in someone else's room."

"No, dear, that's hardly fair," Pet said gently. "She only came in and then realized her mistake."

"Mistake!" Roger grunted. "The room's on a different floor!"

Miss Burreton snapped, "You came in my room—you're always coming in my room. I don't like it."

Mr. Courtney, apparently ignoring this wrangle, said suddenly and clearly, "They're picking up Monty, you know."

Nobody answered, and there was a long silence. Tim, with other pressing matters on his mind, had just decided to tiptoe away when Liz spoke.

"If you only weren't so damned temperamental about your stupid hand!"

"I don't care," Mr. Courtney said defensively. "I can't help it. You'd be angry too, I—"

"Oh, nonsense! Rubbish!" Roger boomed, and Pet said hastily and pacifically, "Please. Let's forget it. Where's Mrs. Johnson?"

"Yes, where is she? Where is she?" Miss Burreton took it up. "I particularly want to speak to her."

"I don't know where she is," Liz said shortly.

Mr. Courtney added, "Nor do I."

"Well, don't look at me," Roger boomed after a short pause. "I don't have her in my pocket. Chances are she found a new admirer and eloped again." His guffaw was killed by an admonishing murmur from Pet.

There was another short silence, and then Pet sighed. "It must be somewhere."

Miss Burreton said, "It's disgraceful."

"There you go again," Roger told her. "You are definitely getting very vague. Isn't she?" he appealed to the others.

"I am not!" Miss Burreton cried shrilly.

"Oh, let her alone," Liz said, and Pet added gently, "She's all right, dear."

Mr. Courtney spoke up, less precisely than usual. "I don't know —Burry, wouldn't you like to go to some nice place—where they'd look after you, you know—take care of you properly if you were ill—"

"I'll go where I like, and I'll do what I like, and I don't like it much here," Miss Burreton said angrily. She left the room so swiftly and quietly that Tim did not hear her coming, but she padded by without having noticed him at all and went up the stairs, chewing furiously.

After a while Roger said, "It's not really fair, Liz being so extravagant like that."

"Just don't bother following up that line," Liz retorted in a flat, level voice, "because it will get you exactly nowhere."

"Suppose we meet in my room after dinner," Mr. Courtney suggested. "I think we must face the fact that poor old Burry needs institutional care, and it's up to us to get her into the right sort of home."

"Yes." Pet spoke on a sigh. "We have other things to discuss too. I suppose poor Monty— Well, anyway, shall we say about nine? I want to take a little nap now before dinner."

The others decided to go upstairs too, and Tim slipped out to the back hall to intercept anyone who might come that way and interrupt George.

But they all went up the front stairs. As soon as they had gone Tim joined George with a reassuring whisper, "It's all right— it's I."

"I don't give a good goddamn who it is," George snarled. "They can all stand around in a circle and watch. All I want is to get this blasted door open. There's somebody else around here who's doing things, and I don't know what's going on, but if anybody around here has hurt that poor old lady, I'll make it hot for him."

Tim peered closer and saw that there was now a hole in the door, and George seemed to be working on it with a narrow little saw.

"Here—hold the damned flashlight," George muttered, and thrust it at him.

Tim took it and asked chattily, "What makes you think anything has happened to the old lady?"

"Ah, shut up, and hold the flash straight, for God's sake."

Tim held the flash straight.

"You seem," he ventured presently, "to care more for this old lady than for the other one—recently deceased."

"She gave me cookies," George said, and then swore hotly when the saw slipped.

"Didn't Grandma Smith ever give you anything?"

George let out a long, sighing breath. "There she comes! God! What a door! Like cast iron!"

Tim, supposing that the job was finished, allowed the light to drop from the vital spot and was fiercely and profanely told to put it back again. He obeyed hastily and then asked, "Was Liz very extravagant?"

"All the way. Sky was the limit," George said grimly.

"What does she live on now?"

"As far as I can make out on the house."

"And who gives her spending money?"

George swore at the saw again and then said impatiently, "I don't know—maybe she borrows from the others."

"Have you seen them giving her money?"

"Oh, for God's sake!" George said explosively.

"Please answer me," Tim persisted. "It's important."

"I haven't seen anything," George told him grudgingly, "but I've heard them all complaining that she owes them money—and Aunt Ellen said Liz owed her money too."

"Why didn't Aunt Ellen put her out?"

"They were old friends."

"Yes, but Aunt Ellen was pretty tough about money matters—that seems established—and so"—Tim tapped a fingernail against the metal of the flashlight and ended triumphantly—"Liz must have known about the skeleton. Blackmail, you see."

George delivered himself of a very rude expression and added, "I don't believe Aunt Ellen ever made a skeleton of anybody."

"Then who started that one upstairs on its way?"

"Plenty of skeletons around."

Tim shook his head. "Not like that one—with bits and pieces still clinging to it."

"Here we are," George said suddenly, and something clattered onto the floor. He fiddled around further for a moment and then the door swung inward.

In his eagerness Tim pushed George against the jamb and was promptly pushed back again. They stumbled into the little room together, and something fell down with a bang. George directed the flashlight downward, and they saw that it was Anne's suitcase.

The room was empty. George threw the circle of light over the walls and floor and did not know whether to be relieved or more worried when there was no sign of Mrs. Johnson. The walls were of stone—ragged, with large indentations, and the floor was composed of wide wooden planks, dusty and scuffed. Tim said suddenly and tensely, "Wait a minute—turn the light over there—over in that corner."

The light wavered for a moment and then steadied, and on the dusty planks of the floor, in the corner, they both looked in silence at Mr. Courtney's artificial hand.

CHAPTER TWENTY-FOUR

GEORGE PICKED UP the artificial hand and muttered, "How the devil did that get in here?"

Tim shrugged. "Perhaps Mr. Courtney wished to keep it in a safe place— he's very temperamental about the thing."

"What do you mean?" George asked irritably. "Matter of fact, he's very sensible about it—uses that hook and keeps this for the stage."

"Yes, my dear, practical George, but he was so angry—"

"You can't blame him," George interrupted, "for getting as mad as hell when other people start using it for practical jokes."

"Do you call it a practical joke when somebody smears it with Paul D.'s good red blood?"

"I don't know anything about it, or what's going on," George said gloom- ily. "All I want now is to find Mrs. Johnson."

Tim moved away. "Play that flash around the wall, George—I want to see something." He passed his hand over the uneven stones and presently added, "Do you know that someone has been digging into the walls with a chisel?"

George examined the chipped walls briefly and nodded. "Someone thought Aunt Ellen had her money hidden here—the money that wasn't in the coat."

"You mean, perhaps, the money that was in the coat—and that, there- fore, was not here."

"No, I don't. If you'd known Aunt Ellen, you'd realize that she'd never have left money in the lining of a coat. She might have put a map in there, explaining where the money was to be found."

"Of course, of course," Tim said with sudden eagerness. "Now we're getting somewhere."

"We are not getting anywhere," George contradicted him sourly, "and fast. Will you be good enough to use your outsize brain to find Mrs. Johnson— at once?"

Tim nodded agreeably. "Now that you ask me—yes. At once."

Vally was sitting in Anne's room, smoking a cigar, and gloomily regard- ing her through its haze. She was sound asleep, and when he'd tried to rouse her she'd said drowsily that she was glad to see him and then gone off again. Doped, like the Depilriattia guy. Young Smith could have done it at lunch. But why? To frighten her off? Vally shifted his cigar to the other side of his mouth and discovered that his left foot had gone to sleep. He'd checked on her, and it was straightforward enough—only her story of how she got here sounded screwy. Vaddison was a good-looking guy, of course—maybe that was what enticed her.

"Oh hell!" Vally said loudly, and stood up, stamping his left foot on the floor. He'd go down and get some coffee and see if he could wake her up with it. He wanted to get home sometime—he was in the middle of a good book.

He went downstairs and through the dining room to the kitchen, where he found Ginny washing up the tea things.

"I want a cup of coffee—strong and black."

"So do I," Ginny said simply.

"O.K. Make enough for two."

She dried her red, soapy hands on a towel and explained, "I don't know how to make coffee—me not being the cook around here. I thought you was going to make some."

"Don't hand me that line," Vally said curtly. "I want strong coffee—now—so get going."

Ginny assumed a sulky expression, but she got going. She never had been able to make decent coffee, and she hoped this would turn out worse than usual.

Vally slumped into a chair and asked abruptly, "Where's the cook?"

"You think I'd be doing all her work if I knew?" Ginny demanded indignantly. "She went up to see Mrs. Smith, and I ain't seen her since—nor anyone else ain't, either."

"Maybe she went out," Vally suggested, without much hope. He'd make it hot for somebody if she had gone out and had been missed—but he didn't really believe it, although he wanted to. It would simplify things.

"She never went out," Ginny declared firmly, "not in her work clothes, leaving her hat and coat in her closet—which I seen with my own eyes."

"Maybe she had another hat and coat."

"Are you kidding?" Ginny demanded, whirling around to face him. "And her with one hat and coat which she brought with her fresh out of the ark when she first come here in the dark ages!"

Vally shifted in his chair and grunted. "How about that coffee? Is it ready?"

Ginny poured dark liquid into a cup and was surprised and pleased to note that it looked and smelled like coffee. Vally took the cup and walked out with it. He went up the stairs, holding it carefully, but by the time he had reached Anne's room most of it had slopped over into the saucer. He lifted the cup, cursing softly, and poured the coffee from the saucer back into it. Then he glanced over at the bed. Anne was no longer there.

At the same moment she was just waking into stuffy darkness. Her head felt woolly and confused, but she knew that she must get up, because she had seen Vally, and she felt a pressing need to speak to him. Only, when she got up, he wasn't there—and she must find him.

It was so close and stuffy—it must be that little room. Oh no, she must wake up—she couldn't be in that room again—she couldn't stand that. She shook her head to try to clear it and stretched out her hands. Why, it was a closet. There were clothes hanging all around her. She stumbled against a wall, cushioned by the clothes that hung against it, and rested her head in folds of cloth that smelled strongly of camphor. But she must not go to sleep again—not now. She began to move, feeling her way with outstretched hands, and thought confusedly that it was a large closet—very large. She fumbled on, her hands feeling for the door—only there was no door. She went on, around and around, interminably it seemed, and there was no door. The sleepy cloud that lay over her mind lifted a little to admit a sharp thrill of fear. How could there be a closet that had no door? All these clothes—they must have been brought in through a door—and all the moth balls. The fumes were choking her, and her shoulder hurt too—hurt terribly. She felt very ill, and she wanted to go to sleep again—only she must find the door first.

Vally, standing with the cooling coffee still in his hand, decided that the girl had wandered out to the bathroom. She'd be back shortly, no doubt, and if she had roused that much, she wouldn't need the coffee. He sat down and drank it himself.

He should have waited and not bothered with the coffee. She'd said she wanted to speak to him, and people who had been doped did queer things. Chances were she'd have come out of it and told her tale without realizing she'd ever been asleep in between. Better go and look for her if she didn't come back in a minute.

George and Tim came into the room, and Vally, rarely given to that emotion, was conscious of a slight embarrassment. "She— er—I think she's in the bathroom," he said stiffly.

"Have you talked with her yet?" George asked.

Tim murmured, "I could do with a cup myself."

Vally handed him the cup, in which a little coffee still remained at the bottom, and said, "Help yourself. As a matter of fact, that girl's been gone a bit too long. I think I'll investigate. She was pretty dopey."

"Dopey?" Tim repeated sharply, but Vally walked out of the room without answering.

"Come on," George said impatiently. "You said we'd search every inch of the house, so let's get on with it."

Tim rumpled his hair fretfully. "I hate this routine spadework—it doesn't suit me. It's for dull plodders like you. However, I promised—and my word is my bond. We have only this floor and the ground floor left to do."

"And the cellar," George amended grimly.

They searched Anne's room, which was an easy job compared to what they had been through on the floor above. Everyone had been taking naps, and there had been hard feelings and harsh words, but George had pushed on doggedly, with Tim sidling along behind him.

They went along to Miss Burreton's room after finishing with Anne's and ran into a snag. The door was locked, and Miss Burreton's voice, from inside, informed them that she was taking a nap and could not be disturbed. No argument had any affect upon her, and they were forced, in the end, to retire.

They went down to the first floor, George shaking his head and muttering on the way, "Who gave her a key, anyway? She shouldn't have one—she's entirely too vague these days. She doesn't know what she's doing half the time, and if anything happened to her, we'd have the very devil of a time getting in there to her. I'm goddamn sick and tired of this place, anyway, and I'm leaving as soon as I can."

"You're too conscientious," Tim said placidly. "You're always willing to shoulder the load, so of course it's always thrown at you—naturally. You must come and share my apartment with me—this is a bona-fide invitation."

"Your apartment?" George said abstractedly.

"Yes, certainly. It is large—really too large for me."

"But aren't you expecting to get married shortly?" George asked. "I mean, don't you think Anne might object to a boarder?"

"Stop showing your claws," Tim said, a little coldly. "You know very well that she won't marry me. But if I can get you to come and live with me, perhaps she won't marry you, either."

"I don't follow you."

"No," said Tim, "a dullard like you could hardly expect to follow a mind like mine. I am the sunshine—a rainbow—the crystal spray of water. You, my dear George, are an earthworm."

"Do you like the sound of your own voice?" George asked, genuinely puzzled.

"Not particularly, but it is necessary for me to practice all the time. My business, you know."

"What is your damned business? If any."

Tim had put his head into the closet under the stairs and emerged festooned with dust and cobwebs. "Don't these people ever go out when it rains?" he asked in an aggrieved voice. "This place is filled with raincoats, rubbers, and umbrellas, but they don't seem to have been disturbed for years."

They finished their search of the first floor and then went on down to the cellar. It took longer to cover the ground there, and Tim acquired more dust and cobwebs, but they found nothing. As a last resort they opened the secret room again, but it was quite empty, and George said somberly, "She must have gone out, after all, because she damn well is not in the house."

"Don't be too sure," Tim objected. "There might be another secret room. That sort of thing becomes a passion with some people, you know—if they built one, they might have built others."

George thought it over and said slowly, "If there is anything of the sort, it would be directly above this room. The construction—"

"Don't bore me with the details," Tim said, his eyes snapping. "Let's go."

They went back upstairs, but in the hall they ran into Miss Burreton, who stopped George with a wavering hand on his arm.

"I'm going to a home, George—a nice old ladies' home, where they will look after me. Will you find me one?"

"Anything I can do—" George began uncertainly.

"You must arrange it now," Miss Burreton said insistently. "Right away. You see, they say I'm getting old and foolish, and I'm afraid—I'm afraid of what they'll do to me."

CHAPTER TWENTY-FIVE

"WHY ARE YOU AFRAID of them?" Tim asked Miss Burreton eagerly. She looked at him, blinking and chewing on her gums, but she made no reply. George took her by the arm and led her back to her room. Tim slipped into the room with them and began to make an unobtrusive, but fairly thorough, search. When he got to the closet, Miss Burreton said suddenly, "What is it? What is he doing in my closet?"

"It's all right," George soothed her, "he lost something and he's trying to find it. You lie down now and have a little nap before dinner."

Miss Burreton padded over to the closet and got her hat and coat. "I had my nap—I had a nice long nap. Now I want to go. You take me, George."

"I can't take you now," George explained patiently. "I'll have to make arrangements for you first—perhaps tomorrow. And you'll have to let me know how much money you have."

"I have money," she said excitedly. "You know my father left me money—plenty of money."

Tim murmured, "Nothing here," and George nodded.

"I'll go and telephone," he said to Miss Burreton. "I'll try to make some arrangement for you. You wait here till I come back."

Miss Burreton was putting on her hat. She said, "I want to go now," but her voice had lost its petulance and became vague. She added, "Where are we going?"

Tim walked out of the room, and George followed, closing the door firmly behind him. An instant later he opened it again and removed the key, but Miss Burreton saw him. She cried shrilly, "What are you doing with my key? You must give it back to me—I want it."

In the interest of peace George was obliged to return it to her and to stand outside while she locked herself in.

"You see," Tim said, "she's badly frightened—and not of Monty. There is someone else here."

"Maybe it's you," George retorted morosely. "I'd hate to have an exhibit like you poking into my closet."

He moved down the hall and then came to an abrupt stop. "I'm cracked," he muttered. "There's no other secret room—this space is taken up by a closet—I think they keep linen and laundry here—things like that. I forgot it because it has a sliding door—looks like one of the wall panels."

"If only," Tim murmured, "your brain could compare with your brawn, my dear George."

Vally came up behind them, his red hair bristling angrily. He was beginning to think that the girl had skipped out on him while he was getting that coffee, and he did not like being skipped out on. He had waited outside the bathroom door for some time, only to have Mr. Courtney emerge and give him a decidedly nasty look. He'd talked to Miss Kalms after that and she'd given him a lot of dope on the Monty guy—certainly looked like he was the one, all right. But the girl had a nerve, dodging him this way, and he'd talk to her, if he had to put these two fools behind bars to get at her.

George gave him a furious look and then turned away and slid open the panel that served as a door to the storage closet. It was a similar arrangement to the one downstairs except that there was no button on the wall to release it.

Anne stumbled out almost immediately. She looked at the three of them, turning her head slowly, and murmured, "How do you do?"

"Darling!" Tim cried, looking stricken, "you've been drinking without me."

George put a steadying hand on her arm and asked peevishly, "What's the matter with you?"

Vally sighed deeply, stepped forward, and removed Anne from George's grasp. He led her back to her room, and George and Tim, after a hasty look in the closet, followed along behind.

"Nothing there," George muttered, "but some old clothes—laundry hamper—linen press."

Vally had seated Anne in a chair, and he looked up and observed curtly, "I don't need you two fellows."

"Quite all right," Tim said, waving a gracious hand. "We can spare the time."

George closed the door after him and leaned against it with his arms folded.

Vally turned his back on them and spoke exclusively to Anne.

"Now, young lady, you found the money, didn't you?"

"What money?" Anne asked drowsily.

Vally shrugged. He was convinced that the Smith boy had the money, but there was no harm in asking.

"Look," he said after a moment, "don't you think you'd better go back to your friends and behave yourself?"

Anne thought for a while, and finally said, "Yes."

"Who else was in this besides you and Paul Depilriattia?"

Anne thought some more and said, "Yes," again.

Vally wrote something in a notebook and closed it with a snap.

"O.K.—I'm off now. The Smith boy is about due, and I want to welcome him home."

"What about Mrs. Johnson?" George asked coldly. "Or don't you consider that any of your business?"

"I'll acknowledge her as a missing person if she hasn't turned up by tomorrow morning," Vally said, and took himself off in a fury. No use trying to get any sense out of the girl now—she was doped to the eyebrows. He'd have to come back, that was all. And to hell with the cook—and those two baboons as well. He went outside and started taking it out on his men.

Upstairs, Tim was hovering anxiously over Anne. He presently succeeded in pulling her to her feet, and started to walk her up and down the room.

"Go and get coffee, George," he said over his shoulder. "Strong and black—and hurry."

George went down to the kitchen, where he found Ginny struggling with dinner preparations and impending hysteria. She had no time to make coffee, and said so, using more words than were necessary.

"All right, all right," George broke in. "Just do the best you can and shut up, for God's sake. I'll get the coffee myself."

He concocted some sort of mixture, swearing steadily throughout, and took a cupful upstairs.

Tim said, "Ah!" relieved him of the cup, and turned to Anne. "Here you are, precious. You must drink it down and you'll feel better. But keep walking."

"Why don't you let her sit down?" George demanded. "The poor kid is practically asleep on her feet."

"My dear George," Tim moaned, "when will you learn to keep your ignorance to yourself ? Many stupid people have gone a long way merely by keeping their mouths shut and looking profound. You must surely realize that this child has been doped. You remember the story that Paul D. told Vally? He had been doped, of course, and was eventually frightened off. Now they hope to get rid of Anne by the same method."

Anne, sipping the coffee, choked a little and asked plaintively, "What is this? I thought you said it was coffee. And no one needs to try to force me out, because I'm going as soon as I can collect my wits."

"Who put you in that closet?" George asked.

"I don't know. I don't believe anybody did. I was looking for Vally and I think I must have wandered in there."

Tim wrinkled his forehead. "But, my darling, how could you? The door slides—it doesn't hang open."

"She might have fallen against it," George suggested, "and perhaps slid it open, and then stumbled in."

Anne put the empty coffee cup onto a table. "I wish you'd tell me what that was—it tasted like some medicine I once had for an upset stomach. And as for that sliding door, I might have pushed it open by mistake, but I wouldn't have closed it after me."

Tim said, "No," and George shrugged.

"Perhaps she went to sleep in there, and then someone passed by and closed it."

Anne said, "My shoulder hurts." At the same time an altercation started, apparently on the floor above, and George and Tim went out to see what it was.

Roger and Mr. Courtney were standing just outside Roger's room, and Mr. Courtney was almost shouting, "I won't have it, do you hear! This is the last straw!"

"I assure you, sir, I know nothing about it," Roger cried indignantly, his face brick-red. "I have told you that I did not touch it."

"Just tell me where it is," Mr. Courtney said shrilly. "I'm going to get a key and lock my door—I'm going to keep it locked. If you didn't take it, you know who did."

"On the contrary—" Roger began, and was violently interrupted.

"I think I should have some control over the disposition of my own possessions! It's an intolerable outrage! Just tell me where it is so that I can get it."

"I assure you, sir—" Roger began again, and was interrupted once more, this time by the refined voice of his wife Pet, who appeared at the door behind him. She spoke so quietly that Tim and George were unable to hear what she said, but Roger and Mr. Courtney dropped their voices at once.

"It's his hand," Tim said. "What on earth did you do with it?"

"I'm saving it to hang on the Christmas tree," George snarled.

"You left it lying on Anne's suitcase—I remember now. You'd better go and get them both."

George went off and presently returned to Anne's room with the suitcase and the artificial hand. Tim was leading Anne up and down the room again, but she stopped and shuddered.

"I wish you'd take that thing out of here—I never want to see it again."

George dropped the suitcase and went out. He was relieved to discover that Mr. Courtney had not yet returned to his room, which enabled him to put the hand in a bureau drawer under a shirt and thus save explanation and discussion.

He wondered a little why Mr. Courtney had accused Roger. While Roger might have wished to get Paul out of the house, it seemed improbable that he'd go to the length of appropriating the hand, dipping it in Paul's own blood, and dangling it before him. Certainly it had been effective in ousting Paul, but if Roger had done it, he must be going a bit queer. And "queer" was too mild a word, at that.

George went downstairs with a worried frown on his face. He'd better do something about getting a lawyer for Monty, although he wasn't too troubled about Monty now. There was something else—some evil in the house that hadn't left when Monty ran away like a frightened kid. And it was just like Monty to run away instead of facing things—that was a lot of his trouble. Well—George heaved a ponderous sigh. When this lousy mess was cleared up, he'd get out—go and live by himself. He wasn't going to live with relatives—or with Tim either.

He did some telephoning and then went back to Anne's room, where he found her alone.

"How do you feel?" he asked her.

"I'm better—at least I think so. Tim's making martinis."

George nodded and asked after a minute, "Did you take anything to make you this way?"

"Not voluntarily," she said a little coldly. "I'm leaving as soon as I feel able to crawl into a cab. And you see Vally didn't pick me up—after all the trouble you had locking me into that room."

"No, but he was going to, before he knew about Monty having been in the hospital."

"Hospital?" Anne repeated, and then gave a little cry. "What is the matter with my shoulder?"

George walked over and asked, "Which one?"

She raised her left shoulder and cried out again, and George put a tentative hand on it.

"It's a brooch," he said slowly. "The pin is open, and it's been sticking into you every time you moved. No wonder it hurt."

Anne looked at it curiously as it lay on his palm. It was rather an ornate thing—old-fashioned—with a large amethyst set in gold.

She touched it and said wonderingly, "It isn't mine."

"No. It belongs to Mrs. Johnson. She's had it for many years, and she's very fond of it."

CHAPTER TWENTY-SIX

TIM CAME IN with a tray of cocktails, muttering something about Ginny and the difficulty of obtaining ice in this barbarous place, but the other two never even looked up at him. George was turning the amethyst brooch over in his fingers, and he asked, "Where did you get this?"

"What?" Tim demanded, setting the tray down.

Anne shook her head, her eyes still on the brooch. "I don't know—I must have fallen on it somewhere. I suppose it got stuck in my dress. Anyway, it kept jabbing into my shoulder."

"In that linen closet," George muttered. "Are you sure Mrs. Johnson wasn't in there with you?"

"How can I be sure?" Anne said petulantly. "I don't remember much about it. I think I slept there for a while, but after I woke up, I know there was no one there—just myself and four walls, and the clothes and the shelves with the linen—and something else, I think."

"The hamper," Tim said, nodding. "For soiled laundry. You two never tell me anything, but I assume that brooch belongs to Mrs. Johnson. I find myself arriving at the conclusion that Mrs. Johnson threw a soiled blouse into the hamper and forgot to remove the brooch first. The open pin caught in the basketwork, and Anne picked it up when she fell against the hamper."

"Let's go and find the blouse," George said uneasily. "Somehow I just can't think of her without this brooch."

He left the room rather abruptly, but Tim lingered to take a swallow of his martini. George realized that he was feeling lousy all over again. For a while he had almost persuaded himself that Mrs. Johnson had merely slipped out without anyone having seen her, but now he knew it wasn't so. Something had happened—something else—and someone in the house had gone mad and was running berserk. Of course if anything had happened to Mrs. Johnson, it ought to clear Monty—but that was a lousy way to look at things, anyway.

Tim caught up with him as he opened the closet and said breathlessly, "Why didn't you wait for me? You really can't handle this without my brain to guide you."

George busily pulling soiled clothes out of the hamper, said, "Aw, shut up," rather absently.

They sorted the laundry carefully, but there was no blouse. They found only sheets, pillowcases, and two bureau scarfs.

"I didn't expect to find anything of the sort here, anyway," George said on a long breath. "But, dammit, she's been here. She was up in Min's room, chatting, and then she left to get the tea—but she never got as far as the kitchen. She must have come in here. Perhaps Min told her to throw the bureau scarfs in the hamper."

"Simple enough to check on that," Tim murmured. "Suppose you go and ask her."

George nodded and started out of the closet. "Just put that laundry back into the hamper," he called over his shoulder.

Tim obeyed reluctantly, shuddering as he handled each soiled piece. When he had finished, he went back to Anne's room and discovered that she had finished the martinis.

"Darling!" he cried, "you've finished them! You must like them."

"I do not," she said coldly, "but I felt the need of something to pull me together."

"My dear, in that case you might have left mine for me."

"You've probably had more than enough today."

"Well—but, darling, that's hardly the point. I don't think all that alcohol can be very good for your present condition."

"Why don't you mix some more?" Anne asked impatiently.

"Precious, I can't. That Ginny creature won't let me have any more ice."

George came in and said gloomily, "Min didn't tell her to put anything in the hamper. She just said she was going down to make the tea, and left."

"George," Tim said, looking desperate, "could you get some ice from Ginny?"

"I suppose so." George glanced at the glasses. "Have you finished that already?"

"Don't quibble, I beg of you. Just get the ice, so that I can make martinis, and then I can think."

"Gruesome threat," George commented, and went out.

He ran into Miss Kalms in the hall, and she asked if she could stay to dinner. He nodded absently, and she proceeded to wonder—with an appraising glance at him—whether she might have just one little cocktail first. It had been a hard day, and although she did not drink as a rule—

George told her to go to Anne's room and, remembering that he had been delegated to get ice, went on down to the kitchen. Ginny was still there, and Min had appeared, dressed, and with her face carefully made up. They were both shedding tears.

George said, "Oh, God!" and Min began hastily to mop at her eyes. She said, "Come on, Ginny. Shut up, will you? We've got to get this dinner finished and on the table."

George went to the refrigerator for ice, and Ginny, after drying her eyes on her apron, said, "I hope there's some left, Mr. George —that crazy fella keeps taking it and I don't know how to stop him."

George put the ice into a pot which Ginny promptly assured him they were going to need. Min produced a bowl, and George took it and departed, flinging over his shoulder the glad news that Miss Kalms would be with them for dinner.

In the front hall he came face to face with Lily, smartly attired in dark green with some jewelry that might or might not have been emeralds, but looked expensive, in any case.

She cried, "George, darling, there you are! I just couldn't stay away. It bothers me frightfully to think that I have lost your scalp."

"Where did you see it last?" George asked courteously. "Maybe it s only mislaid."

"George—*darling!* You left early last night, and I haven't seen you since."

"My dear girl," George said sensibly, "we've been in bad trouble here. Aunt Ellen was murdered this morning."

Lily screamed on a high, lovely note.

George glanced down at the melting ice. "Come on upstairs. That monkey is going to make some drinks."

"What monkey?"

"Mr. Capri."

Lily said, "Oh—oh—Mr. Timothy Capri. George, you shouldn't call him a monkey. Why, Tim's wonderful. He's the biggest—"

"Monkey," said George. "There you are—that door on your right—Anne's room."

Tim seemed to be lost in thought when they went in, and Anne was sitting in an armchair, her head against the back, singing softly, with her eyes closed.

"Ah," Tim said, "the ice. I was sure you had forgotten. And Lily as well. How are you, you gorgeous hussy?"

"Timmy! My dear!" Lily screamed. "What's new? And whatever is the matter with the little Anne?"

"The poor dear drank some martinis that were meant for me."

"Why don't you look after her better, for God's sake?" George demanded. "You'd better take her to her friends."

Tim shook his head. "I couldn't possibly take her in this condition—I'd be ashamed."

"I thought Miss Kalms was coming in for a cocktail," George muttered, glancing around the room.

Tim nodded. "She came—but she couldn't wait. She went out for a quick one, first telling me carefully that she had to post a letter."

Lily had dropped her coat and was carefully pulling off her dark green gloves. "George, you must tell me all about this terrible thing. You say that poor, dear old soul was actually murdered?"

But George was thinking of something else. "I know Mrs. Johnson wouldn't take that pin off—and what reason would she have for going to that closet?"

Tim handed him a glass. "Here's a drink, George—pour it down."

George poured it down.

"I didn't mean it quite as literally as that," Tim murmured.

"Well, next time say what you mean."

Lily gave a peal of silvery laughter, and Anne opened her eyes. Tim went and knelt beside her.

"Feeling better, dear?"

"I'm all right—a little dizzy. I think I'm hungry—I haven't had much to eat all day."

"But, precious—" Tim began, and George interrupted him.

"Dinner will be ready soon. Perhaps you'd better eat something before you go."

"Where's she going?" Lily asked.

Miss Kalms came in and gave Lily a cold stare.

"Here is a martini for you, my dear Nightingale," Tim said. "And now, do please tell us—who keeps clothes in that closet in the hall—the one where the linen is kept?"

Miss Kalms, sipping her drink, said, "For heaven's sake, who wants to know? I kept my things there, and I think there are some old things that no one uses any more."

Anne stood up suddenly, and Tim flew to her side, his arm about her shoulders. Lily said curiously, "She really sends you, doesn't she?"

"Yes—it's strange. I don't quite understand it."

"Why is it strange?" George demanded, with a trace of belligerence.

Miss Kalms sidled up to George and started to speak, but Lily shot a crimson-tipped hand out and crossed it firmly on her arm. "Nurse, dear," she said gently, "this is mine."

George said, "Lily, don't be a damned fool."

The dinner gong sounded from downstairs, and Anne exclaimed, "That's it—that's what I've been waiting for. I need food."

"We really shouldn't let her eat here after what has happened," Tim said, with a glance at George.

"Oh, come on down," George said impatiently. "We'll be there to watch, so that if she gets another dose, at least we'll know it came straight from the kitchen."

Tim shrugged. "Well, I suppose she needs food. But I do not like to have my darling used as a guinea pig."

"Dears," Lily said, "you are all talking in puzzles. It's an awfully dull party."

"This is no party," George said with sudden heat. "My aunt—"

"Yes, George, your aunt. But you haven't told me anything—and I cannot let my hair down and cry for shadows."

"Have dinner with us, Lily," Tim said kindly, "and we'll tell you all about it."

He took Anne's arm and guided her carefully down the stairs.

The others were already in the dining room, including even Mr. Alrian, who sat apart with his usual air of cold reserve.

Tim seated Anne and Miss Kalms, and George produced another chair for Lily, who looked about her in wonderment and said in a clear, carrying voice, "What an absurd time to be having dinner. Surely it can't be much later than six o'clock?"

Several heads turned her way, and Roger said loudly, "For people who get up at a decent hour in the morning, this is a decent hour for dinner."

Lily looked at him and said in a distressed voice, "Oh, dear! Now I've offended one of the inmates."

Roger was infuriated. "Don't you call me an 'inmate,' Miss— I am well known here—and so are you, for that matter."

Lily giggled into her water glass—which was a bit short of ice —but George actually blushed.

Miss Burreton said, "Disgraceful."

"The trouble with George," Tim said critically, "is that he has no sense of humor. Look at the rich color in his cheeks."

"You leave George alone," Lily pouted. "He can laugh like a hyena when he doesn't have all this on his mind."

Tim sighed. "I know. I suppose at the movies when somebody throws a pie at somebody, George rolls in the aisle."

Miss Kalms laughed heartily, and Ginny, who had panted up to the table, said, "I can't serve five here."

George turned a baleful eye on her, and she backed away, stammering, "Well, I'll see—maybe I—er—"

"You see that?" Lily said triumphantly. "That's what I love about George."

Tim curled his lip. "Don't be so obvious, Lily—and stop flattering him. It's constantly amazing to me what prestige a beautiful body brings to a stupid mind."

George ignored them both and said earnestly, "Anne, did you fall against some clothes in that closet or against the laundry hamper?"

Anne shook her head. "I just can't remember what happened in that closet."

"Good heavens!" Lily exclaimed. "Do you mean to say that you haven't a laundry chute in an establishment as big as this?"

George and Tim, both with forks suspended midway between mouth and plate, stared at each other with wide eyes—and George felt a prickling all over the top of his scalp.

CHAPTER TWENTY-SEVEN

GEORGE GOT SLOWLY to his feet, and after an abstracted look around the table said, "You'll have to excuse me."

Tim stood up, and Lily looked at them both in bewilderment. "But what is it now? Surely it can wait until after dinner. George, really!"

Anne, busy with her food, ignored them completely, and Miss Kalms giggled. "That's the way they act all the time—now you see them, now you don't."

Tim caught up to George in the hall. "Is there a laundry chute anywhere?"

"Never heard of one—I'm going to take a look."

They found it in the linen closet, directly behind the hamper. It was a gaping hole in the wall, not visible until the hamper was moved to one side.

"One of old Mr. Smith's little jobs," George said grimly. "It doesn't look very workable, and I know it's never used."

"We must go down to the cellar and find the outlet," Tim breathed tensely. "Perhaps they do throw the laundry down when they get ready to wash."

George shook his head. "They send it all out." He turned abruptly out of the closet and ran down the back stairs.

In the kitchen they found Mrs. Smith eating, and she said rather fretfully, "Your dinner's in there—it'll be getting cold."

George was already on his way to the cellar, but Tim threw her a fleeting smile as he panted along behind.

But there was no outlet in the cellar—nothing but blank walls—and Tim said reproachfully, "You could have asked Mrs. Smith before clumping down here in such a hurry."

They went up and asked Mrs. Smith, and she said carelessly, "Oh, that. It was never finished. Grandma told me all about it. Old Mr. Smith started it, but when he got to this floor, he ran into a snag of some sort—couldn't get through—so he gave it up in a temper."

"You mean it's just a hole that stops on this floor?" George asked. "But that's very dangerous."

Min shrugged. "We keep the hamper in front of it—and nobody ever fell down there yet. Listen, George, when will Monty be back? You haven't told me—"

"I don't know—but you mustn't worry about it. I have a good man down there looking after things."

"He never should have run off like that," she moaned. "It looks so bad—and you know he hasn't done anything wrong."

"Where can I get into the chute from this floor?" George asked.

"Why, I don't know—I haven't any idea."

Tim nudged George and said, "Get a flashlight—we can peer down from upstairs and perhaps see to the bottom."

"But he must have opened it down here somewhere." George went into the pantry and looked at the floor. Concrete—and it was cold—not built over the cellar. He stood for a moment, figuring it out, and then moved slowly around the pantry until he found it. It had been smoothly plastered up, and on the other side was the lobby at the head of the cellar steps. It would be a job to open it up. He sighed, picked up a flashlight, and started upstairs again.

"I told you to do this in the first place," Tim said resignedly.

"That's right, but I'm not as smart as you, so I have to take one thing at a time and not do any skipping."

They were unable to see to the bottom with a flashlight, since the first section of the chute had a shallow pitch and they could not reach beyond it. George considered it with narrowed eyes and then turned to Tim.

"It's pretty obvious that I won't fit in there, so you'll have to crawl in, while I hold your legs."

Tim paled and backed away a step and at the same time he felt George's hand on his arm, firm and unyielding. "I know your usual job is the brainwork, but this time you're going to crawl. Take the flash and get going."

Tim said angrily, "I hate this sort of thing," but he took the flash and crawled gingerly into the chute, while George took hold of his legs.

"Leave me alone," Tim called in a muffled voice. "I won't fall in. What do you think I am?"

"I refuse to answer," George replied virtuously. "Why start a fight?"

Tim began to back out again almost immediately. He brushed himself off very carefully, purposely keeping George waiting as long as possible.

"Well?" George said impatiently. "What's down there? Did you see anything?"

Tim pursed his lips. "There seems to be a pile of old clothes down at the bottom."

"Old clothes? What do you mean?"

"I mean old clothes. There appears to be an old red coat on top, and some darker things underneath."

"Can we haul them out?"

Tim shook his head. "They're too far down—we'll have to get at them downstairs. I don't know who you can get to do it at this time of night, and probably they are just old clothes—"

George turned away. "Stop dithering," he said grimly. "I'll open it up now—myself."

He went downstairs, armed himself with some tools, and started to hack at the wall without any further delay. Mrs. Smith had disappeared, but Ginny, still working feverishly in the kitchen, watched him with one eye and muttered, "For God's sake!" several times as she flew about.

Tim stayed long enough to satisfy himself that it would be a long job and then returned to his dinner.

Anne had finished eating and was smoking a cigarette. Lily was talking earnestly to her—apparently reciting the highlights in the story of her life. Miss Kalms had gone.

Tim sat down, discovered that his dinner had been cleared away, and got up again.

Lily interrupted herself to say, "Don't go, Timmy. Where's George?"

Tim went to the kitchen and asked in an injured voice, "Where's my dinner?"

Ginny spared him a brief look and said, "God knows."

Tim found a plate, filled it from the various pans lying around, muttered, "I don't suppose it's worth it," and wandered back to the dining room.

Anne looked up at him. "Don't we get coffee?"

"Yes, darling, when I have finished this garbage, I shall go out and see to it."

"My dear," Lily said, "don't bother. I know the system here—we all repair to the lounge, and coffee will be served there."

"Ah, yes," Tim murmured. "Crude of me not to have realized."

Anne laughed, and Tim said delightedly, "Precious, I think you are getting your wits back."

"But how did I lose them in the first place?"

"Oh, my God!" Tim exclaimed. "You were presumably doped at lunch—and we were supposed to watch like hawks tonight to see that it didn't happen again."

Lily gave him an oblique grin. "Nice job of hawking. But I have been here all the time—and unless it was done in the kitchen "

"Who would do such a thing to me?" Anne asked, and added plaintively, like a child, "I want to go back to Mary's."

"Right after dinner, my darling," Tim promised. "I shall take you myself. Suppose we go into the lounge now and have coffee. You see, everyone has gone."

They stood up, and Lily said, "I ought to go—I have a party on—but I simply had to know what had happened to George. I expected to hear from him."

Tim looked at her in honest bewilderment. "My dear, I simply don't understand why you give George a thought—he is definitely not your type and must inevitably be a disappointment to you."

"But you're so brilliant, Timmy," Lily screamed. "You're so right. George has always been a disappointment to me. Handsome brute, though."

"Gangway, please," said Ginny's voice behind them.

They stepped aside, and she bore the coffee tray to the lounge, banged it down on a table, and departed without a word.

Lily glanced around the lounge, where the inmates of the house were sitting in silence, and shivered. "Such gloom," she murmured.

Mr. Alrian got up from his chair, poured himself a cup of coffee, drank it without stopping for breath, and left the room without a glance to right or left.

Tim tried to get to the coffee next, but Miss Burreton elbowed him out with a baleful glare. She poured a cup for herself and carried it—slopping into the saucer—to a chair, where she proceeded to drink some, and spill the rest down the front of her dress.

Tim poured two cups and handed them to Anne and Lily and, at the same time, Roger grumbled out something about Mrs. Dimple and Liz Sampson having been there first, so Tim poured two more cups and handed them out. They thanked him politely, and Liz managed to press his hand. Tim sighed, and poured coffee for himself.

Lily drank her coffee standing up and said, from time to time, "I really must go."

Tim presently looked full at her and asked, "Why? Do you expect to be with people who are more entertaining than I?"

Lily gave him a long, slow smile, and slightly raised her shoulders. "Of course, when you put it that way—"

Miss Burreton said clearly, "Hussy!"

Pet laughed nervously and whispered, "Hush."

Lily whirled around. "Oh—hello, Miss Burreton."

Miss Burreton stared in silence, and Roger got up and poured himself another cup of coffee. Mr. Courtney announced that he was tired and was going to bed immediately, and they all made a point of saying good night to him. Tim reflected that he could almost hear them thinking that they'd be seeing him in his room at nine o'clock. He was privately furious at them for having arranged the meeting at nine, since he would be unable to be there. But he must tell George to listen in.

Miss Burreton said suddenly, "I'm going to look for the money again," and the others all spoke at once, in an attempt to drown her out. Roger said it was a pity there had been so much snow, and Pet wondered when they would hold the funeral for Mrs. Smith. Liz said she thought the latest fashions were simply vile.

Anne and Lily were surprised at the sudden spurt of conversation, and Miss Burreton looked a little astonished too. She gazed at them, opened her mouth as though to speak, and then shut it firmly and padded off.

Lily gave Tim a special smile. "Timmy, let's go somewhere together sometime. I really think I could enjoy your company."

"Others have," Tim admitted. "Anyway, we could try. Nothing to lose except my money and your time."

"Where is that wretch George?" Lily sighed. "I want to say good-by to him before I leave."

"Come," said Tim, "I'll show you. Then I'll drop you where you want to go, and Anne at Mary's—I'll just have time."

He took them out to the kitchen, where they found Ginny working at the sink surrounded on every side by dishes. She said feebly, "Will somebody help me? Or would you rather pick me up off the floor later?"

Anne picked up a dish towel, and asked, "What happened to the cook this time?"

"God knows," Ginny said, and broke a plate. She added, "Good—I hadn't washed it. I'm telling you, I'm leaving—what with old Mrs. Smith murdered in her bed, and Johnson disappearing off the face of the earth—and Mr. George breaking down the wall looking for her. Anyways, I guess that's what he's doing—and I'm scared sick."

Lily gave a clear, bell-like scream, and Anne and Ginny ran to the pantry.

Lily, Tim and George stood in silence, looking down at something on the floor. Anne pushed in and saw the head and shoulders of a man—a dead man.

CHAPTER TWENTY-EIGHT

ANNE SPOKE INTO the silence. "That's Spike," she said in a sick voice. "Spike Magraw."

Ginny turned and ran back to the sink, and Lily followed and collapsed onto a kitchen chair.

"Are you sure?" George asked quietly, and Anne nodded, her handkerchief pressed against her mouth.

Tim straightened up from a careful examination. "He seems to have been shot through the head."

"Better call Vally," George said.

"All right—but let's pull him all the way out. There might be—"

"Go away, Anne," George said abruptly.

She returned to the kitchen, her handkerchief still crushed against her mouth and her mind fiercely concentrated on subduing her stomach.

Ginny was leaning against the sink. "Oh, heaven help us," she moaned, "they expect her to be there too."

"Who?" Anne asked sharply.

No one answered her, and they could hear George swearing. Ginny wavered over to the pantry, took a quick look, and stumbled back again. "It's her ,all right—they've got her—she was stuffed in there with him. I'm going home—I'm going to get my hat and coat and leave right now."

"You'll do nothing of the sort." Lily said sharply. "You'll stay right here and help."

Ginny turned to the sink and began to fumble with the dishes, and Anne picked up the towel again.

They heard Tim say, "It's no use—she's been shot through the head too. Dead for some time."

"I'm going to get a doctor," George muttered thickly.

"Right. I'll stay here with them. And you might let Vally know too—or his feelings will be hurt."

George went through to the front hall and picked up the telephone. He arranged for a doctor to come at once and then turned to find that Vally had come into the hall and was watching him.

"The cook," Vally said simply. "Been on my mind. Has she turned up yet?"

"She's turned up all right—the only trouble is, she's dead."

Vally had learned to keep a poker face over the most tumultuous thoughts, so he said merely, "Show me."

George led him through to the kitchen where Ginny was dripping tears into the sink. Lily had the dish towel now, and Anne was sitting down.

Vally looked them over in silence and followed George into the pantry, where Tim stepped aside with a slight downward gesture.

Vally dropped to his haunches, asked a few brief, rapid questions, and then stood up again. "I'll have to do some phoning. See that no one touches them."

He hurried to the front hall, and George and Tim came into the kitchen.

"I'd like a drink," George said wearily.

"No." Tim pulled him to one side and began to whisper, while the three women stared at them. "Don't drink anything now—you must keep your wits sharp. All the old mossbacks are having a conference in Mr. Courtney's room at nine o'clock. You must hide yourself somewhere so that you'll be able to hear every word."

"Why should I waste my time?" George demanded irritably. "I've often listened to them, and they never say anything."

"I *wish* I did not have to go," Tim muttered. "You must listen, George— I assure you that it will be worthwhile this time." He glanced at his watch and sighed. "Come, girls, I'll just have time—"

Lily dropped the towel and said, "I'm ready right now."

Anne shook her head. "I'm staying. We'll all be wanted. If you two are going, you'd better duck out the back door at once, before Vally comes back."

"Darling!" Tim cried. "You're wonderful. I shall see you later."

He went off with Lily clinging to his arm, and Anne picked up the dish towel. "Come on, Ginny, you'll never get through at this rate."

The doctor whom George had called arrived at that point, and Vally followed him out to the kitchen. They went into the pantry, and George asked Anne, "Where did Tim go?"

Anne shrugged, and Ginny said shrilly, "Do you mean to say you don't know—"

Vally emerged from the pantry and interrupted her with a curt gesture. He began to question Anne about Spike Magraw. After she had denied at least six times having had any previous connection with him, Vally asked how it was that she could so positively identify him after having seen him only once. Anne said she didn't know and added that she didn't care, either.

A group of men pounded into the kitchen, and Vally prepared to join them. He said to Anne, "You'll be here when I want you," and left off the question mark at the end.

"Certainly," Anne replied coldly. "Since you put it that way."

She went back to drying the dishes and urged Ginny on with a threat. "I'm getting tired, and if you don't hurry up I'm going to leave you flat."

"You're going to leave," Ginny muttered. "I'm going to leave, and *that's* flat."

George and the doctor he had called were eventually squeezed out of the pantry by Vally's men. "Terrible thing," the doctor said, rubbing his hands delightedly. "Dreadful, dreadful."

George, anxious for a word with Vally, bided his time by the pantry door and caught him, at last, when he was mopping his face with a dusty handkerchief.

"Did you see Monty Smith?"

Vally nodded.

"When is he coming here?"

"As soon as I can strike the fetters from his wrists," Vally said, scowling.

George nodded. "It's obvious that he had nothing to do with Mrs. Johnson's death."

"Actually," said Vally, "I saw that for myself." He added, "I want everyone in the house to assemble in the living room."

"You want me to round them up for you?"

Vally said, "If you please," quite politely.

George glanced at Ginny. "I think the maid is anxious to get home."

"So am I," said Vally. "I want them all."

He went back to the pantry, and Ginny burst into tears. "I can't go and assemble in the lounge, Mr. George—my feet are killing me and I got to get home—not to mention I ain't washed the meat pan yet."

"You've done enough for tonight," Anne said gently. "Come into the lounge with me, and we'll sit down and have a cigarette."

Pet, Roger, and Liz Sampson were still in the lounge, and Roger asked, "What's Ginny doing in here? I say things have come to a pretty pass when the guests are expected to mingle—"

Pet said, "Hush, dear," and Liz asked, "What's going on out there? All those men—and one of them told us to stay here."

Anne hesitated. "It's Mrs. Johnson," she said at last. "She—there's been an accident. She's dead."

Ginny started to weep afresh, and the other three looked at Anne in silence, their faces pinched and frightened.

"What happened to her?" Roger asked at last. "What sort of an accident?"

"She—I guess she fell down the laundry chute."

"Laundry chute!" Liz cried shrilly. "Why, there isn't any."

"Oh, yes, Liz," Pet reminded her. "Mr. Smith built it, but he never finished it—there was trouble about getting it through to the cellar. You must remember that."

Roger nodded. "That's right—that's right. Silly old buster never finished it. But how could she fall down there? Ridiculous!"

They all looked at Anne, who looked back in silence. At last Pet said quietly, "She wasn't pushed, was she?"

Anne dropped into an armchair and rested her head against the back.

"Good God, girl, can't you answer a civil question?" Roger asked nervously.

Anne closed her eyes. "I'm afraid she was."

George came in to see who was there and left immediately, paying no heed to Roger's bellowed command that he come and tell them what was going on.

Anne pulled out a cigarette, and Liz asked for one. Liz turned it over in her fingers for a moment before lighting it and said, "Simply divine—I adore them. But so frightfully expensive."

Anne glanced down at the box in her hand and realized that she had never heard of the brand before. Tim had given it to her, she remembered.

"Heartless of you girls to smoke at a time like this," Roger declared, and added fretfully, "I need a drink."

"Now, Roger," Pet admonished gently, "you don't need anything of the kind."

They fell into a gloomy silence, and presently George came back with Miss Burreton, who looked at Ginny and said fiercely, "That's my chair."

"Now, Burry," Pet protested, "don't be tiresome. Come and sit in this one by me."

Miss Burreton shuffled over and lowered herself into the chair by Pet, but she continued to glower at Ginny, and said, "It's utterly disgraceful."

"Why don't you put on a new record?" Roger growled. "That one's cracked."

Pet said, "Hush."

Mr. Alrian came in and nodded coldly at everyone, including Ginny. He sat down, pulled a paper out from under his arm, and appeared to lose himself in it.

"Just like a dead fish," Liz observed clearly.

Mr. Alrian rattled the paper.

Mr. Courtney came in, followed closely by Min who wore an old dressing robe and looked haggard under a hasty application of rouge. George put her into a comfortable chair and told her in a low voice that she was not to worry—Monty would be home soon.

"Now, George," Roger said firmly, "we want to know what has happened. We have been told that Mrs. Johnson was pushed down the laundry chute."

"That's right."

"But, God almighty, man, can't you give us some details?"

Pet and Liz spoke together—the one anxiously, the other with nervous irritability. Miss Burreton chewed on her gums and stared fixedly at the chandelier.

Vally walked in and quieted them with a glance. "I'll want an account of your activities for the day."

Miss Burreton and Liz at once began an account of their activities for the day. Roger demanded to know by what right Vally asked such a question, and Pet and Mr. Courtney suggested that they be told first what had happened. Min said that she wasn't going to open her mouth about anything until Monty came home and was proved to have no bruises on him, and Ginny told the entire room, three times in quick succession, that she had done nothing whatever all day. Anne remained silent. George paced the room restlessly, and Mr. Alrian put his newspaper away.

Vally let it go for a while, then raised his hand and said, "All right, all right—that will do. We'll take it one at a time. Mr. Vaddison, will you either sit down or stand still."

George stopped in front of Roger, who told him to get out of the way, so he moved over behind Liz.

"Any one of you own a gun?" Vally asked into the silence.

There was a blank pause, and then Miss Burreton nodded her head two or three times.

"Not a gun, you know—no lady would keep a gun. But I have my pistol."

CHAPTER TWENTY-NINE

"YOU HAVE A GUN, Miss Burreton?" Vally asked carefully.

"No," said Miss Burreton, "but I have a pistol."

"I see. And where do you keep it?"

"In the drawer," said Miss Burreton crossly. "In the bureau drawer—but you mustn't be touching my things—you must leave them alone."

"Is it loaded?"

"Of course it's loaded. My father gave it to me so that I would be protected."

"Will you show it to me?" Vally asked.

"No."

Vally raised an eyebrow at George, and the two of them went out and up the front stairs. Everyone in the lounge followed at a discreet distance, with the single exception of Mr. Alrian, who opened up his paper again.

George and Vally went into Miss Burreton's room, and George looked around rather helplessly. "Damned if I know where she keeps anything."

Vally began to go through the drawers, which were cluttered with bits of ribbon and lace, handkerchiefs, letters, and other odds and ends. After a while he noticed that Miss Burreton was right beside him, and he sighed. "Where do you keep your pistol?" he asked patiently.

"Oh," she said, "the pistol? It's right here where I always keep it."

She opened one of the top bureau drawers, which Vally had already searched, and thrust her hand into a tangle of lace and artificial flowers. Vally caught at her arm hastily and, eventually, withdrew the pistol with a handkerchief carefully wrapped around it. He examined it briefly, while the crowd surged in from the doorway, peering interestedly, and then he straightened up and looked at them severely.

"Please return to the living room. I wish to question each of you separately in the dining room. I shall be as quick as I can."

They headed for the stairs, and Roger made his way determinedly to Vally's side. "That gun isn't loaded—we took the bullets out some time ago—thought it wasn't safe."

Vally stopped and eyed him. "That so? Where did you put the bullets?"

"In a trunk in the attic."

"Did you lock the trunk?"

Roger frowned. "No, no—certainly not. We didn't think she'd find them."

"Who's 'we'? Who knew they were up there?"

Roger became a little flustered. "Why—er—my wife and myself—Mr. Courtney and Miss Sampson. Mrs. Smith must have known, since it was she who suggested the attic. I really don't know who else."

"In other words," said Vally sourly, "anyone might have known except

Miss Burreton—and she probably did too. Come on, you'd better show me where you put them."

They went up to the attic, where Roger opened a small trunk in dignified silence. A strong smell of camphor drifted up, and he muttered, "Beastly smell."

Vally shifted the trunk to a better light and went through it thoroughly, but there were no bullets. He got up, dusting his knees, and asked, "Are you sure this is where you put them?"

"Of course I'm sure, man, do you think I'm a dithering idiot?"

Vally forbore to commit himself and went down the stairs, where George was waiting for him on the landing.

"Is that gun loaded?"

"Slightly," Vally said furiously. "Two shots have been fired from it. If I'd been able to find the bullets these people hid so carefully, I could have traced whoever bought new ones. As it is, I merely have to discover who took them out of the trunk." He stared at a stain on the wall and muttered, "It must have been done in the closet both times, so that the reports were a bit muffled, and anybody hearing it would think it a backfire outside."

They all went down to the lounge again, where Mr. Alrian was still reading the newspaper. George began to pace up and down, and Ginny was escorted into the dining room where Vally had established himself. Ann sat a little apart from the others and smoked another one of Tim's fancy cigarettes.

One by one they were taken into the dining room, until only George and Anne were left. George had stopped his pacing to stand by the window, but he came over and sat down beside her.

"Look—do you mind if I go next?"

"Certainly I mind," Anne said, "and maybe Vally will too."

"It's this way. Tim said that all these people are having a conference tonight, and I want to listen."

"All right," Anne said wearily. "Go next, if he'll have you."

"Good. If he insists on having you next, you'd better go up and listen. You can hear very well from the closet in your room—it used to be a connecting door, but it's been boarded up. It's only thin plywood, so you should be able to hear everything."

"Well"—Anne closed her eyes for a moment, and gave her head a little shake—"I'll go if you want me to, but I'm still a little fuzzy. Why don't you simply tell Vally and take him up to my closet?"

George looked at her and then grinned suddenly. "Damned if you're not right. That nosy, overdressed bloodhound has got me trying to keep things from the police too."

"What time are they meeting?"

George glanced at his watch and gave a low whistle. "It's nearly ten, and they were supposed to get together at nine. Chances are they'll call it off."

Anne was called for her session with Vally, and George decided to run upstairs to see whether the meeting were being held or not. Mr. Courtney, the last to have been questioned, had just reached the top of the stairs, and George waited, looking up and whistling soundlessly through his teeth. When Mr. Courtney had disappeared he went up quietly, entered Anne's room, and tiptoed into the closet.

For a while there was no sound at all, and then the door opened, and he heard the voices of Mr. Courtney, Pet, and Roger. They came into the room, and Roger said, "How long will Liz be? The woman never gives a hang how long she keeps people waiting."

"I hope Burry doesn't smell us out," Pet worried. "You know how she is—if she comes in, we won't be able to get anything settled."

Liz arrived and began to talk in a strident voice before the door was well closed behind her. "This is frightful—if they find out about us we'll be blamed for everything. Do you think Burry could have shot those two? You know she's a bit nuts these days."

"If she had, she would have informed upon herself before this," Roger said gloomily.

"We shall have to get rid of her," Pet sighed, "before she informs on us."

Mr. Courtney cleared his throat. "I think she'll consent to go to a decent home—but where will we get the money for it?"

"Well, dammit," Liz said, "hasn't she anything left herself? She never spends a nickel."

"She had nothing to start with," Roger said crossly. "I know she's broke now—like the rest of us. If you hadn't spent yours in such a tearing hurry, so that we had to help you out, we'd all be better off."

"Oh, shut up," Liz muttered. "That other money must be around somewhere—we've simply got to find it, that's all. I'm pretty sure Ellen never got around to telling the girl where it is."

Mr. Courtney cleared his throat again. "No. She was killed neatly, just in time to stop it."

There was a silence, and then Roger gave a sort of bellowing sigh. "Well, I don't know anything about her death."

There was a chorus of similar denials from the others, and Liz said, "You know, Burry was always mean."

"Yes, she was," Pet declared. "I can't see why we should have to give her money now—that is, if we find it, of course."

"And if we don't find it?" Mr. Courtney asked quietly.

"We must tear the place apart," Roger said vigorously. "It must be somewhere—we're bound to come across it. As for Burry, we can—er—deny en masse anything she says."

"Has anyone looked to see how much she has left?" Pet asked.

"She changed the place," Liz said flatly. "She must have caught on that we were checking up on her."

"How much did you take from her?" Mr. Courtney demanded.

"Well, of all the nerve! I'm not a thief!"

"No?"

Liz sounded a little flustered. "Well—that other doesn't count. You know how Ellen got that money—she had no right to it. Anyway, she never knew it, so what difference does it make?"

"I admire your flawless logic," Mr. Courtney said nastily.

"This is getting us nowhere," Roger interrupted. "Matter of fact the thing's extremely simple. Burry's gone a bit potty—she has no money to pay for a nice old ladies' home—but if she's responsible for these murders, they'll put her away anyhow—and that's what she needs. So why all the fuss?"

There was a short silence, and then Pet said, "Roger is right. We—we can easily drop hints."

"Sure," Liz agreed enthusiastically. "And she probably did it, anyway."

Several voices said, "Yes, yes—she must have."

Roger gave a loud rumbling cough. "Right. That's settled. Now, where shall we look next?"

"Perhaps it was in the lining of that black coat," Mr. Courtney said slowly. "Ellen must have said something—you remember that girl said the lining had been ripped open. Someone got in ahead of us—probably Miss Kalms."

"Why not the girl?" Roger asked.

"She would never have talked about it. No. My guess is Miss Kalms. Chances are she has the money."

Liz asked, "What are you talking about? Was the money in the coat?"

"No, no," Pet said. "Ellen would never let money get around like that. Actually, she would put Missy's money in a place where Missy would never find it—poor soul."

"Let's look in the coat," Roger suggested.

Mr. Courtney made a vexed sound. "Of course there's nothing there now. I have the nurse's address, and I shall call on her. If she has the money, I intend to get it."

"Listen to him," Liz said derisively. "What are you going to do? Turn her upside down and shake her?"

Pet's gentle voice broke in. "You all saw a great deal of Ellen before she died. Are you sure she gave none of you a hint?"

There was an uneasy silence, and then Mr. Courtney asked coldly, "Are you insinuating that one of us is holding out on the others?"

"Maybe little Pet knows more than she's telling," Liz said.

Roger came furiously to his wife's defense. "How dare you! Both of you! You know perfectly well that Pet is simply trying to cover the ground thoroughly."

Liz said, "Yeah," and Mr. Courtney observed, "Ellen was not herself during her illness, but the instinct to keep her money hidden was still strong."

"Hidden and unused," Liz muttered sourly.

"Better than spending every nickel and going into debt."

"We are getting nowhere," Roger said patiently.

"Yes, we are, dear," Pet declared. "We have agreed to drop hints about Burry—and then Liz must go into her room, find her money, and see how much she has left. She might have a little something, which would tide us over. I'll go with you, Liz."

"I shall escort you both," Mr. Courtney announced.

Roger said, "You're all very suspicious—"

"We'll get that part of it done tonight," Pet decided. "Roger, you must keep Burry away so that we won't be disturbed. About the other money—I think it's still in the house, and we'll have plenty of time to find it when things quiet down."

"Is it agreed?" Roger asked, and there was the sound of a general movement.

George left the closet and went to the door of Anne's rooms where he peered out cautiously. They were all going down the hall toward Miss Burreton's room, where they stopped while Pet knocked discreetly on the door. George walked out into the hall as Miss Burreton opened her door and looked out, blinking and peering.

"We are having a nightcap in our room, Burry," Roger said genially. "Care to join us?"

She looked at him vacantly for a moment, and then her eyes kindled. "Roger, you must help me—you must find out who did it. Someone has stolen all my money."

CHAPTER THIRTY

ROGER'S FACE purpled. He roared, "What!" and Pet stepped forward hastily.

"You've just mislaid it, Burry dear. We'll come in and help you find it."

They all surged into the room, and George, who had approached quietly, went in with them and was not discovered until they turned to shut the door. They stood and looked at him in silence.

"I thought I heard Miss Burreton say that there had been some money stolen from her."

"Yes, yes," Roger boomed, and winked at him. "Probably mislaid it, you know. We offered to help her find it."

"Very good of you," George said, trying to keep his voice even. "However, I should prefer to look into this myself, if you don't mind. You must all be tired, and I'm sure you want to go to bed. If I find Miss Burreton's money, I shall put it back where she usually keeps it—and then she won't think that it has been stolen."

They departed reluctantly, glancing back uneasily at George, and unable to understand why the tone of his voice disturbed them so much.

George turned to Miss Burreton, who was placidly established in her rocking chair.

"Where do you usually keep it?"

"What?"

"The money."

"Oh," said Miss Burreton, "the money. Yes."

George took a long breath, and began slowly and methodically to search the room.

"I should go to bed," Miss Burreton said, rocking comfortably, "but I'm frightened. I've lost my key."

"I'm trying to find your money," George grunted. "Then you can go to bed."

"I can't sleep—I never sleep now. I have to watch, because I don't know who might come in."

"Nobody here would hurt you."

"Oh yes, oh yes." She stopped rocking and spoke very earnestly to him. "You see, they all took the money—and I did too. But I kept mine for Ellen, because it was her money, and she was saving it. But they all took it, and she never knew about it."

"What happened to Missy's money?" George asked quietly.

"What?"

"You know—the money Ellen was saving for Missy."

"Ellen hid it—she hid the money for poor Missy."

"Where did she hide it?"

"She hid it," Miss Burreton said. "She hid Missy's money and she never would tell. She should have told me—I asked her again and again—but she was very rude and wouldn't tell me."

George sighed and continued to search. He found no money, and, when he had finished with the room, he asked, "Where are your trunks? In the attic?"

She admitted to two, or possibly even three, trunks in the attic, but was unable to produce any keys. She padded along in front of him as he went upstairs, and stopped once to ask, "What are you looking for, George?"

"I'm looking for your money," he said shortly.

"Oh," said Miss Burreton. "But it's in the bank."

"I'm looking for the money you had here."

She said, "Oh," again, and continued on upstairs.

In the attic she identified her own trunks, which were all unlocked. George began to go through them and had started on the second when Anne appeared.

"What are you doing?"

"I'm picking daisies," George snarled.

Anne looked down into the tangle of ancient finery he had turned up and said critically, "That big one on the hat looks more like a rose."

"Hussy," said Miss Burreton.

George finished his search, banged the last trunk shut, and stood up.

"Are these all the trunks you have?"

"These are my trunks," she said. "Did you find it?"

George was in a bad humor and could not resist saying "Find what?"

Miss Burreton nodded. "That's good. Now I can go to bed."

"For God's sake, do," George muttered under his breath.

They went downstairs, and George had the satisfaction of seeing four people beating a hasty retreat from Miss Burreton's room.

"At least they didn't find anything there," he said and Anne looked at him curiously.

"For heaven's sake, what are you all hunting for now?"

"One of them is only pretending," George said curtly.

Tim came up the stairs, and George hailed him. "Go and get Vally up here, will you."

"Vally went home in a snit. How are you, darling?"

"Are you addressing me?" George asked.

"I'm talking to my little precious here."

George glanced down at Anne and said, "Oh hell, let's have—"

"Wonderful," Tim agreed. "Suppose we go down to the kitchen, where we'll be close to the ice."

While Tim made martinis, George told them of the meeting in Mr. Courtney's room. He gave them all the details and had swallowed three martinis before he came to the end. "So you see," he finished, "we'll have to get hold of Vally." He added irritably, "Don't you ever drink anything but this hogwash?"

"It narrows the field," Tim said, his eyes shining with excitement. "It's among those four—and one of them has double-crossed the others and made away with Miss Burreton's pile."

"She has something in the bank," George said. "I think this was only her spending money."

"No, no. She has what she has in the bank—but this is the other fund—

the one for which Grandma killed a man. She took his money and hid it, and the others found it, divided it, and spent it. Apparently Grandma never discovered her loss."

"The man she is supposed to have killed could hardly have had a fortune in his pockets," George said. "Anyway, she would never have kept money around here without running it through her fingers occasionally. She was like that."

Tim thought it over. "He might have carried a fortune around in a suitcase. Some people don't trust banks—I don't like them myself—their monthly statements never agree with mine. Grandma might have run across a man like that and been tempted beyond her strength."

"Murdered him," George said bitterly.

"Not necessarily. He might have fallen downstairs or had a heart attack, and she couldn't resist taking advantage of it. She couldn't put the money in the bank, since it would require some explanation, so she hid it. I think she divided it in some way and hid a pile, separately, for Missy—and I think it was all hidden in this house. She sewed a map or an explanation of some sort into the lining of the black coat, but of course Missy never found it. The gang evidently found the main pile some time ago and have spent it, since they're all broke again. One of them quietly extracted Miss Burreton's hoard, but they haven't found Missy's money yet. And, by the way, George, I think we should get Miss Burreton out of the house—she seems to be in a spot of danger."

"I don't see why Mrs. Johnson was killed—or Spike," Anne mused.

"It does seem a rather extreme measure," Tim agreed. "Grandma was beginning to talk too much and had already given up the secret of the coat—which explains her demise. Mrs. Johnson knew things, though—and Spike, as well. But not Paul. Paul was pushed out, and Anne was to have been pushed out too. Anne, precious, how do you feel?"

"If you mean, was I doped again at dinner—no. But I have felt better."

George stood up, and Tim said quickly, "No, George, don't get Vally. He interferes. Just give me an hour or two—that's all I'll need."

"Suppose something happens in that hour or two," George said aggressively. "Vally will want to know why I didn't tell him about those four thieves—and rightly so. You, of course, could always say you're sorry—that ought to help."

"I don't see why the map she sewed into the lining wouldn't have crumbled away in all that time," Anne said thoughtfully.

Tim looked at her. "Darling, you *are* wonderful—I keep saying so. Now the old lady had trouble sewing the thing in the lining, and Missy's pile has not yet been found. Either the map was lost—or it was too obscure. We'll look at that coat again."

"It would be much better," George said stubbornly, "if I were to get hold of Vally. He'd have the authority to turn those people out of their rooms while he searched for Miss Burreton's money. Whoever has it, is *it*."

"My dear, honest, sober George —"

"Save your breath," George said, heading for the telephone. "I'm getting Vally."

Tim followed him all the way to the telephone, arguing first plausibly, then hotly, but George ignored him. He sat down, dialed, waited, spoke, waited again, and then had to leave a message. Vally was not available, and no one could be induced to reveal his whereabouts.

Tim and Anne had gone to her room, and George followed. He watched gloomily while Tim took the coat and spread it out on the bed, and was unaware of the fact that Tim was ignoring him stonily, because he was mad at him.

Anne and Tim studied the coat together, and Tim said, "Look for white thread sewed into the lining, precious."

"Sure," said George, "waste your time, precious, with a black cloud hanging over your head. Matter of fact if I could give that information about the others to Vally, it would get you out from under—at least to some extent."

Tim looked up and said sharply, "Nonsense! Anne is virtually a prisoner here—she would most certainly be stopped if she tried to go. Lily and I are hardly under suspicion, but we had to wade knee-deep in red tape to get out on legitimate business. We were stopped, you know, outside. Vally thinks Anne is a member of a gang, and the fact that those old crumbs pinched some money they found in the house is not going to change his mind."

"The way I feel now," Anne said, brushing hair back from her feverish forehead, "I no longer care."

"Darling, *don't* be so defeatist. I am here to protect you, and I shall not sleep until this thing is finished."

Anne returned to the coat. "Does it have to be white thread?" she asked wearily.

"No, my sweet—no. I just thought that when she said she sewed it into the lining, she sewed it in—do you see?"

"Very clear," said George from his chair.

Anne straightened up for a moment and rubbed her back. "Well—there seems to be a lot of extra black thread here."

Tim bounded to her side, looked closely at the spot she indicated, and nodded. "Wait a minute," he cried, and flew out of the room.

"Gone to get a magnifying glass and a bloodhound," George murmured, and Anne laughed. He smiled back at her, and she thought that it was the first time she had seen him really smile.

Tim was back immediately, and Anne laughed again when she saw that he held a large magnifying glass.

George said, "You've forgotten the checked cap."

Tim pulled the coat over to the light and began to study it under the glass. He was silent for some time, then he looked up.

"It's sewed right on to the leather," he said slowly, "and somebody has tried desperately to cut it out—but failed. George, do you know what 'one, two—one, two, three means?' "

CHAPTER THIRTY-ONE

GEORGE SAID, "One, two—one, two, three? Certainly. It's a recipe for a sweater—simply darling. I can let you have the pattern if you like."

Tim sighed. "George's wit. We must bear with it, because, though it is a poor thing, it is his own. George, I beg of you— This is most certainly a message."

"If you say so," George murmured courteously. "It's probably in the secret room. They've all been digging around in there, but they didn't know that you had to go one, two—one, two, three."

"We must go down there at once and see," Tim decided.

They started down the stairs, and Tim glanced back along the hall. "So quiet tonight—they must all be asleep."

"I doubt it," George said.

"Probably listening at their doors," Anne added.

Tim nodded. "One of them is, almost certainly."

Anne refused to go into the secret room, but stood just outside the door. She watched Tim and George moving around with a flashlight and counting one, two—one, two, three, over and over again until she had to smother an outburst of hysterical laughter in her handkerchief.

"There are no loose stones," George said after a while, "and we'd need a mason to do anything with this wall—might bring the whole thing down on our heads if we start fooling around with it ourselves."

Tim agreed reluctantly, but continued to tap at the uneven stones, while George came out and joined Anne.

"No luck?" she asked.

He shook his head. "I'm going to try to get hold of Vally again."

They walked through into the front hall and came face to face with Vally himself.

"You called me?"

George nodded. "You'd better come into the lounge and sit down."

They went to the lounge and established themselves in chairs, while Anne stood uncertainly in the doorway.

"The shots were fired from that gun all right," Vally said. "No finger-prints, of course."

Anne decided that Tim might be interested in this piece of news, so she went quietly back to the secret room and gave it to him.

Tim nodded, and then said with restrained excitement, "Come here, dar-ling, and see what I have found."

She stepped gingerly over the sill, and he took her hand and drew her in. "You see, we were concentrating on the blank parts of the wall and didn't bother with the parts that had already been dug out. I found this loose stone—chipped and battered—and the niche behind it."

Anne peered in and gave a little cry. "Why, it's the money— packets and packets of it. Tim, you found it!"

"No, dear, I thought so, too, at first. But you see? Stage money."

Anne let out her breath and said, "Oh," rather feebly.

"Well, that's all, sweet. We'll take this fake money and hand it over to Vally to play with—as long as the honest George is telling all."

Anne help him to carry the packets, and he kept dropping them as he closed the secret room again. They went to the lounge, where Tim dropped the packets on the floor in front of Vally and dusted his hands.

Vally gave him a sour look and asked, "What's this?"

"That is the stage money that those four put into the secret room to fool the old lady into thinking that her money was still intact."

George turned one of the packets over with his toe. "Five," he said after a moment. "Miss Burreton got her cut too."

"Six probably," Tim said, looking smug.

"Why six?"

"Mrs. Johnson."

"How do you figure that?" Vally asked, reluctant to encourage him but unable to restrain his curiosity.

"Mrs. Johnson was cook here for many years, and I cannot believe she did not know what was going on. She very unwisely stated that she knew the identity of the murderer—and so put herself next on the list."

George shook his head. "She meant Monty. I know, because I talked with her."

"Did she actually say she meant Monty?"

"Well—" George was unable to remember that she had. "But she im-plied as much."

"Of course," Tim agreed. "By then she was biding her time."

"Why did she go on cooking, if she had her share of the money?"

"My dear George, the sum could not have been so very great even in the beginning—divided five or six ways, it becomes no more than a comfortable nest egg."

"Why was Spike Magraw murdered?" Vally asked.

"He stumbled across something and was unwise enough to confront somebody. Spike was tough, but this person was frightened and desperate, so Spike got the worst of it."

"I see it this way. Spike made demands, and the murderer went off—ostensibly to get Missy's money—and came back with the gun and the bullets. He took Spike into that hall closet—which looks like a reasonable place for hidden money—shot him, and pushed him down the chute."

Vally said, "Serve him right, trying to make money out of his brother's dead wife and child."

Tim opened his mouth, but George got in ahead of him, "Missy's child is dead?"

Vally wished he hadn't mentioned it. He heaved a sigh and went on, "Yes, Magraw was a crook and hired this girl to impersonate the granddaughter. The girl was picked up in Scranton and spilled it all."

"But the relatives told me she was alive," George said.

"The relatives you contacted were Mr. and Mrs. Henry, alias Spike Magraw," said Vally dryly. "The girl died five years ago." George was silent, and Tim again opened his mouth, but he didn't make it this time, either. George got in ahead of him again.

"I think you're all wrong about Mrs. Johnson," he said suddenly. "She would never have taken anything that did not belong to her."

"A lot of people look honest," Vally commented.

"She might not have been in on it," Tim conceded. "But she certainly suspected something near the truth."

Vally stood up. "I'm going to get those people down here."

"Now?" George asked.

"Right now. I want them collected here, and I want you to keep them here until I get a chance to talk to them. They'll squawk, but I can't help that."

"Mr. Alrian too?"

"Mr. Alrian," said Vally, "and the nurse, and the maid."

"The nurse and the maid have gone home. What about Mrs. Smith? She hasn't been well."

"Mrs. Smith too," said Vally, and walked out of the room with George grumbling along behind him.

"You see what he proposes to do, of course, darling?" Tim said. "He'll sneak in and search all their rooms while they're congregated down here. There'll be no one to stop him."

Anne gave a tearing yawn that ended in a groan. She wandered out into the hall and looked up the stairs.

"You know, 'one, two—one, two, three,' makes me think of stairs."

Tim looked blank for a moment, and then yelled suddenly, "My precious *darling!*"

Vally and George, who had reached the top of the stairs, stopped and turned around, and Tim called up to them, "The stairs—of *course* the stairs—that's where the other fortune is. Third step on the second flight."

Vally said, "That was obvious from the start," and went on.

"He is an infernal, flatfooted liar," Tim muttered to Anne. "He never would have thought of it, and I'm sorry I told him."

Upstairs, George was knocking on various doors, and Vally was staring, fascinated, at the third step of the second flight. Tim came up behind him and murmured, "Carpeting. That makes it a bit more difficult."

There were a few noisy objections to the gathering in the lounge, although Pet and Mr. Alrian went quietly. Roger raised the biggest fuss, but was induced, in the end, to accompany his wife downstairs. They were in various states of undress, with the exception of Mr. Alrian and Miss Burreton, who were attired about as usual.

George, mindful of his promise to keep them in the lounge, talked of irrelevant things, and felt like a fool. Tim whispered to Anne, "I'm going to enjoy this. George will have to stand on his head to keep them all amused."

George handed out some drinks after a while, and Pet, Mr. Alrian, and Miss Burreton refused. These three were correspondingly restless, and Miss Burreton took to padding around the room—stopping to peer into the hall and out of the front window.

Roger stood it for a while and then exploded. "For God's sake, Burry, come to roost somewhere, will you?"

Miss Burreton ignored him, and Liz said, "Let her alone, for heaven's sake."

They all became restless in the end, and Roger shouted, "Why the devil were we roused out of our beds to sit here for nothing?"

"He'll be here soon," George said, looking a bit desperate. "Would—er—anyone like some crackers and cheese?"

"That's a good idea," Min agreed, tightening the cord of her wrapper. "And some coffee. I'll get it."

George held her back with a hand on her shoulder. "Stay where you are. I'll get it. We don't need coffee—only keeps us awake all night."

"It looks as though we were to be kept awake all night without the aid of coffee," Mr. Courtney said acidly.

They were silent for a while after that, and even Miss Burreton sat down and stared at nothing.

"Do you suppose he's snooping through our things?" Liz asked presently.

Roger swelled and started to bellow, and Tim said hastily, "No, no—it's nothing like that. Something to do with the laundry chute, you know. He'll be here in just a minute."

Miss Burreton slid out of her chair and began to pad up and down the room again. Roger glared at her, and Min tried to distract his attention.

"We'll have breakfast later in the morning," she said nervously, "and you can all catch up on your sleep a little."

"Madam," said Roger, "if the breakfast is to be left in Ginny's hands, we shall most certainly have it later."

Anne thought they all looked worried and frightened—except Mr. Alrian, and, of course, Miss Burreton. Mr. Courtney was in possession of his usual poise, but she thought he looked haggard in spite of it.

Mrs. Smith began to worry—out loud—about Monty. No one listened to her, but she droned on until a sound from upstairs stopped her in mid-sentence. Tim cocked his head and realized that Vally was removing the carpeting from the second flight of stairs.

He felt cheated for a moment, then he set his jaw, jammed his hands into his pockets, and concentrated fiercely. I should know by now, he thought—it's all there in front of me—I *must* know.

"What's all that hammering upstairs?" Liz asked, and Tim looked up suddenly.

Suppose this murderer who was among them thought that Vally was finding the money for which he had already killed three people—wouldn't he want to go up there and look? But, then, so would the others, since they'd been after the money too. Of course only one of them had really examined the coat, although the others knew more or less about it. Anne had spoken to Vally of it at lunch, and they had all listened. But even though Anne had supposed the money had been in the coat, they were all still looking for it. So they knew it was in the house—Grandma must have told them.

One of them, however, had read the message in the coat and had put the bill there to stop Anne from further searching.

Tim sat up and glanced around the room. "That noise," he said carefully, "is Vally investigating the one, two—one, two, three business."

This brought forth a barrage of questions, and Tim tried to look embarrassed. "I thought you knew," he stammered. "Perhaps I should not have mentioned it, but I thought Vally had told you."

They fell silent, and Tim leaned across and whispered against Anne's ear, "In less than two minutes the murderer will get up and leave the room."

CHAPTER THIRTY-TWO

ANNE LOOKED around the room, and then lowered her eyes with a feeling of sheer terror. Except for Miss Burreton, who continued to pad around, they were all silent and still. Even Mr. Alrian had lowered the magazine behind which he had been hidden.

Tim waited with his eyes half closed. He was convinced that one of them knew what one, two—one, two, three meant—and that that one would have to go up and see Vally take the money for which he had risked so much.

The silence was so absolute that Miss Burreton's soft shoes seemed loud on the carpet. Tim turned to look at her and saw her peering out first one window and then another. At last she sidled behind their chairs to the archway and padded out into the hall.

Tim blushed, and Anne gave a hysterical little giggle. "Better run and catch her."

"Somebody had better get her," Roger said morosely. "It's downright revolting, upon my word. I don't believe she even undresses to go to bed any more—her clothes look that way. Putting on weight, too, isn't she?"

"Don't let her get on your nerves so, dear," Pet murmured. "We should have started a game of bridge—that would have kept her quiet."

"Shall I get her?" Anne asked. "I'll play with you."

Tim stood up. "No. I'll get her."

He went out, and saw that Miss Burreton was near the top of the stairs. Bridge, he thought—did she play bridge with her mouth hanging open? Why hadn't he thought of it before? Anne had told him of the game she and George had played with Pet and Miss Burreton. He should have realized it then. You can't play bridge, or read, or anything of that sort when you are as vague as Miss Burreton appeared to be.

He reached the second floor, and saw her standing at the foot of the second flight of stairs. As he watched, she drew back into the shadow of a doorway, and he saw Vally and another man working on the third step. Vally was swearing, and muttering about damned fools who hide things in old houses. The carpet had been flung off the stairs, and they were lifting up the stair tread.

Tim backed into another doorway and watched avidly.

Vally said, "God's sake, look out, or the whole damned thing will cave in. Wild-goose chase—goddamn amateur detectives—"

"No, sir," said the helper suddenly. "Look—there's a bag."

Vally handed out a small canvas bag and held it up, looking almost disappointed. "Heavy," he commented, and, a moment later, after he had opened it, "Gossake! Nuggets!"

"Geez," said the other man. "Gold nuggets!"

"O.K., keep an eye on it, and try to get these stairs back into some sort of shape so that nobody breaks a leg." He spoke to another man and added, "Don't miss anything—I'll give you another half-hour. I'm going down to keep them in line."

Miss Burreton and Tim flattened themselves against their respective doorways as Vally passed. The helper on the stairs put the bag down and turned to the broken step. The other man went into a room, and at the same time Miss Burreton emerged from her doorway, picked up the bag, and headed for the back stairs, without making any sound at all.

Tim followed quietly, but he had to hurry, for she was going very swiftly. She sped down the stairs through the kitchen and to the darkened dining room, where she landed on a chair that was near the lounge. She immediately said, "Disgraceful!" in a loud voice.

Tim heard several people say, "There she is," and Vally's voice rang out above them. "I thought you said she'd gone upstairs."

Tim backed into the kitchen as Vally pounded into the dining room and put on the light. Tim was fascinated by Miss Burreton at this point, and he walked through the hall and on to the dining room again. When he got there, the old lady was staring up at Vally, saying, "What is it?"

"Where have you been?" Vally roared.

"Well—I came here, you see. They're all here."

"Come into the lounge," Vally said curtly. "I want everyone's fingerprints."

"You have some prints?" Tim asked eagerly. "Where did you get them?"

Vally said, "Kindly mind your own business."

Miss Burreton went into the lounge, where she immediately became interested in a plate of cheese and crackers that stood on a table. She ignored the crackers but smeared cheese over her hands and mouth with great gusto.

Tim watched her carefully. She probably doesn't know, he thought, where Vally might have got prints that would mean something, so she's smearing her fingers in the hope that he'll get disgusted and push her to one side—figuring that she couldn't possibly have done all this, anyway.

Vally was taking fingerprints, and Tim sidled up and looked over his shoulder. "If you'll tell me where you got those prints," he murmured, "I'll tell you who to take next, and then you won't have to do them all. You'll be able to go home and get some sleep."

"Will you go away?" Vally snarled. "Go and unravel some other mystery. Why should I get it all, and leave all the other guys out in the cold?"

"I know where you got those prints," Tim said suddenly. "On the wall in George's room—where that cord was taken from the curtain. Walls are always dusty in a place like this. It must be a marvelous print."

Vally sighed, ground his teeth, and sighed again. The jerk was right, of course, and he'd been right before, and he'd probably be right again. It was a lousy case, and he wanted to go home, finish his book, and go to bed.

"Tell me," he said evenly.

Tim whispered Miss Burreton's name in his ear, and he backed away, indignant and incredulous. "Are you crazy?" he roared, and could not keep his eyes from sliding around to Miss Burreton, who was still eating cheese.

The man who had been repairing the broken stair tread chose to appear at this moment with an embarrassed confession that the bag of nuggets had disappeared. Vally's face darkened to an almost purple shade, and Tim hastily whispered in his ear again. Vally threw up his hands and walked over to Miss Burreton.

"Have you got that bag of nuggets on you?" he asked quietly.

Miss Burreton sat very still, and Vally added, "I can have you searched, you know, so if you have it, you'd better produce it now."

Miss Burreton blinked at him and said, "Eh?"

"Give me the bag you found upstairs."

Miss Burreton pulled it out from somewhere in the recesses of her skirt, and said, "It's mine, you know—I found it."

Vally threw the bag on a table and ran his trained hands over Miss Burreton's skirt. "Where'd she buy a dress like this?" he muttered. "Pockets as big as a potato sack on each side."

Miss Burreton said, "This is disgraceful," and Pet explained, "She makes those skirts herself."

Vally drew a package of money and a small kitchen knife from the second pocket, and the old lady snapped, "That's my money."

"O.K., O.K., come and have your fingerprints taken."

This took time, since the cheese had to be wiped off first, but when it was done at last Vally stood for some time, comparing the prints with those from George's room. He glanced up after a while and encountered a smug and superior smile from Tim, and thought wistfully that it would improve his feelings tremendously to wipe it off by force.

He turned to Miss Burreton and asked sternly, "Did you kill your friend Ellen Smith?"

She chewed on her gums excitedly. "Yes—oh yes. You see, she told me to."

"Did the man Spike Magraw tell you to kill him too?"

"Eh?" said Miss Burreton.

"The man—the one you shot and stuffed down the laundry chute."

"Yes—the man. My father told me, you know—he said I must always defend myself. That man—he thought I had a lot of money in the bag, but I didn't."

"Did he catch you listening at Grandma's door?" Tim asked.

Miss Burreton flicked him a swift, odd look from her pale eyes, and Vally said angrily, "Kindly allow me to handle this." He cleared his throat and added, "Now, Miss Burreton, why did you kill Mrs. Johnson?"

"Eh?"

Vally repeated the question, and she blinked at him. "That was the cook— she was the cook—and she saw me take the little knife. She said I killed Ellen, and she wanted the knife back. I told her I had it in the closet. I put the pistol back in my pocket, and then I put it back in the drawer. They hid the bullets, you know, and they were my bullets, but I found them. My father—"

"Why did you take the knife?" Tim asked. "So that you could cut that man's arm?"

"Yes, yes, yes—he was always looking through my room, and I didn't like it. I took the hand and put it in his blood—I didn't like him. I tried to keep the hand—I put it down in the room, but somebody took it. I was frightened. They're all against me, and they frighten me."

"You come along with me, Miss Burreton," Vally said quite gently. "I'll take you to a place where you'll be safe and they won't frighten you any more."

"Oh yes." She smiled. "A nice home for ladies."

"You'll have to stop playing bridge," Tim said sardonically. "Give the show away."

"Shut up, will you?" Vally said in complete exasperation. He turned to George. "About the thefts—"

George shrugged. "It's hardly up to me."

Vally departed with Miss Burreton trotting contentedly along beside him.

CHAPTER THIRTY-THREE

"SHE'S MARVELOUS, isn't she?" Tim said. "Even Vally won't suspect that she's in full possession of her senses, until she escapes from where they put her, of course."

Mrs. Smith said, "Isn't that awful? How were we to know that she was as mad as a hatter?"

Liz murmured diffidently, "George—er—what did Vally mean? I mean, he said something about thefts."

"Well, you'd better all sit down. Except Mr. Alrian, of course."

Mr. Alrian bowed and departed, and George cast a speculative eye over the rest of them.

"There's a skeleton in the attic, and there's a secret room with stage money in a hole in the wall, and this young lady—Miss Anne—was doped today at lunch."

Liz put a dramatic hand on her bosom and said, "I'll tell you everything, George, and I'm sure you'll not blame us."

She pulled her girdle down, started in, and made quite a good job of it. They had never known who the skeleton was—he was just lying there, with clothes on him, when they first discovered the secret room. Well, not clothes, exactly—old rags—and he must have been there for a long time—it was simply ghastly. They had found out about the room by seeing Miss Burreton go in there, and Miss Burreton had been most upset. She had made them promise not to tell Ellen, and had told them that Ellen had killed the man. However, if there were anyone who liked money better than Ellen, it would be Burry. In the beginning they had divided a portion of the money, but Miss Burreton had run out and had started to come down and pick up a bit more now and then. In the end Mr. Courtney had proposed that they divide the entire amount and put some stage money in its place, since Ellen liked to look at her money, but never wanted to spend it.

Mr. Courtney interrupted at this point to declare emphatically that the idea had not been his.

"You supplied the stage money," Liz said accusingly, and he fell silent.

Liz drew a long breath. Miss Burreton had fiercely resisted the division of the money, but they overruled her. Then Ellen fell ill and got the odd notion that she wanted her granddaughter. George started making inquiries, and contacted some Magraws. Then, while some of them were talking with Ellen, she let slip the fact that she had some money hidden away for her granddaughter. And so—well—they had started looking for it. "You see— er"—Liz stammered—"we felt that the girl didn't have any real right to it. After all, she'd never seen her grandmother."

They concentrated on the secret room, but the presence of the skeleton had been so hideous that, in the end, Pet and Roger had cleaned him up a bit, thrown the rags in the furnace, and removed him to a trunk in the attic.

More troubled followed. The man Paul appeared, and they found him looking all over the house. They were uneasy, since they did not know who he was, and they determined to drive him out. They started feeding him their sleeping pills, which they put in his drinks, and they put the light on and off in his room while he was sleeping. It was Liz herself who thought of Mr. Courtney's hand. They did not tell Mr. Courtney because they knew he would object—and Miss Burreton insisted on handling this aspect of the matter entirely by herself. They had no idea, naturally, that she would cut the poor man's arm and dangle the bloody hand in front of him! Liz shuddered. But, in any case, it had sent him away—and then they started in on the supposed granddaughter. They merely wanted to drive her away, because why should she come in for all that money? She had no claim—

"You hung that beastly hand up in my room?" Anne asked.

"Why, yes." Liz pulled her girdle down again. "Roger did that. And I was waiting around to take it down again and return it to Mr. Courtney's room. I always stay up late, anyway, and we figured you'd run out of the room, screaming. I thought I could get it down before you came back with anybody, and then you'd think you had a haunted room, and maybe go away—"

"That was before you doped me?" Anne asked coldly.

"Well—not exactly. We started right away, actually, but those things sort of take time and mount up."

Pet stood up, her face crimson and her dainty lace handkerchief in ribbons.

"That's enough, Liz, I think we should all go to bed—we need sleep very badly. Min dear, you look deathly tired. Can I get you anything?"

Min looked surprised and pleased at this unexpected and unusual solicitude, and they moved out of the room in a body.

George, left with Tim and Anne, raised his eyebrows. "Mrs. Crimple is the smartest—she's sucking up to Min already in the hope that the money—stolen and spent—will be overlooked."

Tim laughed and, stretching his legs out before him, murmured, "Isn't old Miss Burreton marvelous?"

"She's not right in the head," Anne protested. "Why would she admit to everything at once like that?"

"You too?" Tim sighed. "The old girl is as smart as a whip. She knew her fingerprints would show up, and she knew I'd seen her pinching the bag of nuggets, so she went on pretending to be soft in the head so as to end up in a comfortable berth. It was the only way out."

"I can't understand Aunt Ellen and that skeleton," George said in a bothered voice.

"I wonder who he was?" Tim yawned.

"Old man Smith went on a gold rush once," George said thoughtfully, "and friends he'd made out there used to turn up here from time to time—some of them broke—some with money. This one evidently had it, and had it with him. Miss Burreton didn't find it, I suppose, and Aunt Ellen hid it away for Missy with a key message that only Tim could figure out."

"Thank you," Tim said formally. "Precious, suppose we go out for food and drink, now that it's all over. I feel rather flat."

"Go on out by yourself," George said with sudden heat.

Anne yawned. "I'll have to go and look for a job in the morning."

"Oh, for heaven's sake, darling," Tim exclaimed, "didn't you know? I am almost the biggest name in radio and George is only a stodgy lawyer. In any case, you hardly need to go looking for jobs."

"You mean I have to choose between you?" she asked, laughing a little.

"Yes, darling—a woman's crossroads, you know. Please get it over with."

Anne sighed. "Then I'll take the earthy George, so that when he spurns me, I can go and look for a job with a clear conscience."

"Precious!" Tim threw up his hands. "He is not going to spurn you—and you *know* it."

THE END

Murder is a Collector's Item by Elizabeth Dean. "(It) froths over with the same effervescent humor as the best Hepburn-Grant films."—Sujata Massey. "Completely enjoyable."—*New York Times.* "Fast and funny."—*The New Yorker.* Twenty-six-year-old Emma Marsh isn't much at spelling or geography and perhaps she butchers the odd literary quotation or two, but she's a keen judge of character and more than able to hold her own when it comes to selling antiques or solving murders. Originally published in 1939, *Murder is a Collector's Item* was the first of three books featuring Emma. Smoothly written and sparkling with dry, sophisticated humor, this milestone combines an intriguing puzzle with an entertaining portrait of a self-possessed young woman on her own at the end of the Great Depression.   **0-915230-19-4 $14.00**

Murder is a Serious Business by Elizabeth Dean. It's 1940 and the Thirsty Thirties are over but you couldn't tell it by the gang at J. Graham Antiques, where clerk Emma Marsh, her would-be criminologist boyfriend Hank, and boss Jeff Graham trade barbs in between shots of scotch when they aren't bothered by the rare customer. Trouble starts when Emma and crew head for a weekend at Amos Currier's country estate to inventory the man's antiques collection. It isn't long before the bodies start falling and once again Emma is forced to turn sleuth in order to prove that her boss isn't a killer. "Judging from (this book) it's too bad she didn't write a few more."—Mary Ann Steel, *I Love a Mystery.*   **0-915230-28-3 $14.95**

Murder a Mile High by Elizabeth Dean. When Emma Marsh is asked by her old pal Mary, a visiting diva at the Central City, Colorado, Opera House, to desert the summer heat of 1942 Boston to help her with a little romantic problem, Emma smells trouble. After all, Mary of all people ought to know better than to get involved with a tenor. But Emma dutifully kisses her boyfriend Hank Fairbanks goodbye, reluctantly turns over the running of J. Graham Antiques to its owner, and boards a train for the Rockies. Besides it just might help her get over the pending loss of Hank—who enlisted shortly after Pearl Harbor—to Army Intelligence. Soon after she arrives in Central City, Emma stumbles across the body of the tenor, encounters a very strange old man who seems to run the town, and spots what she thinks could be a nest of German spies. The old man offers to help catch the murderer but Emma can't help but think he just might be covering his own guilty tracks. There are also plenty of candidates for murderer among the members of the opera company, including Mary, who appears to be keeping company with yet one more tenor—one with a decidedly Germanic bearing. If only Emma could account for the movements of all the suspects—but that, unfortunately, would require that she stay awake through one entire performance of the opera, a feat that seems beyond her abilities. Imbued with the same sparkling humor that made *Murder is a Collector's Item* and *Murder is a Serious Business* a hit with readers and critics alike, *Murder a Mile High* was first published in 1944 and is one of the earliest detective novels to fully utilize Colorado as a setting.   **0-915230-39-9 $14.00**

Common or Garden Crime by Sheila Pim. Lucy Bex preferred Jane Austen or Anthony Trollope to the detective stories her brother Linnaeus gulped down but when a neighbor is murdered with monkshood harvested from Lucy's own garden, she's the one who turns detective and spots the crucial clue that prevents the wrong person from going to the gallows. Set in 1943 in the small town of Clonmeen on the outskirts of Dublin, this delightful tale was written by an author who was called "the Irish Angela Thirkell." Published in Britain in 1945, the book makes its first appearance in the United States here. The war in Europe seems very distant in neutral Ireland, though it draws a little nearer when Lucy's nephew, an officer in the British army, comes home on leave. However, most of the residents are more interested in how their gardens grow than what's happening on the Eastern Front or in Africa. It's a death a little closer to home that finally grabs their interest. The Irish Guard is called in to investigate but this time it may take someone with a green thumb to catch the murderer. Pim's detective stories were greeted with great critical acclaim from contemporary reviewers: "Excellent characterization, considerable humour."—*Sphere.* "Humor and shrewd observation of small town

Irish life."—*Times Literary Supplement.* "Wit and gaiety, ease and charm."[1]—*Illustrated London News.* "A truthful, humorous, and affectionate picture of life in an Irish town."—*Daily Herald.* **0-915230-36-4 $14.00**

A Hive of Suspects by Sheila Pim. Jason Prendergast built his fortune taking minerals from the earth near the Irish town of Drumclash, but bees became the real passion of his life once the mines gave up the last of their riches. When he dies after dining on honey from one of his own hives, village beekeepers suspect local bees are feasting on poisonous plants and infecting hives with deadly nectar. Prendergast's solicitor, Edward Gildea, consults his fellow beekeepers, who think rhododendrons the most likely source of the poison. But why is it that only Jason Prendergast's hives were infected? And why should bees suddenly take a liking to this particular plant? The Civic Guard prefers to look for a human hand and suspicion falls upon those locals who stand to benefit from the old man's death, including several servants and an aged distant cousin who deliberately hacks her own rhododendron plants to bits in a crazed frenzy. The chief suspect, however, is Phoebe Prendergast, a niece who gave up a promising career on the stage to look after the old man. Gildea can't believe in Phoebe's guilt and conceals from the police the fact that Prendergast was about to add a codicil to his will disinheriting her should she return to the stage—even after his death. Nor does the Phoebe's odd behavior following the old man's death bode well for her innocence in this 1952 novel, Pim's only mystery to be published in the U.S. in her lifetime. **0-915230-38-0 $14.00**

Black Paw by Constance & Gwenyth Little. Thanks to some overly indulgent parents, Callie Drake was "brought up soft" and doesn't know the first thing about doing housework, which makes it a bit of a stretch for her to pretend to be a maid in the Barton household. She's there dressed in the skimpiest maid's outfit this side of Paris to snatch some compromising love letters written by her friend Selma, who's afraid that her brute of an estranged husband just might use these adulterous missives to lower her alimony. Altruism isn't a big part of Callie's makeup and she agrees to the scheme only after Selma offers to hand over the keys to her hot little roadster in exchange for this bit of petty larceny. But when murder erupts in the Barton mansion, the police think it's a little odd that the bodies started falling only hours after Callie's arrival. Even worse, Selma's soon-to-be-ex is on to Callie and seems to take perverse enjoyment in forcing this spoiled debutante to continue her domestic chores. In between long hot baths and countless cigarette breaks, Callie stumbles across mysterious pawprints in a house without animals and comes upon rocking chairs that move even when there's no one in the room. It's enough to make this golddigger start digging for clues in this 1941 charmer. **0-915230-37-2, $14.00** Other Little books available from The Rue Morgue Press: *The Black Gloves* (0-915230-20-8), *The Black Honeymoon* (0-915230-21-6), *Black Corridors* (0-915230-33-X), *The Black Stocking* (0-915230-30-5), *Black-Headed Pins* (0-915230-25-9), *Great Black Kanba* (0-915230-22-4), and *The Grey Mist Murders* (0-915230-26-7) ($14.00 each).

Brief Candles by Manning Coles. From Topper to Aunt Dimity, mystery readers have embraced the cozy ghost story. Four of the best were written by Manning Coles, the creator of the witty Tommy Hambledon spy novels. First published in 1954, *Brief Candles* is likely to produce more laughs than chills as a young couple vacationing in France run into two gentlemen with decidedly old-world manners. What they don't know is that James and Charles Latimer are ancestors of theirs who shuffled off this mortal coil some 80 years earlier when, emboldened by strong drink and with only a pet monkey and an aged waiter as allies, the two made a valiant, foolish and quite fatal attempt to halt a German advance during the Franco-Prussian War of 1870. Now these two ectoplasmic gentlemen and their spectral pet monkey Ulysses have been summoned from their unmarked graves because their visiting relatives are in serious trouble. But before they can solve the younger Latimers' problems, the three benevolent spirits light brief candles of insanity for a tipsy policeman, a recalcitrant banker, a convocation of English ghostbusters, and a card-playing rogue who's wanted for murder. "As felicitously foolish as a collaboration of (P.G.) Wodehouse and Thorne Smith."—Anthony Boucher. "For those who like something out of the ordinary. Lighthearted, very funny."—*The Sunday Times.* "A gay, most readable story."—*The Daily Telegraph.*   **0-915230-24-0**   **$14.00**

Happy Returns by Manning Coles. The ghostly Latimers and their pet spectral monkey Ulysses return from the grave when Uncle Quentin finds himself in need of their help— it seems the old boy is being pursued by an old flame who won't take no for an answer in her quest to get him to the altar. Along the way, our courteous and honest spooks thwart a couple of bank robbers, unleash a bevy of circus animals on an unsuspecting French town, help out the odd person or two and even "solve" a murder—with the help of the victim. The laughs start practically from the first page and don't stop until Ulysses slides down the bannister, glass of wine in hand, to drink a toast to returning old friends.
0-915230-31-3   **$14.00**

Come and Go by Manning Coles. The third and final book featuring the ghostly Latimers finds our heroes saving an ancestor from marriage and murder in a plot straight out of P.G. Wodehouse.   **0-915230-34-8**   **$14.00**

The Far Traveller by Manning Coles. The Herr Graf was a familiar sight to the residents of the Rhineland village of Grauhugel. After all, he'd been walking the halls of the local castle at night and occasionally nodding to the servants ever since he drowned some 86 years ago. No one was the least bit alarmed by the Graf's spectral walks. Indeed, the castle's major domo found it all quite comforting, as the young Graf had been quite popular while he was alive. When the actor hired to play the dead Graf in a movie is felled by an accident, the film's director is overjoyed to come across a talented replacement who seems to have been born to play the part, little realizing that the Graf and his faithful servant—who perished in the same accident—had only recently decided to materialize in public. The Graf isn't stagestruck. He's back among the living to correct an old wrong. Along the way, he adds a bit of realism to a cinematic duel, befuddles a black marketeer, breaks out of jail, and exposes a charlatan spiritualist. In the meantime, his servant wonders if he's pursuing the granddaughters of the village maidens he dallied with eight decades ago.   **0-915230-35-6**   **$14.00**

The Chinese Chop by Juanita Sheridan. The postwar housing crunch finds Janice Cameron, newly arrived in New York City from Hawaii, without a place to live until she answers an ad for a roommate. It turns out the advertiser is an acquaintance from Hawaii, Lily Wu, whom critic Anthony Boucher (for whom Bouchercon, the World Mystery Convention, is named) described as "the exquisitely blended product of Eastern and Western cultures" and the only female sleuth that he "was devotedly in love with," citing "that odd mixture of respect for her professional skills and delight in her personal charms." First published in 1949, this ground-breaking book was the first of four to feature Lily and be told by her Watson, Janice, a first-time novelist. No sooner do Lily and Janice move into a rooming house in Washington Square than a corpse is found in the basement. In Lily Wu, Sheridan created one of the most believable—and memorable—female sleuths of her day.   **0-915230-32-1**   **$14.00**

Death on Milestone Buttress by Glyn Carr. Abercrombie ("Filthy") Lewker was looking forward to a fortnight of climbing in Wales after a grueling season touring England with his Shakespearean company. Young Hilary Bourne thought the holiday would be a pleasant change from her dreary job at the bank, as well as a chance to renew her acquaintance with a certain young scientist. Neither one expected this bucolic outing to turn deadly, but when one of their party is killed during what should have been an easy climb on the Milestone Buttress, Filthy and Hilary turn detective. Nearly every member of the climbing party had reason to hate the victim but each one also had an alibi for the time of the murder. Filthy and Hilary retrace the route of the fatal climb before returning to their lodgings where, in the grand tradition of Nero Wolfe, Filthy confronts the suspects and points his finger at the only person who could have committed the crime. Filled with climbing details sure to appeal to expert climbers and armchair mountaineers alike, *Death on Milestone Buttress* was published in England in 1951, the first of 15 published mysteries in which Filthy solved murders on peaks scattered around the globe (a 16th novel has yet to be published)..   **0-915230-29-1**   **$14.00**

Murder, Chop Chop by James Norman. "The book has the butter-wouldn't-melt-in-his-mouth cool of Rick in *Casablanca*."—*The Rocky Mountain News*. "Amuses the reader no end."—*Mystery News*. "This long out-of-print masterpiece is intricately plotted, full of eccentric characters and very humorous indeed. Highly recommended."—*Mysteries by Mail*. Meet Gimiendo Hernandez Quinto, a gigantic Mexican who once rode with Pancho Villa and who now trains *guerrilleros* for the Nationalist Chinese government when he isn't solving murders. At his side is a beautiful Eurasian known as Mountain of Virtue, a woman as dangerous to men as she is irresistible. Together they look into the murder of Abe Harrow, an ambulance driver who appears to have died at three different times. There's also a cipher or two to crack, a train with a mind of its own, and Chiang Kai-shek's false teeth, which have gone mysteriously missing. First published in 1942. **0-915230-16-X $13.00**

Death at The Dog by Joanna Cannan. "Worthy of being discussed in the same breath with an Agatha Christie or Josephine Tey...anyone who enjoys Golden Age mysteries will surely enjoy this one."—Sally Fellows, *Mystery News*. "Skilled writing and brilliant characterization."—*Times of London*. "An excellent English rural tale."—Jacques Barzun & Wendell Hertig Taylor in *A Catalogue of Crime*. Set in late 1939 during the first anxious months of World War II, *Death at The Dog*, first published in 1941, is a wonderful example of the classic English detective novel that flourished between the two World Wars. Set in a picturesque village filled with thatched-roof cottages, eccentric villagers and genial pubs, it's as well-plotted as a Christie, with clues abundantly and fairly planted, and as deftly written as the best of Sayers or Marsh, filled with quotable lines and perceptive observations on the human condition. **0-915230-23-2, $14.00**. The first book in this series is **They Rang Up the Police** by Joanna Cannan. "Just delightful."—*Sleuth of Baker Street* Pick-of-the-Month. "A brilliantly plotted mystery...splendid character study...don't miss this one, folks. It's a keeper."—Sally Fellows, *Mystery News*. When Delia Cathcart and Major Willoughby disappear from their quiet English village one morning in July 1937, it looks like a simple case of a frustrated spinster running off for a bit of fun with a straying husband. But as the hours turn into days, Inspector Guy Northeast begins to suspect that she may have been the victim of foul play. Never published in the United States, *They Rang Up the Police* appeared in England in 1939. **0-1915230-27-5 $14.00**

Cook Up a Crime by Charlotte Murray Russell. "Perhaps the mother of today's 'cozy' mystery . . . amateur sleuth Jane has a personality guaranteed to entertain the most demanding reader."—Andy Plonka, *The Mystery Reader*. "Some wonderful old time recipes...highly recommended."—*Mysteries by Mail*. Meet Jane Amanda Edwards, a self-styled "full-fashioned" spinster who complains she hasn't looked at herself in a full-length mirror since Helen Hokinson started drawing for *The New Yorker*. But you can always count on Jane to look into other people's affairs, especially when there's a juicy murder case to investigate. In this 1951 title Jane goes searching for recipes (included between chapters) for a cookbook project and finds a body instead. And once again her lily-of-the-field brother Arthur goes looking for love, finds strong drink, and is eventually discovered clutching the murder weapon. (out-of-print as of June 2001, reissue likely sometime in future.) **0-915230-18-6 $13.00**

The Man from Tibet by Clyde B. Clason. Locked inside the Tibetan Room of his Chicago apartment, the rich antiquarian was overheard repeating a forbidden occult chant under the watchful eyes of Buddhist gods. When the doors were opened it appeared that he had succumbed to a heart attack. But the elderly Roman historian and sometime amateur sleuth Theocritus Lucius Westborough is convinced that Adam Merriweather's death was anything but natural and that the weapon was an eighth century Tibetan manuscript. **0-915230-17-8 $14.00**

The Mirror by Marlys Millhiser. "Completely enjoyable."—*Library Journal*. "A great deal of fun."—*Publishers Weekly*. How could you not be intrigued by a novel in which "you find the main character marrying her own grandfather and giving birth to her own mother?" Such is the situation in this classic novel, originally published in 1978, of two women who end up living each other's lives. Twenty-year-old Shay Garrett is not aware that she's pregnant and is having second thoughts about marrying Marek Weir when she's suddenly transported back 78 years in time into the body of Brandy McCabe, her own grandmother, who is unwillingly about to be married off to miner Corbin Strock. Shay's in shock but she still recognizes that the picture of her grandfather that hangs in the family home doesn't resemble her husband-to-be. But marry Corbin she does and off she goes to the high mining town of Nederland, where this thoroughly modern young woman has to learn to cope with such things as wood cooking stoves and—to her—old-fashioned attitudes about sex. In the meantime, Brandy McCabe is finding it even harder to cope with life in the Boulder, Colorado, of 1978.   **0-915230-15-1**   **$14.95**

About The Rue Morgue Press

The Rue Morgue Press vintage mystery line is designed to bring back into print those books that were favorites of readers between the turn of the century and the 1960s. The editors welcome suggestions for reprints. To receive our catalog or make suggestions, write The Rue Morgue Press, P.O. Box 4119, Boulder, Colorado 80306 (1-800-699-6214).